'This book tells the story of Rose and her mother, Natalie, who are trying to cope with Rose's newly diagnosed, and very serious, illness. With the help of a diary she discovers, Natalie begins to tell Rose the tale of a group of men battling to survive on the Atlantic ocean in a lifeboat with limited food and water. This is a moving and richly drawn novel, and fine storytelling in its purest form. With lilting, rhythmic prose that never falters *How To Be Brave* held me from its opening lines. I found myself as eager to return to the story of Colin, Ken and their companions on their boat in 1943 as Rose herself was! Louise Beech masterfully envelops us in two worlds separated by time yet linked by fierce family devotion, bravery and the triumph of human spirit. Wonderful' Amanda Jennings, author of *In Her Wake*

'One of the books that has really struck a chord with us this year is *How to be Brave* by Louise Beech. It is truly 5*, uplifting and compelling. This is a haunting, beautifully written, tenderly told story that wonderfully weaves together a contemporary story of a mother battling to save her child's life through the medium of storytelling with an extraordinary story of bravery and a fight for survival in the Second World War' Trip Fiction

'A wholly engrossing read, *How To Be Brave* balances its two storylines with a delicate precision. I loved the dynamic between Natalie and Rose, and Beech manages to convey an awful lot about Rose's condition without ever setting foot in dreaded info-dump territory. The epic survival strand, as the shipwrecked sailors fight against the odds, is engrossing, and the connections are seamless. Bravo!' Sarah Jasmon, author of *The Summer of Secrets*

'Beautifully written, intelligent and moving, this book will stay with you long after you reach the end' Ruth Dugdall

'Two family stories of loss and redemption intertwine in a painfully beautiful narrative. This book grabbed me right around my heart and didn't let go' Cassandra Parkin

'An amazing story of hope and survival ... a love letter to the power of books and stories' Nick Quantrill

'Louise Beech is a natural born storyteller and this is a wonderful story' Russ Litten

'This is a yellow brick road of a novel that when it delivers you home will have you seeing all the people you care about anew, in glorious Technicolor. The stories are authentically told, in fact they are rooted in the author's family history, and the characters are so real that they speak to anyone who knows what it is to be alone and what it means to be connected to others. *How To Be Brave* shares the same magic that Ray Kinsella's *Field of Dreams* possessed. It makes you want to snuggle up with your own children in a book nook and hold them close' Live Many Lives

'The two threads of the story are cleverly interwoven, the historical aspects are stunningly intuitive and with a highly engaging sense of place and time – a novel of two intensely emotional halves creating an incredible whole. It is emotionally resonant – you will cry – but it is also brave, true and utterly compelling, a cliff's edge read where you are waiting for that moment then realise that the whole darn thing is *THAT* moment' Liz Loves Books

'Exquisitely written with storytelling of pure beauty, this debut novel is like nothing I've read before. Highly engaging and compelling, Louise's writing is sharp and astute, wise to the emotions built through a mother-daughter relationship. *How To Be Brave* is a truly unforgettable novel. An extraordinary debut – emotionally driven, finely written and highly compelling' Reviewed the Book

'Every so often a book will come along and will seep its way into your heart right from the very beginning. You'll instantly connect with the main protagonists and it will leave you feeling completely overwhelmed by how much it has affected you. This was the effect that *How To Be Brave* had on me' Segnalibro

'Wow, I have just this minute finished *How to be Brave* and I am just in an emotional state trying to process and express how much I loved this book, which is definitely a contender for my Book of the Year even in September! Even if you have to beg, steal or borrow, read this book – it is truly spectacular' Louise Wykes

'Ms Beech has written an amazing story. A story of survival, of struggle, of bravery and hope. But mostly, it is a story of unconditional love, the best cure for every pain and disease ... I hope that this book won't stand alone on Ms Beech's bookshelf, there will be many more from her writing pen in future' Chick Cat Library Cat

'The writing is simply beautiful – quite effortless prose, full of emotion, totally engrossing whichever strand of the story you may be immersed in. The relationships are perfectly drawn ... It's a wonderful story about what bravery really is, the power of words and stories, full of immense sadness, but full of hope and suffused with love. I was absolutely enthralled by this book from beginning to end, with scenes that will stay in my memory for a very long time – whether it's Rose injecting her bruised flesh, Natalie and her mallet, the lead shark following Colin's lifeboat, or the simple reading of the daily prayer. Quite wonderful' Being Anne Reading

'With a hint of ghost story, mixed up with contemporary, up-to-the-minute narrative and a good dose of wartime history, *How To Be Brave* is a very special, unique and quite beautiful story. The stories are blended to perfection, the author masterfully and seamlessly knits them together resulting in a hugely satisfying, intelligent and emotional creation' Random Things through my Letterbox

'Prepare for tissues. You would never think that a story of illness merged with a story of sailors abandoned at sea would work but this does and more. Remarkable. The power of stories really can change the world' The Booktrail

'It's not enough that the story is (almost) true though. It's also beautifully, poetically written' Louise Reviews

'I adored this novel. I don't think I've cried so much over a book since reading *Charlotte's Web*, when I was about six years old! *How To Be Brave* will definitely be one of my top ten books of the year. It's a hard act to follow' Book Likes

'The writing is incredibly evocative, I felt like I was sitting alongside Rose and Natalie's relative. I could feel the boat rising and falling on the waves, taste the thick flesh of the all too rare raw fish on my thickened thirsty tongue and feel the intense heat of the sun as I lay exposed to the elements with the other crew members, as they grew weaker with each passing day' Pam Reader

'This book made me cry – for the right reasons. A triumph of love and hope over adversity, of knowing that "we don't get less scared, we just find it easier to admit it when we have been as brave as we can"' Thinking of You and Me

'*How To Be Brave* is a heartwarming and heart-wrenching story all mixed in together ... beautiful storytelling; it's amazing that this is the author's debut!' Claire Knight

'*How To Be Brave* tackles the subject of grief and hardship in such a wonderfully unique way. Each word feels magical and makes the story more captivating. Even in describing something ugly, Louise manages to use such beautiful, captivating language. For example: "One wound cut his face almost in two, like a forward slash dividing lines of poetry." This kind of writing appears throughout the book and adds to that bittersweet undercurrent that runs throughout. Louise couldn't have written a more perfect debut novel' Words Are My Craft

'I think it's impossible to encounter this story without being affected by it. I'm finding it difficult to convey how fabulous the writing is – as Louise Beech has left me, to quote her, "speechless, full of silent words" and not a few tears' Linda's Book Bag

'Stunning, penetrating' The Discerning Reader

The Mountain in My Shoe

ABOUT THE AUTHOR

Louise Beech has always been haunted by the sea, and regularly writes travel pieces for the *Hull Daily Mail*, where she was a columnist for ten years. Her short fiction has won the Glass Woman Prize, the Eric Hoffer Award for Prose, and the Aesthetica Creative Works competition, as well as shortlisting for the Bridport Prize twice and being published in a variety of UK magazines. Louise lives with her husband and children on the outskirts of Hull – the UK's 2017 City of Culture – and loves her job as a Front of House Usher at Hull Truck Theatre, where her first play was performed in 2012. She is also part of the Mums' Army on Lizzie and Carl's BBC Radio Humberside Breakfast Show. Her debut novel, *How To Be Brave*, was a number-one bestseller on Kindle in the UK and Australia, and a *Guardian* Readers' Pick for 2015. *The Mountain in My Shoe* was longlisted for Not the Booker Prize. Louise is currently writing her third book.

You can follow her on Twitter @LouiseWriter and on Facebook at www.facebook.com/louise.beech, or visit her website: www.louisebeech.co.uk.

The Mountain in My Shoe

Louise Beech

ORENDA
BOOKS

Orenda Books
16 Carson Road
West Dulwich
London SE21 8HU
www.orendabooks.co.uk

First published in the UK in 2016 by Orenda Books

A catalogue record for this book is available from the British Library.

ISBN 978-1-910633-39-7

Typeset in Garamond by MacGuru Ltd
Printed and bound by CPI Group (UK) Ltd, Croydon CR0 4YY

SALES & DISTRIBUTION

In the UK and elsewhere in Europe:
Turnaround Publisher Services
Unit 3, Olympia Trading Estate
Coburg Road,
Wood Green
London
N22 6TZ
www.turnaround-uk.com

In the USA and Canada:
Trafalgar Square Publishing
Independent Publishers Group
814 North Franklin Street
Chicago, IL 60610
USA
www.ipgbook.com

In Australia and New Zealand:
Affirm Press
28 Thistlethwaite Street
South Melbourne VIC 3205
Australia
www.affirmpress.com.au

For details of other territories, please contact *info@orendabooks.co.uk*

This book is dedicated to my son Conor. Though the character in the story is not you – and not supposed to be you – aspects of you did inspire him, especially you as a child. So I love him the way I do you, and named him after you.

Also to Suzanne, the young girl I befriended while she went through the care system. She came out a survivor, and has a permanent place in my life and heart.

For the late Muhammad Ali.

And Baby P.

'It isn't the mountains ahead to climb that wear you out; it's the pebble in your shoe.'

Muhammad Ali

1

The Book

10th December 2001

This book is a gift. That's what it is. A gift because it will one day be your memory. It will soon contain your history. Your pictures. Your life. You. Isn't it a lovely colour? Softest yellow. Neutral some might say, but I like to think of it as the colour of hope. And I'm hopeful, gosh I am. I hope this book is short because that's the best kind.

But now – where to begin?

Bernadette

The book is missing.

A black gap parts the row of paperbacks, like a breath between thoughts. Bernadette puts two fingers in the space, just to make sure. Only emptiness; no book, and no understanding how it can have vanished when it was there the last time she looked.

The book is a secret. Long ago Bernadette realised that the only way to keep it that way was to put it on a bookshelf. Just as a child tries to blend in with the crowd to escape a school bully, a book spine with no distinct marks will disappear when placed with more colourful ones.

So Bernadette knows absolutely that she put the book in its spot between *Jane Eyre* and *Wuthering Heights* three days ago, as she has done for the last five years. She peers into the black space and whispers, 'Not there', as though the words will make it reappear.

She was waiting by the window when she realised she'd forgotten to pack it; when it occurred to her that the first thing she should have remembered was the last. Bernadette viewed the community of moisture-loving ferns and mosses in the garden below – as she does most nights – and the evergreen leaves had whispered, *the book, the book*. At the front of the garden, the trees appear to protect the house from the world – or do they protect the world from the house? Bernadette is never sure. She often thinks how sad it is that they must die to become the paperbacks she prefers over electronic reading, and vows then to change her reading habits; but she never does.

She waits in the window every night for her husband, Richard, to return from work. He always arrives at six. He is never late or early; she never needs to reheat his meal or change the time she prepares it. She never has to cover cooling vegetables with an upturned plate or call and ask where he is.

Where on earth is the book?

The thought pulls Bernadette back into the moment. Books don't get up and jump off shelves; they don't go into the sunset seeking adventure, with a holdall and passport. It has to be somewhere. It *has* to be. If she doesn't find it she can't leave.

Push away the anxiety and think calm solutions; this is what Bernadette's mum always says.

Maybe she left it somewhere else. Perhaps the panic of preparing to pack for the first time in ten years had her putting things in the wrong place – a toothbrush in the fridge, milk in the fireplace, her book in the laundry bin. So, just to make sure she hasn't misplaced it, Bernadette decides to explore the flat.

She starts at the main door. The room closest to it has a fireplace dominating the right wall and this is where she and Richard sleep side by side, him facing the door, her facing the wall his back becomes. Often the distant foghorn sounds on the River Humber, warning of danger in the night. It's never been replaced by an electronic system and it has Bernadette imagining she's slipped into some long-gone time when people used candles to walk up the house's wide stairs. Then she's happy Richard is at her side; the anxiety his presence often brings is cancelled by her gladness at sharing the vast space of the flat with another person.

Their bedroom enjoys late light from its west-facing window. Richard let Bernadette decorate how she wanted when they moved in and she painted the walls burnt orange to enhance the invading rays.

If she left the book in here it can only be on the bed. Sometimes, when she's absolutely sure Richard won't be home, she lies there and reads it. But never has she *left* it there – and she hasn't now. It isn't by the bed or under it or in the bedside table. Searching for it is like when you pretend to show a child there aren't any monsters in the wardrobe – Bernadette half knows the book won't be there but she checks anyway.

She goes into the wide corridor of their purpose-built flat. It starts at the main door, ends at the kitchen and tiny bathroom, and looks into three high-ceilinged rooms that their things and her constant attention don't fill or warm. Last winter's coldness drove the remaining residents away. Being on a river means the air is damp and the rooms difficult to heat. Low rent attracts people initially. It appealed to Richard. He hates wasting money on unnecessary luxury. It had a roof and walls and doors; it was enough.

Now – with everyone gone – the Victorian mansion called Tower Rise is just theirs. The four other flats are vacant. Their apartment beneath the left tower, with rotting bathroom floorboards and sash windows that rattle when it rains, gives the only light in the building. Cut off from the city and choked dual carriageway by trees and a sloped lawn, soon it will just be Richard's home.

Tonight Bernadette is leaving.

If she closes her eyes she can picture him parking the car perfectly parallel to the grass and walking without haste into the house. She can see his fine hair bouncing at the slightest movement. Physically Richard is the opposite to his personality; it's as if he's wearing the wrong coat. All softness and slowness, pale skin and grey irises and silky hair. With her eyes still shut Bernadette sees him enter the lounge and fold his jacket and put it on the sofa and kiss her cheek without touching it. She imagines her planned words, her bold, foolish, definite words – *I'm leaving*.

But not without the book.

Bernadette has always been fearful of Richard discovering the one thing she has carefully kept from him for five years. When she got it she knew she would have to hide it from him. Coming home with it that first time on the bus, she wondered how. With its weight numbing her lap, she had noticed a young girl across the aisle; a teen with a brash, don't-mess-with-me air. A girl in a yellow vest with clear plastic straps designed to support invisibly and make the top look strapless, her breasts pert without help.

It occurred to Bernadette that when you half hide something you draw more attention to it. The straps stood out more than the girl's pearly eye shadow. *The book must go where all books go*, Bernadette thought. And so when she got home, that was where it went.

Now she continues her game of prove-the-monster-isn't-there and looks for it in the second room. She hasn't been in here for perhaps a month, so what's the point? It's empty. The book has never been here. This room she had once hoped would be a nursery and had painted an optimistic daffodil yellow. But children never came. Richard said they had each other. He said that was all they needed.

Bernadette closes the door.

Richard decided the third room should be the lounge. A fraction smaller than the others, it's easier to heat and the two alcoves are home to his computer desk and Bernadette's bookshelf. She put their table and chairs by the window so she could look out when they ate. It overlooks the weed-clogged lawn and the gravel drive that leads through arched trees to the river. Over the years, during their evening meal, she has often stared down at the stone cherub collecting water in its grey, cupped hands. A wing broke off years ago and a crack cuts its face in two. Birds gather to drink, their marks staining the grey.

'We'll tear that down,' Richard said when they moved in.

But they never did.

Instead Bernadette filled the lounge with plants in brick-coloured pots, gold candles, dried flowers, homemade cushions, and books. In the window she has read *Anna Karenina,* and true accounts of survival at sea and travelogues that took her to Brazil and India and Russia.

Still it feels somehow like Richard's flat. Her choices of wall colour and curtain fabric make little difference because even when he's not here his presence surrounds her, like when wind rushes down the chimneys sending black dust into rooms and the trees sway together like an army united against some invisible enemy.

Bernadette looks in the desk and under the sofa and through Richard's magazines. She searches behind the bin and through the cabinet drawers and on the wall shelves. There's a damp patch near them that no amount of scrubbing will erase. She once said it looked like a streak of blood at a murder scene. Richard shook his head; he always tells her she sees too much in things. She wonders if he will say it tonight when he gets home and finds out she's leaving. The thought chills her. She's not brave or brash and doesn't have a don't-mess-with-me air. She would never wear see-through straps or pearly eye shadow.

It has taken everything for her to bring herself to leave.

What if Richard doesn't let her? What if he shuts the door and won't let her out? What if he talks about locking her away in the dark again? Puts a finger on her lips to shush her? Will he cry when she says she's going? Will he be sorry? Will he just be angry she ruined his evening?

Bernadette goes back to the bookshelf. She spent a long time this afternoon deciding whether she could carry her many beloved hardbacks and paperbacks out of the door, concluding sadly they were too heavy. She is surprised she didn't remember to pack the one book that matters most. She can leave the others with Richard, wordy reminders that she once existed – but not the yellow one.

Perhaps if she closes her eyes and opens them again it will appear by magic, like a Christmas gift sneaked into a child's room while she sleeps. But no, the gap between *Jane Eyre* and *Wuthering Heights* seems bigger now. She puts fingers between them to check again.

How long has it been gone?

When did she last definitely see it there?

Is it possible she didn't slide it into its usual spot at all?

3

The Book

Begin at the start is what they say. Begin at the birth is what we're supposed to do. And I will. But first, welcome to your book.

I'm trying to write as neatly as I can because I'm the first, and also so you'll be able to read my handwriting – it's just terrible. Everyone tells me I should have been a doctor (they're renowned for their bad writing, you see), but I'm not clever enough to cure people and I'd rather help them in other ways.

I've only written in one or two of these books so forgive me if I get it wrong. I believe the idea for them started in the USA. Whoever thought it up was just great. I've seen adults read the words in pages like these, lost for hours, smiling and crying and finally somehow changed. That's what these books do – give a chronological account; although I'm already meandering, aren't I? They're supposed to help you understand the why and the where and the how and the who – that's how I like to put it.

Gosh, I should introduce myself, shouldn't I?

4

Bernadette

Outside, the late-September sun drops behind the trees. The clock reaches six-fifteen. Richard is late. Bernadette frowns at the clock like it might have rushed ahead. He has never been late, not in ten years. No, that's wrong. There *was* one time – but she won't think about it now.

He's so predictable in his punctuality that she can prepare a meal so he walks through the door and is greeted with the aroma of his favourite beef and herb stew at just the right temperature. She can abandon what she's doing at five-thirty, cover the table with a white cloth and place on top a napkin folded twice, polished silver knife and fork, and glass of chilled water.

Tonight there is no food. Instead of peeling potatoes and preheating the oven, she packed clothes, toiletries and money into two suitcases she has never used. She cleaned the kitchen and bathroom, and changed the bedding, feeling it wasn't fair to leave the place dirty. Really she was trying to keep busy. Block the thoughts. The *why don't you just stay*? The *it would be much easier*. The *he isn't going to just say, yes, fine, off you go, Bernadette*.

Sometimes – mid chopping onions or polishing the mantelpiece – Bernadette stops and pauses to wonder what she feels exactly. Sad? Happy? Tired? Scared? Angry? Have her emotions run off like a bored husband?

When she and Richard first wed she could list every single emotion. There was pride that this strong, sweetly succinct man wanted to be with her. Excitement when he came home after work. Confidence that giving up a career to be a wife and eventual mother would reward Bernadette as much as it had *her* mother.

Six-nineteen now. Should she call Richard's work phone? No, she'll have to pretend everything is normal and isn't sure she can. Anyway, the rare times she has called it she got his answering service, an accentless woman who says he's busy. All she needs to know now is that he's coming home; it doesn't matter what the delay is, what has messed up his schedule.

Bernadette doesn't have a mobile phone. What would be the point? Who would call it? She's rarely anywhere but Tower Rise and there aren't many friends who might call to arrange a coffee, no colleagues to discuss work. So Richard can't leave a message explaining his curious lateness.

Just find the book, she thinks, *and you're ready to leave when he turns up.*

Maybe she *did* pack it after all. Maybe she did it without thinking, just took it from the shelf and walked in a daze to the case. Of course – that's where it is. She goes to the luggage by the door and rummages, imagining she'll see the buttery cover, neutral like a blanket for a baby not yet born. But it's not there. Now an emotion: confusion. And another: fear.

The telephone rings. As though startled, birds flee the treetops in a flap of wings and a shrill of squawks. If it's Richard with his reasons then she doesn't want to talk. Let the machine answer, though this will infuriate him. At least she'll know he's on his way.

Bernadette's own soft voice fills the room – *We're sorry we can't take your call but if you leave a message we'll ring as soon as we return*. We. She always speaks in we; not me or I.

It isn't Richard – it's Anne. Anne knows not to call when Richard is there because he doesn't know about their situation, so for her to ring after six means it must be urgent. Bernadette picks up the receiver.

'He didn't come home,' says Anne, tearful.

For a moment Bernadette wonders how she knows. It isn't possible. Anne has never met Richard. The women have become close recently and despite not being the most forthcoming person, Bernadette opened up once about her marriage worries. She didn't share any spe-cifics but admitted she felt isolated at Tower Rise. It was good to share with someone – a someone completely separate.

'Is he there with you?' asks Anne.

And now Bernadette realises she doesn't mean Richard.

She's talking about Conor.

Conor is missing too? Everything is missing. How is it possible? Perhaps they are all in the most obvious place, like books in a library. But where would that be? If everyone were where they're supposed to be, Richard would be eating his beef and reading the paper, Conor would be with Anne, Anne wouldn't be on the end of the telephone, and Bernadette would be measuring out Richard's ice cream so it has a few minutes to melt slightly.

And the book would be in its designated two-inch slot on the shelf.

'You're the first one I've called,' says Anne.

Bernadette takes the phone to the bookshelf and pulls everything off to make sure the no-distinctive-markings book isn't there, just off centre. Perhaps *she* is off centre. Perhaps this is a dream, one of those she often has where she's trying to do a jigsaw and every time she adds a piece the picture changes. What was it Conor said last time, about the centre of the universe being everywhere?

The book isn't there and Bernadette sinks to the floor. She touches the titles she has read over the years to avoid thinking about her own, about the name she once had, the name Richard then gave her, one she might soon discard. She loved signing her new marital name, once upon a time; the S and W permitted her to swirl and curl the pen with flourish. Richard had smiled at the pages and pages of practice signa-tures, asking, was she expecting to be famous?

'Is he there with you?' repeats Anne, more urgently.

'No,' says Bernadette, and Anne's sobs confirm that she knew this would be the case. 'What do you mean he didn't come home?'

Conor is part of the reason Bernadette has finally decided to leave a marriage she has done everything to nourish for a decade. Now he's missing too. Richard and the book barely matter anymore.

'You're stronger than you think,' Anne said, the time Bernadette opened up. They were in Anne's kitchen; it was a few months ago but it feels like a lifetime now. They drank tea and waited for Conor, and Bernadette admitted she didn't know if she loved her husband anymore. Said she wasn't even sure what love was, but that the thought of anything or anyone else was alien.

I'm not strong, Bernadette thinks now.

That she's planning to leave her marriage after ten years might make her so. Memoirs about men surviving months adrift at sea define them as strong. People who cope with losing children are definitely strong. But she is just a woman walking away from a man who isn't what she hoped for. A year ago if anyone had said she'd do it, she'd have said never. A year ago during a phone call home, Bernadette's mother had asked how things were and she paused a moment, didn't answer with her customary, 'Yes, everything's good.'

Instead she asked her mum, 'What if everything *isn't* good?'

Silence on the other end of the line, and then her mum said, 'Well, you make the best of it, don't you? No marriage is perfect and too many people give up these days. My friend Jean from aqua aerobics just left her husband Jim after twenty-five years. She was bored and he'd had a fling. But you work at it, you talk, you do what it takes.'

A year ago Bernadette would have done what it took. Now her belongings are packed in two bags and the flat is as clean as a show home. But without the book or Richard and with Conor now gone, she's trapped in the house where no one else lives. She can't play her game of prove-the-monster-isn't-there anymore.

'He didn't turn up,' says Anne now. 'And you know that isn't like him.'

Bernadette pictures Conor last Saturday, closing the door as she departed, the autumn sun bouncing off the glass as though to cut them in two. She had grit in her shoes from the foreshore and he said that when she took them off at home she'd make a mess 'all over the joint' and remember him. He said other words she can't think of now or she'll cry; ones about mountains and pebbles and Muhammad Ali.

No, Bernadette is not strong. *But he is*.

'Can you come?' asks Anne. 'If anyone knows Conor, you do.'

The words come out despite Bernadette's fears. 'Yes, of course.'

She is afraid that if she opens the front door to leave, all the monsters will jump out.

But she's going to have to.

5

The Book

So my name is Jim Rogers and I'm your social worker. You might have other social workers through your life. (It all depends how things turn out.) No one can know what will happen when a baby is born in circumstances like yours. By the time you read this you'll probably know what a social worker is, but I'll write it in here anyway.

Very simply, social work is about people. Social workers help children and families who are having difficulties. It can be any kind of difficulty – illness, death, emotional problems, circumstances, or other people. We try to do what's best for all concerned. (Sadly this doesn't always work.) Occasionally families have to be split up. Usually it's for a short time but sometimes it can be for much longer. And sadly there are times when it is for always.

I helped decide what was best for you. You were made what is called the subject of a care order, where the local authority has responsibility for you. (I have printed out some information about that and will stick it in your book after this.) We had to decide quickly what would happen and where you would go.

Your mum, Frances, was ill when you were born. She had been ill for a long time. She has an illness that is hard to explain because it's her head that is poorly not her body. It's much harder to fix heads. (Sometimes it's impossible – even for the best doctors.)

Your mum agreed to let you go – not because she doesn't love you but because she does. That's what I think, anyway. It often makes it easier for us to help if this happens. She had to let your older brother Sam go too last year. A lovely family took him in and he's still living there.

We felt you would also be better off living with another family until your mum is well. She couldn't hold or dress you when you were born because she was too sad. She couldn't even take you home, even for a short while, so she let someone else take you.

We usually try and put a child with a relative or family friend if we can but in your case it wasn't possible. You have an Uncle Andrew who wanted to have you, but he has some complicated problems that meant he wasn't able to.

The next option was short-term care while your mum got help.

Gosh, I must tell you, while I think of it, that she chose your name. I thought you'd like to know that, because names are important aren't they? Your name means dog lover. It's nice because your mum said she named you after someone special. I don't know who it is but I doubt there can be any better name than that.

I can't tell you anything about your father, sadly. I don't even know his name. For whatever reason, your mum hasn't told us who he is. (Maybe she'll share it with you one day herself. Or maybe later in this book we'll be able to tell you.) I realise it is hard having only half of the picture, and I'm sorry about that.

So for now you're staying with a lovely couple called Maureen and Michael. They have looked after lots of babies, sometimes more than one at a time. They have a bedroom where there are four cots, just in case. At the moment two are being used. You sleep in one and a baby called Cheryl Rae sleeps in another.

Maureen and Michael keep pictures of every baby they've looked after in a scrapbook. You are the newest. I gave them the first picture of you after you were born. (I've also stuck a copy of it at the bottom of this page.)

I was supposed to start with your birth, wasn't I? Oh well, here goes now. There were no blue or pink blankets on the ward the day you were born so you're wrapped in lemon in this photo. You were the only splash of yellow next to rows of pink and blue. So we knew who you were right away.

I imagine you want to know what kind of baby you were, don't you?

Well, the nurse said you were born last thing at night and it had been stormy but then it got very quiet when you arrived. You took so long to cry that the staff thought you were very happy to arrive in the world but then you screamed so loudly they thought you had changed your mind. You were actually due on Bonfire Night but came five days late. But there were still a few fireworks going off somewhere far away.

There's a copy of your birth certificate over the page so you can see your birthdate, which of course you'll already know when you read this. But also on there is the name of the hospital you were born in, when and where you were registered, and your mum's full name.

Your hair was dark and spiky (I stuck some of it in here too, at the top) and your eyes were blue. Most babies have blue eyes at the start. Then, after about six weeks, they can change to brown or green, and the baby's hair can fall out too. So we will see how you look in a few more months.

Maureen and Michael say you're always hungry and you sleep well. You like it best when they put your pram under the trees at the end of the garden. The wind in the leaves seems to soothe you.

You're a good baby, they say. No bother, they say.

They write a small three-page Baby Book for each baby they have. They're going to photocopy some of yours and I will stick it on another page. So everyone is writing about you.

I'll be checking on you a lot in these first few months. I'll visit every week and write all sorts of dull but necessary reports. We have to constantly monitor your life and investigate anything that needs checking and then present whatever we find to the courts. This could last until you're eighteen, or it might end when your mum is well and you're living with her again. (We'll visit her too.)

But this entry in your book is the most important thing I'll have written this week – much more interesting and special than my other reports.

So, gosh, I suppose it doesn't really matter what the handwriting is like (as long as you can read it!) or if any of us spell things wrong. It just matters that you have a little piece of your history. When other kids have forgotten their childhoods or been told by their parents that they can't quite recall those early days you will have it here in black and white, in this book.

And I'm proud to be the first to write in it.

Jim Rogers

6

Bernadette

Bernadette opens the apartment door to leave Tower Rise. Despite repaints, its wood peels as though sunburnt. Fingers on the handle, she realises how similar this feels to when she first entered the place with Richard ten years ago. Her right hand forces the knob roughly anticlockwise – the only way to free the latch – and the other hand dangles by her thigh with two fingers crossed.

What is Bernadette hoping for?

What did she hope for back then?

Richard didn't follow the tradition of lifting her over the threshold; he carried their luggage instead, letting her be the first to enter their new home. They arrived even before the furniture and Bernadette opened the doors to every room, her icy breath the only thing that filled them. She sniffed the air the way she used to when she was a child and she went somewhere new.

Richard dumped the bags in the corridor, grumbled about the lateness and inefficiency of the removal company, and set about calling them. Bernadette knew he'd soon have the place full of the things family had donated, along with his belongings and her books. She knew he'd make it right; he had so far. So she rubbed her goose-pimpled arms and listened to her new husband's soft voice telling someone he hadn't expected not even to have a kettle yet, and she knew she'd soon be warm, because he'd see to that too.

Back then she had expected Richard would always find the kettle; now she knows it's up to her to find it.

The door hinge squeaks. Bernadette's fingers are still crossed. A draught from the hall below tickles her ankles. Conor is missing and that's the main concern. Anne needs her too. For now she can put aside Richard's rare tardiness and the book's disappearance, but the thought of Conor not being where he should be is too much. She can either stay here – imprisoned by her old routine – or she can go and help Anne.

Bernadette glances back at her two bags by the lounge door, just like their luggage ten years ago. She'll return for them. This isn't the departure she planned yesterday. How can you leave a man who isn't there? Abandon a ghost that follows wherever you go?

Bernadette closes the door.

Dark stairs lead down to a large hall that she knows was once grand; a local history book she read described polished tiles and ornate double doors, and black-and-white photographs showed fresh flowers on a glass table and family paintings the size of windows. Now an economy bulb barely lights the sparse, dusty area; it flickers like a lighthouse warning boats about rocks.

Outside the taxi Bernadette called has arrived. Bob Fracklehurst – the driver who often takes her to meet Conor – finishes a cigarette and stubs it out in a takeaway coffee cup. He never throws his tab end on her drive, yet she's seen him do it in other places.

It's twilight now. The gravel crunches underfoot like spilt crisps. The trees are a black mass, in which Bernadette imagines ghosts and monsters. She gets into the passenger seat, enjoying the blast of warm air-conditioning. Taxis have always taken her to places where more than two buses would otherwise be required. Richard never saw the point in her learning to drive and she agreed that it made no sense; it was costly, and they'd only ever be able to afford one car anyway. While waiting for the children that never arrived Bernadette simply stayed at home, never using her Health and Social Care Diploma to help other families, never travelling to St Petersburg as she'd dreamed of since the age of six, never learning to swim.

'Usual place?' asks Bob.

'Usual place,' she says.

But tonight it isn't usual at all.

Having used Top Taxis for five years Bernadette has met most of their drivers. Some she talks to a little, in her shy and agreeable way – most she doesn't. A driver called Graham is kind and embarrassed about his size and asks thoughtful questions rather than talking over her few words with opinionated ones. Bob lets her daydream. He hums softly and doesn't badger her with demands for weather talk or a discussion of the local news, chatting only if she begins a conversation.

Then, between, for a smoker, curiously melodic hums, he occasionally enquires about Tower Rise's history and her husband's job and her love of reading. Bernadette always relaxes because he reminds her of her father, a gentle man who never raises his voice or hand.

'This isn't your normal time,' Bob says now, and after a thought, 'or day.'

No, it isn't. None of this is normal.

Since getting married Bernadette has never been alone in a taxi after six. She has never had anywhere to go at that time that didn't involve Richard. But for the last five years – two Saturdays a month – she has gone in one from the door of Tower Rise to meet Conor. Saturday is his convenient day and fortunately Richard works six days as a computer engineer so Bernadette can sneak out. The word sneak makes her feel guilty; she does not sneak, she escapes. Just for a few hours.

'Bob,' says Bernadette. And then she can't think of anything.

'Everything okay?' he asks her.

'Not really,' she admits.

'Shall I sing and let you be?'

'I really don't know,' says Bernadette.

'Shall we go?'

Yes, they should. Every minute that passes is one more that Conor might be in some sort of trouble. And what if Richard turns up now? She won't be able to leave. He'll demand to know what's going on and all her planned words for why she's going have changed now. Now there are only three – *Conor is missing* – and Richard doesn't know about him.

'Please, yes,' Bernadette says, and the car pulls away.

They drive under an umbrella of trees, where leaves and bark are gloomy faces watching them escape. What if Richard's headlights now illuminate the evening? Will she tell Bob to put his foot down? Will she open the window and tell Richard she'll explain everything later? What would infuriate him more – her leaving without telling him, or her telling him she's leaving?

She won't wait and find out.

7

The Book

28th November 2002

My name is Maureen and I've been looking after you for a full year.

Jim Rogers said I could write a letter that you'll one day be able to read and I was so very pleased because I never get to talk to any of the babies after they are gone. Not all our babies have a book like yours because most are going back to live with their mummies. Their mummies just need a break and yours did too, but she still does and so you'll go and live with a foster carer now.

I saw the first part of your care plan and it made me so very sad. There were different options for your future and just one had to be ticked. Someone had ticked the box that said Eventual Return to Birth Family (Within Unspecified Months). At least it wasn't the other box, Permanent Placement with Foster Carer until Eighteen.

So you may go and live with your mummy again in the future.

I really do hope so.

We were very sad when you had to leave us, but you see we only take babies up to a year old. Sometimes I think I'm too emotional to keep saying goodbye to babies but I love it so much when they arrive. Every time one of you leaves we wish we could have you for longer. I try and imagine how you'll turn out. They have those really clever computers nowadays that can age you, like when kids go missing and they need to show what they might look like when they're older. I wish we could do that with all the photos of our babies. All we have is a book of pictures of them when they're small.

I think you will be a very curious child. By that I mean I think you'll be into everything. I don't mean you'll be odd and weird! Though maybe you'll be that too in a so very unique way.

You were walking at ten months, which is early, and we just couldn't keep up! You got into the plants and the washing machine and even into the street a few times. My neighbour Charmaine brought you back one day when you'd got out the cat flap, so we have to keep it locked now. I could never turn my back for a minute.

But your smile lit up the house. I'll so miss that toothy grin and how you ran away every time I tried to catch you. You were rough with the other babies sometimes. I don't think you meant to be. You were just hugging them. Like you were grabbing onto them so they couldn't get away.

I've sent your favourite dungarees with you. I loved you in those. They were the only clothes sturdy enough to last for all your adventures! And I also sent the stuffed black cat you like so much. It came with a baby called Ben. He never seemed bothered about it, but you were. You walked around with its nose clamped between your teeth!

You're so very brave. You didn't even cry when they took you from us, but I did. I always cry a bit when the babies go but I try and wait until they've left. I cried as you stared out of the car window and your blue eyes seemed to forgive me. As if you knew I'd have kept you in a flash if I could. I would. God I would. But it doesn't work like that.

I hope you're happy wherever you are. I hope they treat you well and warm your milk to room temperature. It upsets you when it's too cold. I hope Jim passes all that stuff on to whoever has you and I hope he tells them loud, sudden noises scare you and that you like that TV advert for home insurance with the singing phone.

I miss you so very much already.

I'll never wash your gooey red handprint off my wall.

Love
Maureen xxx

PS – Here's a page I've copied from the Baby Book we did for you. The rest got ruined, I'm afraid, when milk got spilt on it.

MY BABY – A record of your baby's milestones

Early Developments

Recognises mother at – Not applicable

Recognises father at – Not applicable

Turns head to one side – Birth

Eyes follow moving object – 3 weeks

First smile – 5 weeks

Laughs out loud – 6 weeks

Plays with hands – 10 weeks

Sleeps all night – 3 months

Eats solid food – 4 months

Notices strangers – 2 months

Sits unsupported – 6 months

Crawls – 7 months (like lightning!)

Stands unsupported – 9 months

Walks at – 10 months

Runs at – 11 months

First word – 12 months – said Mo for Maureen and B for Bye.

8

Bernadette

Bernadette glances back at Tower Rise as though she might never see it again, but her view is denied. No residents, so no lights. The building is a shadow. Not like her first sight of it a decade ago when snow brightened every windowsill, tile and archway. An urgent need for work was disguised by December's white. Christmas lights and tinsel eventually cheered its melancholy corners, until spring revealed the truth – that nothing could save the long-unloved house.

When their furniture finally arrived that first day, and Bernadette and Richard put desks into alcoves and beds into corners, he suggested she bring it to life with her keen eye for colour and charming way of pairing things. She loved his faith in her; yes, she would bring Tower Rise to life for them. She would furnish it with items that hid the damp and enhanced the high ceilings and tall windows.

And one day she would bring it to life the way she really wanted to; with a child.

'Might take longer,' says Bob.

'Sorry – longer?' Bernadette thinks she must have missed a previous conversation.

'Longer to get to east Hull. With rush-hour traffic and all.'

Of course – they have only ever travelled when it's quiet. Conor and Anne live eight miles away. It usually takes twenty minutes to get across town. The first two miles are along the river. Lights twinkle on the opposite shore as though things are so much better there. Bernadette imagines this every time. What lies over the water? What do people in the little villages that line those banks do?

'I'm concerned about you,' says Bob, and it touches her. 'I don't mean to intrude but we've known each other, how long now? A few years. I get a feel for people. You do in this business, with regulars. Barbara in the office said you sounded upset when you called. Not like yourself.'

'I'm okay,' says Bernadette. 'I will be.' She pauses. 'Do you think coincidence is more than mere chance?'

The day's strange occurrences feel linked; two people and one book missing, within hours. She supposes how she met Richard was such a twist of fate, as the tired cliché goes.

Bob chuckles. 'I don't know, but my wife would have plenty to say about it. She always says – what is it now – oh, yes: coincidence is the universe's way of giving you clues that you're on the right track. Quite spiritual is my Trish.'

Clues. Did Bernadette miss any? Were there signs that Richard wouldn't come home? She thinks back to that morning. It was just like any other; he couldn't have guessed from her actions that she planned to leave. If he *was* aware he didn't show it as he went about his morning ritual – shower, shave, shirt.

While he was in the half-tiled corner bathroom, added to the flat as an afterthought, Bernadette ironed his white shirt and considered leaving while he was at work. She paused with the iron mid-air as she thought of it. She could write a note and simply go. Leave it on the table where he'd look for his dinner. Steal down the stairs like a refugee, get Bob Fracklehurst to drop her at the train station. Richard would come home and have to vent his frustration at an empty room as she travelled out of his life for good.

Common sense urged her to do the easier thing. But what Conor had said the previous Saturday still rang in her head: it meant she had to tell her husband the truth. Didn't Richard deserve to hear why she couldn't stay any longer? Bernadette continued ironing. She would leave with honesty.

Richard had walked back into the living room then, bare-chested and cleanly shaven. 'Is my shirt ready?'

She studied him, wondering if she would forget him in such detail. No desire stirred now, despite his good skin and a chest covered in golden hair. The physique that once excited her now left her cold; the opaque eyes that only coloured in rage were dim. He was handsome and would probably age well. But she wouldn't be there to see it. The thought was odd. Picturing a future without him was difficult, if only because she'd always expected him to be there. If Bernadette thought of how he used to bring home a single flower in their early days, she could remember how it felt. How she warmed.

Now, nothing.

Richard was looking at her. 'Can I have my shirt then?'

'Yes.'

She stood the iron upright and handed him the crisp garment. He liked it done well, the pleats ironed with precision, the collar stiff. Not displeased, he fastened it before the mirror. He smoothed down his hair in the way she knew he would. Despite the softness of the strands, there was a part that always refused to flatten and today was the same. He wet and combed it in vain.

'Here, let me,' she said.

Grunting, he did. She knew he was in an obliging mood as she applied mousse to the rebellious strands and made them respond to her wishes.

'How do you do it?' he demanded, talkative for once.

Don't be nice, she thought. *Don't remind me of the man you can be – just sometimes – because I've fallen out of love with the one you mostly are.*

'I can never manage. A woman's touch, I suppose.' He went to the computer desk and gathered his things. 'I'll be on time tonight,' he said, unnecessarily.

Was that a clue? Did he state the obvious? In drawing attention to his usual prompt homecoming was he trying to deceive, like a secret book among the others?

'What will you do today?' he asked.

Bernadette paused while folding the ironing board. Did he know her intention? He never asked what she did all day.

Then she saw him packing his laptop without a glance her way and knew he hadn't expected an answer – he was merely making conversation, was not genuinely interested. She didn't suppose it mattered much to him what she did all day, as long as she was here to greet him on his return. At the start of their marriage she'd done it because she wanted to. Now she did it because it was easier.

Today I will be leaving you, she thought as she watched him search for some elusive item in a drawer. *Today I'll wander this flat for the last time, counting the minutes until you come home, and I tell you that I don't feel anything anymore. Today I'm going to pack the few things I brought into this marriage. I'm going to wash the pots and do the cleaning and the clothes. I'm going—*

'See you this evening,' Richard broke into her thoughts.

When he paused before walking to the door and looked into her eyes in a curiously sad way she thought for a strange second he would kiss her mouth. He hasn't kissed her like a lover for a long time. But he turned and left, his sweet odour lingering on the air afterwards. Relieved, she watched him open the door with hands that could be as cruel as they were graceful. The clink concluding his exit was the last thing to mark that he'd ever been there. It echoed inside her head for some time. She stood with the ironing board at her side for ten minutes.

So what were the clues? His good mood? Letting her tame his hair? The almost kiss? He thought of kissing her, she's sure. He studied her longer than usual. Why? And where the hell *is* he tonight?

'I don't know if I believe in it though,' says Bob.

'In what?' Bernadette jumps.

'The universe and all that. Signs.'

They are in the city centre now. Late-night shopping has the pavements still busy. Some stores are already advertising Christmas bargains. It's not even been Hull Fair yet – the annual travelling fairground that visits the city for a week in October – but already displays of Santa and elves warn shoppers of their imminence. The world seems to want to get everywhere faster.

'Is it trouble at home?' Bob asks. 'Tell me if I'm being nosy. Tell me to bugger off. I'll hum and you can daydream.'

He never asks much about her marriage. He knows how long they've been together and he said once that he thought he knew Richard, asked was he Richard Shaw from Simpletek Solutions? Bernadette said yes. Bob said he'd built a computer system for the taxi firm years ago. Good system – never let them down. He'd left his card and a few of the lads had used him again, for home computers and such. Bob said he was a bit of a brusque so-and-so but who cares if the work is good?

'I'm leaving him,' says Bernadette suddenly. The words jump out like they're escaping a burning house. She regrets the statement and is glad she said it at the same time.

'Tonight?' asks Bob kindly. 'Without anything?'

'I had bags ready. But something happened. It's complicated.'

'Did he hurt you?'

'Oh no,' says Bernadette. 'Not tonight. I mean – not in the way *you* mean. No, he's not violent. I mean, not all the time. Hardly. Only once really.'

'Once is enough,' says Bob, gently.

'I know,' says Bernadette. 'But that isn't...'

'My daughter had a chap once,' says Bob. 'He hit her a few times – it was *her* fault, she said. She antagonised him, she said. But there's never an excuse.' Bob pauses. 'Sorry. Perhaps I shouldn't go on. Are you okay?'

Bernadette nods.

'I only saw him last week,' says Bob.

'You did?' This surprises Bernadette. 'Richard?'

'Saturday it was. Did a bit of a guvvy job for me. My lad's laptop was stuck on this stupid screen. Clicked and clicked but nowt happened. Anyway I called the number on the card Richard left us and he said he wasn't working and he could pop over there and then because he happened to be in the area.'

'Which area?' Bernadette is confused. Richard works on a Saturday, always has. He leaves a little later than on a weekday, just after nine-thirty, but otherwise his routine never wavers.

'Greatfield Estate,' says Bob.

This is nowhere near Richard's office. Perhaps he went at lunchtime. Perhaps he'd gone with colleagues for lunch in a different part of town than usual and so when Bob called he *was* in the area.

'Was it lunchtime?' asks Bernadette.

'No, early. I was off to football, so he came at ten-thirty. Seemed glad of the cash. Brought his sister.' Bob slows to allow a gang of kids to cross the road; they jeer and wave beer cans at him. They are only five minutes away from Anne's house now.

Richard doesn't have a sister. The city's shops and theatres and pubs have morphed into council estate houses and Boozebuster off-licences and working men's clubs. Richard doesn't have a sister.

'Are you sure?' Bernadette asks.

'About what?'

'The sister.'

Bob looks like he realises he's said something not quite right. He sucks in his lips and frowns. Then he opens the window and rummages for a cigarette. 'I'm sure that's what he said. Sorry if I've put my foot in it. He said she was staying for the weekend. I did think they looked nothing like each other. It's odd, but you look more like him than she did.'

It was a common observance. Richard said when they met that Bernadette reminded him of his mother. Most women would likely find this an insult – and Richard's mother was certainly not ideal – but Richard meant physically. He said Bernadette's coppery hair and white-unless-embarrassed skin were just like his mum's – girlish, inno-cent and fresh.

'He doesn't have a sister, does he?' says Bob softly.

Bernadette doesn't speak.

They are near Anne's street. Teens gather at the chip shop on the corner. What on earth was Richard doing with another woman? Who is she? A colleague? It's confusion not jealousy that fuels the questions.

Does this woman have something to do with his not coming home? Does Bernadette feel better or worse for this new information? Might it be easier if he loves someone else?

Smoke from Bob's cigarette snakes through the half-open car window.

'Maybe I do believe in coincidence,' he says. 'Tonight's shift is cover, I wasn't even meant to be working. Wife's not happy, says I'm never home, but I'm glad I agreed to do it. Glad I was here tonight. It's like I *should* be. Hope everything works out for you.' He pauses. 'You'd have got bloody Brad tonight if he wasn't ill.'

Bernadette smiles at Bob; Brad is a bulbous-nosed ex-drinker who swears at everyone on the road and drives like he's in a tank.

They are at Anne's house. Bernadette has never seen it in darkness. The curtains are closed like sleeping eyelids, and the red and yellow and purple border flowers appear grey. Anne opens the door, her face not visible because she's backlit by the hallway lamp. Yvonne is behind her with a file. Often Conor waits in the window but of course tonight he isn't in. Bernadette has almost forgotten why she's here, but now it all comes back.

She closes her eyes and takes a breath and sees the moment she first met Richard, like edited video footage showing the important bits. It was an accident. Not the kind that injures, like a car crash or spilling boiling water on someone's body, but the kind that alters your route.

In the footage it is raining, a torrent that floods streets. She enters a tearoom called Cup and Saucer to meet a man called Richard. Reluctantly she has agreed to a blind date set up by her friend, Shannon, who reckons she's sick of Bernadette moping around and saying she's lonely. Richard is apparently an equally shy and sensitive friend of Shannon's, the perfect match for Bernadette.

The footage slows down when she sees only one person in the café, a fair-haired man who reads a paper and sips tea. It must be him; he looks gentle and ready and appeals to Bernadette's protective side. Looks like he'd let her look after him.

She dares to approach him and says, 'You must be Richard.'

He looks surprised, but says yes, he is.

She sits, bold for once, and they talk. About her recent college course and his mum and their love of this intimate café where you feel you've gone back in time.

The footage speeds up. When Richard asks why she was looking for him, how she knew him, Bernadette thinks he's being playful. Later, when she tells Shannon about how well the date went, and that they're meeting up again, her friend says, 'But Richard couldn't make it, didn't you see my message? He was ill.'

She met the wrong Richard. By some curious chance another Richard happened to be there instead. And, even more curiously, Bernadette – a shy twenty-one-year-old with little dating experience – felt brave enough to make the first move. When she married him a year later she was sure he was the right Richard.

Now she isn't sure who he loves or where he is or if she cares.

'Will you need a lift anywhere later?' Bob asks.

Bernadette opens her eyes. She doesn't know yet.

Anne comes to the gate; Yvonne lingers in the hall. It occurs to Bernadette that she doesn't even know where she'll end up tonight. She didn't even have a plan, only a vague idea of checking into a hotel until she thought about her next step. But now she has fewer clues and nothing but the clothes she's wearing and the things in her handbag. The thought is both terrifying and exciting.

Richard could be at Tower Rise now. It will be the first time he's walked in to find it empty. How will he feel? What will he think? Who is the strange woman he called his sister? Does *she* think he is the right Richard?

'I'm on until midnight if you need me,' says Bob. 'Do you want the usual receipt writing out?'

Bernadette doesn't. Again, there is nothing usual about tonight.

'I guess I'll call if I need to go anywhere else.' She gets out of the car.

'Be safe,' says Bob, and pulls away.

That's all she wants – safety, but for Conor, not herself.

Meeting him could not have been more different to meeting Richard.

9

The Book

14th February 2003

Messy handwriting alert! This is Jim Rogers again.

Gosh, I've been filling in lots of your reports and care plans so I haven't written in your book for a while. I have seen you lots though and you are doing very well in spite of the circumstances.

Since you left Maureen and Michael's home you have been staying at a children's home called Redcliffe. This is a temporary thing until a suitable foster placing can be found. We know all of this can take such a long time.

Next week you are going to stay with a lovely lady called Julia, who is a new foster carer and very keen to look after a child under ten years of age. We hope you will be with her until it is decided whether you can return to your mum. Your care plan is open (which means you might still go back to your family) and this can be good, but unfortunately it also means lots of change.

We don't include all the endless reports in these books, but sometimes I do make copies of ones I think might matter to you in the future. There are ones that give you information you might need as an adult and ones that might explain better than I could how or why something in particular has happened to you.

As I promised and didn't get around to doing (gosh, I'm forgetful sometimes!) I have printed out some more information about what we hope this book will do. I've stuck it in below.

I will see you very soon.

Jim Rogers

Lifebook – Principles and Aims

Every Looked-After Child is entitled to an accurate and chronological account of his or her early life. It should have enduring value and can be given to them when they reach adulthood, or sooner if preferable.

A Lifebook helps every child to:

Understand the background and history of their birth family.

Know where they came from and develop a sense of identity.

Understand why they are separated from their birth family, know who has cared for them and put their past into perspective.

Build self-esteem.

Express feelings.

Help any care worker understand who/what is important to the child.

The principles of the Lifebook are listed below:

The child's Lifebook belongs to them and should be readily available once they are of an age to read it.

From the time a child becomes looked after they should have a photograph of their parents and siblings and important others.

The best people to write in the Lifebook are those caring for them.

The gathering of information and writing of history needs doing throughout the child's time in care.

Overall the responsibility should be with the social worker to ensure that accurate information is gathered and that Lifebook work is undertaken. Foster carers should provide memories for children they care for, and this practice needs to be extended to children in residential care. The Lifebook of a Looked-After Child should begin at birth and continue indefinitely, whether the child is returning home or not.

10

Bernadette

Bernadette and Conor were chosen for each other. Matched like two dominoes. Something so predetermined probably shouldn't work. Years ago, before Richard, Bernadette knew a girl whose marriage was arranged by her strict parents. It was a wretched partnership. The girl was unhappy, the husband brutal and rigid in his belief that she should bend to his will. Divorce was not an option. Nothing was an option – choice didn't come into it. But whoever had joined Bernadette with Conor had startlingly perceptive judgement.

Now Anne comes out of her house like a thin shadow and for the first time in five years hugs Bernadette. She surrenders to the affection and finds she is crying. Years of buried emotions flood out. They cry together.

Then they go inside

Despite the circumstances, it's calm in Anne's house. Not the calm people describe before a storm but the calm that comes when people are doing the things they should be.

Even though September has been pleasant so far, a log fire burns in the hearth, flickering and spitting wood. Hand-crocheted blankets hang over worn sofas and pictures of children Bernadette knows are not all Anne's line the mantelpiece. A box filled with Lego and cars and *Star Wars* characters sits near the TV, and in a neat pile – as though carefully placed – are a variety of Muhammad Ali DVDs.

Bernadette has always loved how homely Anne makes her modest council house, how she caters to simple needs and so provides much more. It's a place that has housed numerous children during the last fifteen years, many of whom have gone on to find permanent homes, either with their own families or via adoption. There is no better refuge for ten-year-old Conor, who's lived everywhere; it is a respite from his travels, at least until his destination is known.

'I just don't know where he is,' says Anne.

'We'll find him,' insists Bernadette.

Yvonne, Conor's current social worker, is on the telephone. She's steadily telling whoever it is that yes, they've done all the necessary searches – they have looked in every room and cupboard and loft, in outhouses and sheds and garages, knocked on doors in the street, and called all friends and family. Hearing the list, Bernadette realises she was more thorough about looking for the book than about considering where Richard might be.

'It's the police,' Anne tells Bernadette.

They go into the kitchen, which is just as welcoming as the lounge. Mismatched mugs hang from rows of hooks and frilled nets block the view of a concrete garden, the only place Anne's touch hasn't reached. Bernadette knows why. Anne's second husband, Sean, died there seven years ago. While tending his beloved pigeons he had a huge heart attack. Anne found him, frozen like a garden statue.

She and Bernadette only see each other alternate Saturdays, their friendship a result of Conor's existence. Anne spoke of her late husband one day while they watched Conor chalking on the fence. She said that what was most cruel was how she'd had to wait so long for Sean, having been married previously to the wrong man. Since his death she has ignored the garden, not planted a flower or placed an ornament.

What if Richard is dead?

The thought comes to Bernadette like a news headline. What if death prevented his homecoming? Might the police be at the Tower Rise doors now? If they are, what can she do? Nothing. It will have to wait. Conor is just a child. She must stay here until he returns and absolutely not permit the dark thoughts about where *he* might be.

When Conor is back she will return to whatever her life might be now.

'We had to ring the police,' says Anne, her voice soft, as if too much volume will make her cry again. She fills the kettle and switches it on: tea, always the comforter.

'Of course.' Bernadette touches Anne's arm.

'Conor's just not anywhere. He left school as normal – I rang them and they said he did get into a bit of bother, messing about in lessons. But we all know that's nothing out of the ordinary. He never went to Sophie's house afterwards, like sometimes. She's been ill, off school with a nasty tummy bug. He doesn't go anywhere else, does he? He has other friends but they don't invite him around.' Anne pauses and says with effort, 'He just didn't come home.'

'What about his mum?'

'We tried Frances' house but there's no answer.' Anne stirs the tea in the pot and replaces the lid with a gentle clink. 'He wouldn't be there, would he? He doesn't know the way. He's never gone without someone. You were the first one I called after I rang the people I was supposed to – the school, Sophie's mum, Yvonne. You're the one who really loves him.'

Bernadette thinks back to that phone call – her confusion, all the missing things, her plan to leave in chaos. Now the strange calm of Anne's home infects her and she says, 'We'll find him. I know it. I promise you we will.'

Yvonne comes into the kitchen as Anne pours tea into one flowered, one blue and one checked mug.

'The police are on their way,' she tells them. Then to Bernadette, 'Have you let BFL know?'

'No, I...' Bernadette didn't think of it. It's one of the things she should do. A thing that, like making tea and calling the police and knocking on neighbours' doors, will keep her busy and stop negative thoughts. She must let the agency know one of their children is missing.

BFL is Befriend for Life, a local voluntary organisation that sets up willing, police-checked adults with children who are in care, so they can befriend and take them out occasionally. It offers respite to foster carers and home workers, but most of all it gives a vulnerable child a person who just focuses on them. People come in and out of the lives of children in care, but a BFL volunteer is a constant, meeting them regularly wherever they live. Bernadette has been such a friend to Conor for five years.

'The office is closed now,' she says. 'But I'll leave a message and they can call me here if they pick it up. Can I use the phone, Anne?'

'Use my mobile,' says Yvonne. 'We need to keep the landline free. Just in case. Anne, did Conor have a phone with him?'

'He doesn't have one,' says Anne, the regret apparent in her face. 'I was going to get him one in a couple of months – for his birthday.' She wraps her hands about the mug. 'I shouldn't have waited.'

Bernadette leaves a quick message for Carole, the team leader at BFL, and gives the phone back to Yvonne. They drink their tea in silence.

Bernadette thinks about all the times she's been there, the cups of tea she's had with Anne while Conor finishes getting ready or brings some drawing to show her before they go out. He's exceptionally good; he shades and sketches like a much older child and copies images line for line. He always wants her to take something home, but of course she can't.

Richard knows nothing about Conor, her voluntary work.

Five years ago, when Bernadette first heard of BFL and knew that befriending a child was exactly what she wanted to do, she also knew Richard well enough to imagine his response to the idea. He'd have said that it would be too much for her – especially after their recent loss – or that she belonged with him and not to a handful of unruly and needy children. Had she suggested that the God he trusted in said people should help others, it would have made no difference. Richard didn't like his God used against him.

So Bernadette trained as a volunteer in secret.

Last week Conor gave her a sketch he had done of his class and she pretended to take it to hang on her wall. But secretly she gave it to Anne to put away, hoping that one day she'd get it back and be able to display it. That day is now here. She is leaving Richard, the ghost who isn't there. Leaving the man who pretended a strange woman was his non-existent sister. Leaving her home of ten years. She'll be able to hang whatever she wants on walls soon.

'I should make more tea,' says Anne.

Bernadette asks a question that none of them want to face. 'Where the *hell* do we think he is?'

The coarse language surprises her. Richard doesn't like swearing, says it is ugly and lazy, that Bernadette is not. She didn't particularly swear when she met him, and after they married he chipped away at the remaining words, like a sculptor fashioning his latest piece. Now the words feel necessary and she feels free to say them.

'Where the hell *is* he?'

Like an answer, there is a knock on the door. Anne rushes to it, knocking her cup over in the dash. The spilt tea drips onto the kitchen lino like tears.

A voice in the hallway. Female. Not Conor.

Bernadette mops up the spillage and follows Yvonne into the lounge, where a uniformed woman is sitting on one of the sofas. She makes Bernadette feel old because she looks as though she's barely finished secondary school. Her hair is neatly swept up and pinned, but one curl escapes behind her ear. Bernadette is sure she's not aware of it.

Anne is poking the fire and it flares again, angry. Her cheeks are damp and her hands tremble.

Yvonne shakes the officer's hand. 'I'm Yvonne Jones – Conor's social worker.'

'PC French,' the policewoman says.

'I'm Bernadette Shaw – I volunteer for BFL.'

They all sit, stiff and awkward as though on a first date. Bernadette is near enough to Anne to squeeze her hand in comfort. Conor's favourite *Star Wars* character – Luke Skywalker – sits on top of all the toys as though he has climbed there.

'So Conor is ten, yes?' asks PC French.

'Yes,' says Anne. 'Is his age relevant?'

'Well, because he's younger than twelve,' says PC French,

'he's immediately classed as missing, not just absent. With an older child we do a risk assessment to see if they're absent, as in they've gone off with friends or are just late home. But the risk levels for a vulnerable child are of course much higher.'

Bernadette imagines the risk assessment for Richard, a young man in good health who – apart from one other time – has come home bang on six o'clock for the last ten years. What are the odds of him not doing so? That he has just gone off with friends or is late? That he has vanished with a strange woman?

She mustn't dwell on his absence, must concentrate on Conor. She's not sure why she can't push Richard's image away, after having been so resolutely ready to leave him.

Then Bernadette realises she is angry – angry that he ruined her moment. Had he simply come home and she'd said she was leaving, no matter what his reaction, she'd at least now be able to put it behind her enough to focus on Conor.

PC French opens a folder to write and says, 'So I just need to ask a few questions about Conor first, okay?'

Everyone nods, a Mexican wave of assents. Anne asks if anyone would like tea, but no one does. Bernadette thinks they're wasting time, time that could be spent actually looking for him, but she knows a report will help.

'How long has he been missing?' asks PC French.

Bernadette sees Anne look at the gold-edged clock; it is seven-twenty. She catches her eye and knows they're thinking the same – it's dark, it's getting late, they should be out looking.

'He didn't come home from school,' says Anne. 'Even when he pops to his best friend Sophie's he's always home by four-thirty. I called the school and they told me he'd been there, left as normal. Then I waited until five-fifteen, thinking he was just taking his time. I started ringing people after five-thirty. So he's been gone nearly three hours now.' The words *three hours* come out as though untrue, like Anne wishes to cancel them.

'Do you have any idea why?'

'Why?' Anne repeats the word like it's repulsive. 'I have no idea at all.'

'Has Conor ever gone missing before?'

'Never.' Anne thinks about it hard, shakes her head. 'Conor's lived here more or less since he started school. He was almost six when he came. I've always known where he was. He always tells me where he's going. This is *so* out of character.' Anne stands. 'Shouldn't we be out looking for him? It gets cold at night now and he's only got a thin jacket on.'

'We will, I promise,' says PC French gently. 'But we need this information to do the best job we can of locating him.'

'You're right.' Anne sits again, wringing her hands. 'I can't bear that he might be frightened somewhere.'

'Did he pack anything?'

'No, not that I can see,' says Anne.

Bernadette thinks about her luggage still waiting by the lounge door at Tower Rise, how she carefully decided what to take. What does one take when leaving forever? That Conor apparently took nothing is either a good sign, or a terrible one.

'I can check again?' says Anne.

'Yes, that would be good. Let's just finish these questions. Might he be testing boundaries, pushing you, playing around?'

'No, not Conor. I mean, he likes to play tricks, you know, hide your things. Glasses, knitting needles, things. But *he* would never hide to worry us!' Anne's voice reaches a pained crescendo.

Yvonne interjects with, 'Look, he really hasn't ever gone missing.'

'Okay.' PC French looks back at her notes. 'What would you say his state of mind was this morning? Did anything happen before he left for school, even something really small and seemingly non-important?'

Anne perches on the arm of the sofa and stares into the fire as though she can see Conor there. Bernadette has always thought his hair is like a fading flame, not quite red, more orangey-golden, soft and floppy and made to be ruffled. She imagines his freckled face, pictures him standing in the kitchen doorway as he did last Saturday, wearing slightly too-small jeans and a Spiderman T-shirt.

'He just got up as usual,' says Anne, eyes closed now. 'He was a bit grumpy at first, but he often is. He had Coco-Pops and a cup of tea. When he came round he was in a really jolly mood, to be honest. Yes, quite happy. He was chatting about our holiday this year – we went to Bournemouth, stayed in a caravan with my daughter Rose and her two children. He lo—'

'Have you checked that he isn't at your daughter's house?' interrupts PC French.

'Yes,' says Anne. 'My daughter lives in Sheffield; he isn't there.'

'Why do you think he was talking about holidays? Is that usual?'

'Not really, but there was a thing on the morning chat show about cheap last-minute deals. Conor saw the images of the beach and said how much he loved Bournemouth. Asked if we could go again next year.'

Bernadette anticipates the next question from PC French, and is right. 'Do you think he might have gone there?' she asks.

'To Bournemouth?' Anne half-laughs. 'Of course not.'

'I doubt he could even get there,' says Yvonne. 'He's not quite as mature as your average ten-year-old.'

'Does he have any sort of disability or medical condition?' asks PC French. 'Any learning difficulties?'

'No,' says Anne, sounding put out. 'He's just emotionally quite young, that's all. Which is understandable, given his history.'

Yvonne leans forward, says that Conor lived in a variety of homes before being placed with Anne five years ago, so he has some issues with security and gets quite clingy and attached to people at times. Bernadette hates how Conor is summed up in such broad strokes, like a bad drawing. They're never going to find him if they go out looking for a caricature.

What time is it now? Seven-forty. Is this how they search for lost children? Writing information in a report? Shouldn't they be at train and bus stations, in shops and on the street, asking people, showing his picture, knocking on doors?

'Have there been any arguments recently, either here or with other family members or friends? Any trouble at school?'

'No,' says Anne. She's clearly losing patience with the interview and paces the floor. 'Just the usual messing around at school. That's nothing new, just attention seeking and totally understandable. Oh!' Anne remembers something – they all sit forward. 'God no.'

'Tell us,' says PC French.

'Well, they were going to have a Stranger Danger talk at school today – it appears a man has been pulling up outside the school in a red car and talking to the kids. God, it couldn't be that could it? *No.*'

Bernadette puts her face in her hands. The thought that some stranger has him is unbearable. She runs to the kitchen and throws up.

11

The Book

Hull Social Services Report – Lisa Donkin (Social Worker)
Record of recent change of placement   **Child: Conor Jordan**
Date of Birth: 10/11/2001   **Date: 15/07/2003**

It's never nice picking a child up at midnight when it's raining and he's asleep and you have to settle him in a new place in a fold-up cot that smells foreign and wrong. This is the hardest part of being a social worker. But I always tell myself it's harder for the child.

I tried to keep you asleep when I carried you but you became distressed. You still have the black cat Maureen gave you and that gave you comfort. You had it clamped between your teeth and wouldn't let go.

We try to keep children in one secure place if we can. We hope when we set them up with a foster family that it will be until they're adopted or go back to their own family home, but it's not always possible.

You had been with Julia five months so you were settling into life there. You had just begun calling her Mum – she tried to stop it but you heard a child in the street saying it to their mum and latched onto it. Mum, Mum, Mum, you said. Even to the lady next door.

Even though you'd heard the word Dad too (Julia is close to hers), you didn't pick it up. But I suppose you have at least some memory of your mum, while you've never met your real dad. Julia found it hard to hear you saying Mum. She didn't stop you to be unkind, but to set you straight. Because one day you might live with your real mum.

I know you're going to be confused that there's another 'mum' and

another home. None of it was your fault. Jim Rogers insisted I include a
report for you so one day you know this.

Julia was a new foster parent, you were her first child and it didn't work
out. She didn't want to do it anymore. This sometimes happens. It can be
hard taking a strange child into your home. It's not always what people
expect. Everyone says it's a good way to make extra money, but unless you
do it to give a child a home and that's the primary reason, you will end up
regretting it. It takes a big heart and an open mind.

The burns on the back of your legs were not your fault either.

Here is what happened:

You were playing in the kitchen while Julia was on the phone in the
hallway. She said she had one eye on you and could see you through the
door crack. But you're an able and fast climber, Julia told us. It seems you got
a hold of the kettle wire. Because it was a sunny day and you were only in a
nappy the water hit your bare legs. It had only boiled a few minutes before,
when she warmed a bottle for you. You wouldn't drink your milk unless it
was warm.

Julia ran in when you screamed. She was upset she'd let it happen. She
screamed for the neighbour and they got an ambulance. You had to stay
in the hospital a few days because it was a second-degree burn and they
needed to keep you hydrated and stop it from getting infected. The doctor
said it might scar. I don't know if it will but if it does you can read this and
know what caused the redness on your legs. The kettle is what did it.

And Julia didn't let you go because she thought you were naughty or
because you did anything wrong but because she could not forgive herself.

She called my phone late one night, upset about it. She was close to
walking away and leaving you in the cot. It wasn't to be unkind but because
she felt terrible about it all. She couldn't cope. It's hard for a parent or carer
to look after a post-burns child. They need extra care for a while. She was sad
at how you cried. She thought she was making it worse even though she did
a great job of helping you heal.

We had to intervene.

So you're with an emergency family now until we can find a more
permanent place. There is still hope that your mum might get better, which

means there'll be one place you'll live until you grow up. And maybe you'll find out about your real dad. She's trying. She won't sign you over to be adopted, which is maybe because she can't part with you permanently. But that means we can't find you an adoptive family.

In the meantime I will be doing my best to secure a home for you.

PS – This info about being a Looked-After Child from Jim got lost, so I've stuck it back in your book.

Placing a Looked-After Child (LAC) on a Care Order
Under Section 31 of the Children Act 1989 the local authority can apply to the court for a child or young person to become the subject of a care order. Care orders can only be made by the court. When an application is made, the local authority must prepare a care plan for the future of the child.

The court will only make a care order if it believes that it is better for the child or young person than not making an order. It can only be made on young people below the age of seventeen and cannot be made on a young person who is sixteen years old and married.

To make a care order, the court must be satisfied:
That the child concerned is suffering or is likely to suffer significant harm.
That the harm, or likelihood of harm is attributable to:
The care given to the child, or
Likely to be given to him if the order were not made, or
The care not being reasonable, or if
The child is beyond parental control.

Once a care order is made, the local authority obtains parental responsibility. The child's social worker will update the care plan and ensure that it is subject to review as required by legislation, regulation and departmental policy and procedure.

Note from foster carer Julia Stevens

15th July 2003

Dear Conor,
I am so sorry. I am so sorry. Your lovely. I hope you will be happy. I am so sorry.

Julia

12

Bernadette

Bernadette grips the sink and waits for the nausea to pass. For a split second she recalls the sickness she felt that one, brief, happy moment. Anne is behind her, saying that Conor would never get into a car with a stranger, that she has warned him over and over never to.

PC French comes into the kitchen, shaking her head. 'No, no, the man outside the school in the red car – we arrested him this morning. So he *can't* have taken Conor.'

'Why didn't you *say* then?' demanded Anne.

'It's fine,' says Bernadette. 'She didn't have chance.'

'I'm sorry,' said PC French. 'The man outside the school had learning difficulties and was more a nuisance than a threat. He'd borrowed his brother's car and kept asking for the library.' She pauses. 'Are you okay?'

Bernadette nods, drinks some water, and they all resume their places in the living room.

'Has Conor's birth mum been contacted?' asks PC French. 'All friends and family?'

'She's the only person we can't get hold of,' says Yvonne. 'We should try again.'

'Yes,' agrees PC French.

Yvonne goes into the kitchen with her phone. Bernadette wants to wrap her arms around Anne, who suddenly looks about half the size she was when Bernadette arrived. The fire is dying again but Anne seems no longer to care. The room cools. The calm from everyone doing what they should be has faded. The questions continue.

'What's Conor's relationship with his mum like?'

That's something that can't be summed up here. Bernadette doesn't want to listen to them paint a lazy picture, using jargon like *difficult background* and *emotional issues*.

'Probably not the kind of relationship you or I have with our mothers,' says Anne, and this is the truth, succinctly put. 'Frances ... she has problems.'

'And what about the relationship with his dad?' asks PC French.

'Sadly,' says Anne, 'there isn't a father. I mean, well, of course there *is*, it's just that Frances has never told anyone who he is. She's referred to him – said something about him giving her a false name and not being sure of his identity. So I'm afraid there's no relationship there.'

Yvonne returns from the phone and shakes her head to let them know there was still no answer at Frances' house.

'So do you think Frances is the key?' asks the policewoman.

'Possibly,' says Yvonne. 'It is curious that she's not in. She has a young daughter so she can't have gone far.'

'We'll need her address – it's somewhere we should go first. I'm nearly done here and then we can implement a search. I just need a photo, preferably as recent as possible. And tell me, does he have any distinguishing marks?'

Anne says she will find a photo and goes upstairs. Yvonne describes the burns that Conor has up the back of his legs, scars he is self-conscious about and reluctant to reveal. His school was approached and asked that he be allowed to wear jogging bottoms rather than shorts for PE, even in summer. Bernadette always thought this was merely drawing more attention to the scars, that his black-trousered legs next to rows of skin ones would cause more issue. But Conor told her once that at least they didn't know what was underneath and that he could invent some brave story in which he was injured while saving a cat from a tree.

'He's left-handed,' says Bernadette. 'That's quite unusual.'

'I mean the obvious things,' says PC French. 'Things that might make him stand out.'

'I think he'll stand out,' says Bernadette. 'He's not of this world, as my mum used to sometimes say.'

PC French uncrosses and re-crosses her legs.

Anne comes back into the room with a photo, which she gives to PC French, and a miniature metal *Doctor Who* Tardis tin, rusting at the corners. Bernadette recognises it; it's Conor's savings tin. He's been putting away every bit of money he gets, whether for Christmas, birthdays or for washing Anne's car. Anne shakes it – nothing.

'It was full last night,' she tells PC French. 'His money is the only thing that's gone. He had about ninety pounds, I think. What does it mean?'

'It could be a good sign,' says PC French. 'It rules out that he's lost or has been abducted. If he took his money this morning then he was intending to go – we just need to find out where.'

Bernadette thinks of how she hid the book among all her others. Where would Conor go if he didn't want to be found? Where would he feel that he fit in perfectly? Is there such a place?

Or what if he wanted to be seen?

'Do you have any idea what he was saving for?' asks PC French.

Anne shakes her head. 'He just said it was for a rainy day. God love him. It's what my mother always says. Put your pennies away for a rainy day. He used to ask why we don't need money when the sun's out.' She begins crying again and Bernadette hugs her.

PC French closes the report with the finality of a fairy-story ending. 'I know that was slow and difficult, but it *will* help. I think someone should go to Frances' home, and someone else should stay here in case he returns. I'll get back to the station and we'll coordinate a search of the local area.'

'I can stay,' says Yvonne, 'answer the phone, wait and see if Conor comes back.'

'Well, should I stay too? Or go?' wonders Anne.

'I don't drive.' Bernadette feels inadequate.

Anne nods. 'Why don't I drive and Bernadette can come with me? She's one of Conor's favourite people. No one knows him like she does.'

'Perfect,' says PC French. She gives them her number, says they should contact her for anything, no matter how small. 'I'll get back. He'll turn up, you know. Most kids do after a few hours, just tired and hungry and tearful about causing so much trouble.'

'I just had an idea about what might help you,' says Yvonne as PC French heads for the door. 'Conor's Lifebook.'

'His what?' PC French pauses by the lamp as though she's under interrogation.

'It's quite a new thing,' says Yvonne. 'It's a book for LACs – sorry, that's our term for Looked-After Child. All the adoptive or foster parents and social workers and carers write things in it. So the child has memories and a record of important life events when they grow up. Conor has one. We've all written in it over the years. I think his mum has as well. It'll have everything you need to help with the search. Anne probably has it here. Don't you, Anne?'

Bernadette drops into the chair with a sickening plunge. She knows that soon they will all turn to her, that Anne will be eliminated when she tells them she passed it over on Saturday, and they'll be left with Bernadette as a suspect.

She looks at Anne's bookshelf, lined with DVDs and photo albums and paperbacks, half wishing the Lifebook to be there. Suddenly – like that effect in movies where the camera zooms in on the character's face while pulling away from the background – Bernadette wonders if she actually did put the book on her shelf at Tower Rise.

Was it ever even there to go missing?

She definitely had it when she was last with Conor, having borrowed it from Anne to write up their recent trip to Ferens Art Gallery while it was fresh in her mind. Now, thinking back, she doesn't recall even writing that memory up. No, her hands have never recorded those words.

'I gave it to Bernadette,' Anne is saying. 'She often takes it to write in after she's taken Conor out.'

The Lifebook was in Bernadette's bag when she took Conor for a burger on Saturday. She wouldn't have taken it out. He knows it exists but Anne thinks it's best left for when he reaches eighteen, so he hasn't read it. Some Lifebooks are written with a child in mind, tame and using carefully chosen verbs and kind adjectives. Some of Conor's book is like that – some not. So Bernadette was careful to keep her bag shut. But did he look in it when she went to the toilet?

Did he take his book? Is it possible?

'Do you happen to have it with you now?' asks PC French. 'It might help.'

'No,' Bernadette says softly.

'She wouldn't,' says Anne. 'It'll be at home. We can get it and drop it off at the police station on our way to Conor's mum, can't we?'

'I...' Bernadette shakes her head.

'What is it?' asks Anne kindly.

'I don't have it. I don't think I know where it is.'

'What do you mean?' Yvonne frowns.

'I mean ... look, I *had* it. Definitely on Saturday with Conor. And I always put it on my bookshelf in a certain place. But when I went for it earlier today it wasn't there. It wasn't anywhere. I really just don't know.'

'Do you think there's a chance Conor has it?' asks Yvonne.

'No. Maybe. I don't know.'

'What if he does?' asks PC French. 'Could it have a bearing on why he's missing?'

Yvonne sighs. 'Well, maybe, if he read it. There are some quite traumatic life events recorded there. We didn't want him to have it until he's fully grown up and more able to deal with it all.'

Bernadette wonders why people always think you can deal with trauma just because you're grown up. Doesn't the child live on inside you? Then she thinks of Conor's words the last time she saw him, the profound things he said that separated the before it from the after it.

'You have no idea where it is?' asks Yvonne. 'That's quite a problem.'

'I'll find it,' insists Bernadette, and Anne nods, trusting her.

On Saturday Conor sat with Bernadette on the wall outside Anne's for a bit, until her taxi came. He'd been talking all afternoon about this

programme they'd watched in school, where a scientist was looking
for the smallest thing in the universe. Conor was fascinated. Said this
thing was so small that no magnifying glass could see it. It was string-
shaped and stretchy, like the elastic band that held all his pens together,
and the universe itself had started that way long ago.

'Like the smallest thing has become the biggest thing ever,' he said,
bouncing around while still sitting down. 'So, like, if that was you I
could hide you away in my pocket and you'd still be the biggest thing
I have.'

Bernadette choked back tears. This was his way of expressing love
without using the actual words. And yet she hid him away in her
pocket. She met him in secret, like he was something illicit, wrong,
forbidden. For a long time Bernadette had been feeling more and more
guilty about this. She was angry that she'd given everything up for
Richard, quite happily and willingly. Now she felt sick.

How could she have done this?

The taxi arrived then. She ruffled Conor's hair, said goodbye and
walked over to it. He remained on the wall, grinning still at his clever
analogy.

In a moment Bernadette marched back to him and hugged him
tightly. She knew it would have taken him by surprise. The boundaries
put in place by BFL to protect children mean no touching beyond what
is necessary, like preventing a child falling over or wiping up a spillage
on a shirt. So over the years she has pushed Conor on the swings and
held his hand going over the road. But never has she cuddled him; not
until last Saturday.

Conor hugged back, sniffed her collar.

'You don't know what you mean to me,' she said to him. 'You've
saved me.'

He had. A small boy with the strength to pick himself up again and
again after being let down, who had lived in place after place, showed
by example that Bernadette too could leave her home, her husband,
and go on.

Now it is up to her to save him.

13

The Book

28th August 2003

Welcome to our family. Its big and noisy. We like kids. When we first met you you was twenty one months old and didnt want to come in. But our oldest kid Chantelle got out the Lego and you was fine for a bit. In this foto you was with us for ten days and look like you was there much longer. You fit in quite good but you dont like going to bed. You cry and cry. You dont like playing with the kids. You just hug your black cat. Dunno what its called. Blackie I call it. But you do eat your tea.

Jayne Smith

19th September 2003

Dr Howard, Mill Practice

Dear Jim Rogers,

After his appointment I conclude that Conor Jordan (10/11/01) is showing signs of Post Traumatic Stress Symptoms in Children after Mid-to-Moderate Paediatric Trauma, more generally known as PTSD. I attribute his sleeplessness, his losing previously learned toilet training ability, and his inability to be left in a room alone, to the trauma he experienced after being burned. Unless addressed, these symptoms may continue for years, or decrease and return later when events trigger unpleasant memories. I recommend that Conor receive some form of cognitive therapy counselling. My colleague Elena Vella (B.Psych Hons) specialises in this area.

That Conor Jordan lives between homes, and has no permanent caregiver, must also be considered. Please contact me at the above number should you wish to discuss this matter further.

Regards,
Dr James Howard

14

Conor

Sophie MacArthur is my best friend because she can turn her eyelids inside out. That's not the only reason. It would be crazy to have a friend just cos of that. She's funny too and dead clever and she likes *Doctor Who*. And she can beat up Stan Chiswick. She did twice. Once when he called me a faggot and the other time cos he stole her lunch money.

Today Sophie was off school and when Stan did my head in I really missed her. Also I had something to tell her. Something I haven't told nobody.

Sophie lives in a house with her mum and dad and baby sister. She always has. I've lived in eleven different places. That's a whole lot for ten years. Ten of those places was before I was six. I know people as old as forty who've lived in only two houses ever. Anne my foster carer is one of them people. She said her first home was white and looked out at the sea and on Sundays she helped her mum make lemon tarts. I'd love a bedroom with a window that sees the beach and to have lemon tarts to make my tongue all blasty. My room looks out onto a square of concrete and bins.

When Sophie didn't meet me at the school gates this morning I was annoyed. I've got other mates. Loads of them. But she's the only one I really talk to. I think girls keep secrets better. They're always whispering and hiding stuff in books. And Sophie's never told anyone that I wet the bed loads until I was eight. She only knows that cos she slept over once and saw. But she didn't laugh or anything. She just gave me a hug. Boys don't do that. I don't neither.

So when she never came to school I was in a bad mood cos I knew I'd have to carry my secret round all day.

First lesson we did Art. We had to make pictures where the words show what they mean. It's called some long crap word I can't remember. *Smile* can be curved like a mouth and *tree* can be all tall and pointy. I already knew that. Been drawing all my life. Mrs McCartney said we could be free and write whatever we wanted. Just like that graffiti on the walls in town. She said we should close our eyes and let what was on the inside of our eyelids appear.

So I did THUNDERSTORM in wavy black lines. Made the Ts into evil scarecrows and the S into an angry snake. Nearly tore the paper with the pen. Normally drawing soothes me but I was real moody. Then Stan Chiswick started punching my arm and daring me to write something on Mrs McCartney's back. Fuckface, he said.

The other kids always get me to do stuff because they know I will. I'm not a wuss or owt. I just love how it feels when they brag to the rest of the year group what I've done. Like I'm a hero or something. Like I'm Muhammad Ali. Float like a butterfly, sting like a bee.

Today I tried to ignore Stan. I've already had two detentions and we've only been back at school two weeks. One was for locking myself in the art paper cupboard and the other was for putting Suzy Kendal's hamster in with the snake we had on loan from some museum knob-head. The kids still talk about Skitty the hamster and Monty the snake's fight. They kind of laugh at first cos of how funny it was when Skitty leapt in the air and squealed. Then they wrinkle their noses and look sad because he died. I feel bad he died. I only wanted to make them laugh. But I killed Suzy's pet.

So today in Art I told Stan I couldn't be arsed with another detention. I said my foster mum Anne said she'd kill me. She didn't – she's too nice. Really it was because of my secret. I couldn't get kept behind today. There's somewhere I need to go.

But Stan kept nagging me to write something on Mrs McCartney's back. Do it, do it, *do it*, arse-face, he kept saying. In the end she sent us out for disrupting the class so I never finished my THUNDERSTORM sheet. O, R and M were missing. It would've made a great work of art too.

There were plenty of black names in my head when we got marched into the corridor and told to stay there until lunchtime. Stan kept hissing at me from his bench but I ignored him. Closed my eyes to see what was on the inside of my eyelids.

Mr Grimshaw the headmaster got us in his office and told us off for being unruly and said if he saw us again today he'd keep us behind after school all week. Fuck it, I thought. Need to stay away from Stan.

In last lesson we had another Stranger Danger talk. We're way too old. We had that in like year two or something. Some of the girls got upset. There's been this man outside school in a red car trying to get the younger kids to show him where the library is. The police have been there looking out for him. Mr Grimshaw said we should come straight in and tell an adult if we see this man. If our parents can't meet us we should walk home in pairs.

I'm not scared of strangers. I've met loads of them. I've lived with them all my life.

I was first out of school when the bell went. I never mess about. But I wasn't going home. Home is Anne's house. My eleventh, her second. It's ten minutes from school and she always has a pot of tea ready when I get in. I've never told anyone. Tea's for old crinkly people. But it's so good with Anne's jam tart. She always asks what I've been doing and I tell her the good stuff like beating Sophie at conkers or being on the first sitting at lunch.

I wasn't thinking about Anne when I got out of school today. I was thinking about my real mum. I always start thinking about her when I try to be good and mess it up. When I get detentions even if it wasn't me. When I plan not to join in the larks but I still get blamed.

For the first five years of my life I never saw my mum at all. She had these problems that meant she couldn't look after me or my brother. My brother's a year older than me and called Sam. I had one that was younger called George but he died two years ago. I only ever seen George twice and Sam three times cos we were at the funeral together.

Everyone tells me my mum's problems are the kind that never go away. I've got those too. They use all nice words instead of sandshoe-black ones. I've never really understood. And even though I do more now cos I'm older it kind of makes it even more confusing.

Mum got better for a while and had another baby that she's kept. So I have a little sister called Kayleigh. She's three. Mum's nice to Kayleigh. And that was when I started seeing her every four weeks instead of just sometimes on supervised visits. Supervised visits means a social worker comes with you.

Imagine that. You get two hours with your mum. Once a month. Some knob of a social worker has to come. It's not the same. You can't be with your mum like that. You can't ask about stuff you really want to know and you can't tell her you hate being away from your brother and you can't say it's not fair that Kayleigh gets to live there and you don't. Supervision is stupid. Like I'm not capable of doing stuff myself when I'm ten. Yeah, right.

Lots of stuff can happen in ten years so I'm much older. I know more than them after all the places I've been. All the houses and rooms I've lived in. And I know exactly which train to get on to go to Mum's house. I've gone on it a few times with Len cos he can't drive. Yvonne is my main social worker and she drives us to Doncaster. But Len gets us two return tickets from the machine in the station and we get on the train at platform three.

I've never gone alone but I reckon I'm old enough to do it. Anyway if I want to tell Mum about my surprise I'll just have to. Don't want social workers interfering. But I really wanted to tell Sophie first. I really wanted her to come with me.

The sky was ashy black like my THUNDERSTORM words when I got out the school gates. I could hear kids coming out behind me. I pictured Anne waiting for me at home and felt a bit bad that I wasn't going there. Her tea would get cold and she'd worry and wring her hands and call people. I really thought about just going home then. Telling Anne my plan. But then it wouldn't be special. Wouldn't be just me and Mum. And she might stop me.

Maybe it was stupid of me to go on a journey without provisions. In survival stories they always take provisions. They pack a compass and warm clothes and food. When they get lost and stuff they make do with what they can find, like berries and weeds and coconut milk and fish. But I won't get lost. I was excited when I got up this morning. I hate morning normally. I scrunch the covers up and put them in the bin. That gets rid of a bit of my grumpiness. Anne makes me a cup of tea with two sugars and ruffles my hair and sings 'Jingle Bells'. Even in summer.

I've been saving my money for ages and I've got a surprise planned for my mum. I didn't bring food or a big coat or a compass or owt. I'll just make do.

Just as I was going left towards the station Stan Chiswick grabbed my arm. I thought he wanted to fight but he said, *look there's that stranger mister they warned us about*. And there was a black car parked at the kerb. Not red. Maybe he switched it to trick everyone. Clever.

But it didn't trick me. Didn't frighten me neither.

The policeman who sometimes walks up and down wasn't around. I've heard Anne's friend say they're never around when you need them. I didn't need one. The man in the car was looking at us. He didn't look evil or anything. Just dead normal.

Then he waved me over. It was definitely me he wanted. Stan went goggle-eyed. Coward. Said he was going to look for the copper or get a teacher. I was curious. No one could get me in a car if I don't want to go. I decided I was going to tell the man to bugger off and stop harassing the kids. I'd be a hero again. They'd stop saying I was a hamster killer.

So I went to the car.

15

The Book

5th October 2003

Hi Conor,

Messy handwriting alert! This is Jim Rogers again.

I have something nice to share with you but first I wanted to explain why I included a copy of a doctor's referral I received. (Some social workers don't think such things should be included in these books but I feel that one day you'll need to know about it.)

Lots of things in life shape us. Gosh, I think about that a lot, especially in this work. Things like genetics, circumstance, our history, our family, our surroundings, and our unique personality. I've read Lifebooks that are gentle and full of generalities and so not awfully truthful. I've also read ones that are brutal.

In the USA they are very much intended to be simple so a child can read them. I tend to write that way at the start. When I read back over my entry from when you were born, I see I spoke as though you were very small, but since you'll be an adult when you read yours I'm not sure why I did that. (I still do at times.) I suppose I'm trying to make sure yours is both gentle <u>and</u> honest.

So I have decided to include various documents that might make you sad but that will be helpful one day in explaining things that happened. I'm going to include a report by psychologist Elena Vella.

But before that here is something from your family.

I got a letter from an Aunt Rhona that I'd like to stick in here. She is actually your Great Aunt, which means she is your grandma's sister. She's an aunt to your mum, Frances. Sadly Aunt Rhona died recently but her husband made sure this letter got to us. I think you'll enjoy reading it one day. It's definitely one of the things that should be included in here. It's your history and I hope it's one of the things that shapes you.

Jim.

1st October 2003

Dear Conor,

I hope you are well. I hope this letter finds you. I hope I have done the right thing. I'm your great aunt even though I've never met you. I don't even know your mum now. Since they all left Belfast I've hardly heard from her or any of them. I hear her life has not turned out very well. I don't know much about that. But anyway I don't want to dwell on it too much. We all make mistakes and she had a tough start. They never had much money you see. Not with ten children. I never had no kids. It's like my sister had them all. But anyway. She had it hard bringing up ten. I helped where I could. If I'm real honest little Frances was my favourite. I know you shouldn't have favourites. But I couldn't help it. Your mum was the kind of little girl who tugged on your heartstrings as they say. My heart nearly broke when they all went to England to be with her dad's lot. She was about fifteen then. She was what they call wayward. Not the cute little thing she once was. The devil was in her they said. Well, her dad did but he could be nasty. He didn't do much to help and had a bad temper and liked to drink. So all the kids got into bother and stuff. They were left to roam wild you see a lot of the time. But when she was little Frances would come and sit quietly with me and put her head on my knee and not say much but just be there. It was nice. She sometimes couldn't stand all the noise in the house. She had to share her bedroom with two sisters and a brother. That was her twin, Andrew. Them two were like light and dark. When she was good he seemed to be bad. He stole from his mam's purse once. Then when Frances grew up a bit and got with the wrong boys Andrew went all good. Tried to stop her. I think Andrew is the only one Frances still sees. Twins can never be parted for long. I'm ill now and have been told by my doctor I'll be lucky to live a year. My sister, your grandma, died a few years ago. Your granddad is still alive but lost most of his memory through alcohol. He drinks and brawls. So I'm writing to you and your other brother Sam before I'm gone. Just to say I'm sad I never knew either of you. I should have maybe found a way to see you somehow and do regret it. But at least you might read this when you're big and know we were all thinking of you. They tell me Frances had a kid die. Never knew till after. They said it was a real tragedy. Never should've happened. But she didn't have the best start. Remember that. She was a sweet sweet girl once upon a time. Keep that in your heart.

Love Aunt Rhona

16

Bernadette

Outside Anne's house, darkness disguises the area. Streets that by day are a mixture of both well-maintained and rundown properties are made uniform at night, becoming rows of identical shadowy squares.

Anne lets Bernadette in the car and then gets out again without a word and goes back into the house. Perhaps she has changed her mind and cannot cope with this night. Perhaps she needs a moment. But she returns with a cloth and wipes bird droppings off the car's back window, before dumping the rag in the bin and getting back in the car.

'If Conor were here,' she says, sadly, '*he* would have cleaned that off. Then he'd say, Anne, if you've only got a quid instead of two I don't mind.'

Bernadette squeezes her hand. 'Where on earth *is* he, Anne? Where did he go? Why did he take all his money?'

'God, if I knew.'

'It makes no sense. He's happy at the moment, doing well.'

Bernadette remembers one of her favourite survival stories, where a man lasted three weeks on a mountain ledge, with a broken leg and only two days' worth of food. He said it was the thought of his daughter at home that kept him going. Once rescued, he recovered well, until ten months later when he collapsed in a shop and died. Has Conor now given up the battle after five years in a safe place?

'I think Frances is the key somehow,' says Anne. 'He's not with any of the people who matter to him – you, Sophie, me. The only other person he talks about is his mum.' She starts the car. 'I think we need to get there fast, see where she is and then perhaps find out where *he* is.'

They travel in silence through the estate. Only when they pass the city centre and drive parallel with the river does Anne ask gently, 'Is Conor's Lifebook really lost?'

'Yes,' says Bernadette.

'I wondered if you were maybe protecting him or something,' says Anne. 'His privacy. I would've understood. That book – it's not to be bandied about by just anyone.'

'Anne, I haven't told you everything.'

Bernadette watches the lights bounce on the water. She finds it easy to talk to Anne. She doesn't have anyone else; friends drifted away when they had babies and Bernadette didn't, when she stopped joining them on evenings out, when she didn't work in the offices or shops they did.

'I didn't want to say in front of Yvonne and PC French – it's private. It's not just the book. I was leaving Richard tonight.'

'You were?' says Anne, softly. 'You mean, when I called? You sounded upset and I thought you'd had a psychic hunch about Conor. I know you've been unhappy for a while – that's been easy to see. How did Richard take it?'

'I haven't done it yet. I mean, I couldn't, because he didn't come home.'

As they drive onto the motorway she tells Anne about the curious evening. She has started at the end, at Richard not turning up. That's the cliffhanger, like when you tune into a soap opera just before the credits roll. She needs to explain how it came about and what happened with the Lifebook and what Bob Fracklehurst told her in the taxi about Richard's so-called sister. She needs to go back even further.

She needs to talk about it.

Bernadette has never been a big talker. As a child she was happiest with her nose in a book and had just one school friend, Shannon, with whom she lost touch after college. Bernadette's mum always said, 'We hardly know we've got her.' If Bernadette was worried about something, she would keep it inside; it wasn't that her parents didn't care or want to know – they are both loving people – but Bernadette couldn't stand to upset them or cause trouble. And yet loneliness frightened her; the thought of never finding a partner, someone to share a home with, kept her awake many nights during her teens.

'Do you want to tell me about it?' asks Anne kindly.

Bernadette does. She needs to make room in her head, but there is so much to share. It starts to rain and the windscreen wipers swish-swash the water, like waves after a zigzagging boat.

'We've got an hour,' says Anne. 'Talk to me. It'll distract us both and get us to Conor faster. It'll clear your head to help you concentrate on him and it'll give me something to listen to while I drive. Tell me, Bernadette.'

How should she tell it? Should she just speak as though reading lines in a book, like they're sharing a favourite chapter? Should she pretty the truth with gentle adjectives or go with precise verbs – the things he did, the things he said. A sort of verbal Lifebook. Anne is waiting and Bernadette knows she won't ask questions or interrupt.

Who better to tell?

'What is a husband supposed to be?' Bernadette asks, not sure if the question needs an answer.

'What do you mean?' Anne looks over and the car swerves very slightly.

Bernadette doesn't voice the other questions racing through her head.

Is a husband a man who ignores you for two days because you asked why his mother has to decide what you do every Christmas? Is he a man who tells you your inability to carry a baby to term is because you're not pure? A man who says he loves you after breaking your arm, that you shouldn't have questioned his decision to move the furniture in the bedroom so you'd not hear the couple on the other side having sex? Is he a man who puts a cheap gold band on the wrong finger at a tiny wedding service blessed by his mother's priest, one who kisses you chastely and promises to honour but not obey? A man who says you don't need a honeymoon because you've got each other for the rest of your lives.

Is a husband someone you forgive and stay with because you loved him so much at the start, because your own mother gave up everything for your father and they're happy, because now you have no one else and no money and no bravery?

Yes. That is a husband; that is Richard.

'It was the milk,' says Bernadette.

'The milk?' asks Anne.

'Yes. Last week.'

*

'Did you leave the milk out?' Richard's voice came from the kitchen, distance not softening his tone.

Bernadette froze with a silk pillowcase in one hand. Richard always slept restlessly, leaving sheets everywhere. As every morning, she tucked corners beneath mattress, puffed up pillows and smoothed down dishevelled duvet. She'd spilt milk on her pillowcase last night and removed it now to replace it with another. But Richard's words stopped her.

'Did you leave the milk out, Bernadette?' Slightly louder, but still slow.

'Yes.' She softly pressed her fist against her lips and closed her eyes. When she opened them again his words had not gone away.

She left the unfinished bed and went to the kitchen; if he came looking for her it would only add to his annoyance. In the kitchen he stood barefoot and crisply suited for work, with a half-empty carton of milk in his left hand: semi-skimmed, for their health.

'You *know* I hate lukewarm milk on my cereal in the morning.' Richard looked at the space above her head like he couldn't bear to look at her face. He often did this. 'You left it out all night. How hard is it to remember to put it away?'

Bernadette didn't respond. She knew from experience that he didn't want any sort of answer. It was best to listen. How quickly she had picked up and acted on signs so their marriage ran more smoothly.

'Now I'll have to go to work on an empty stomach. Do you know how little time I get to eat?' The milk carton swilled at every jerk of Richard's arm.

Still he stared into a distant place beyond her existence. Often she wondered if she existed at all when he glared at that elusive spot above her head. Was she here? Was *she* the ghost in a house she often felt was haunted? Noises at night on the stairs often had her creeping down to check things. Rattling in other rooms had her running to catch some intruder.

Perhaps *she* was the poltergeist.

'Are you listening, Bernadette?' Richard's voice crept up a few decibels. Now he required an answer. Now he looked directly at Bernadette and she existed again, but it really didn't matter what she said.

'Yes. Sorry, I had some milk in bed last night and I must have forgotten to put it away.' It was so unlike her. She knew he liked order.

'Because you have *so* much to think about, I suppose? Because you have endless deadlines to meet and you're competing with a hundred others half your age? You're in charge of our home. That's all. You deal with the small things and you can't even manage that.'

Bernadette listened as the words span faster, like Conor freewheeling on his bike, knowing where it would lead and unable to prevent the crash. She could have said that she'd love to go to work like he did. That the small things of home were not enough and by mid-morning she had only her books and the trees.

But she didn't. On and on went Richard's voice. She tried to listen and anticipate what he wanted from her, but the slap punctuated his sentences with an exclamation mark.

Bernadette fell back but quickly caught her balance. She avoided his eyes; if even a flicker of anger stained hers he would continue ranting. Such violence was a shock. He had only struck her a handful of times; usually the stream of words was enough to quell his rage.

He hurled the milk at the wall. The plastic carton bounced and landed on the table and then the floor, spraying milk like liquid fireworks. Rancid milk dripped onto her feet.

Richard then touched her cheek tenderly. 'You make the small things pure,' he said softly. He often used the word pure. He meant perfect. Right. His. 'Most of the time. No one does it like you.' She still didn't meet his eyes. Finally he walked past her, avoiding the milk. 'I love you for those reasons,' he said, and went into the lounge.

Kneeling where the lino was dry, Bernadette mopped up the milk and squeezed the sodden cloth into the sink three times. She wiped the wall where it had splashed, and polished the floor with a different cloth until it gleamed and there was no risk of anyone slipping.

Down the passage, the front door slammed and she knew the place was hers again. Bernadette changed out of her wet clothes. Her throat was so full of trapped words, it ached more than her cheek. Richard would say sorry later – he always did after losing his temper. He'd explain that he only got angry because he cared, because he loved her so much.

In the quiet she tidied the kitchen. There were no dishes from the night before so it didn't take long. Pots were never left overnight; Richard thought it slovenly so Bernadette always did them last thing. Usually she put the milk away too. She wouldn't forget again.

He'd said she made the small things pure. Was this all she wanted from life? The small things; mopping up milk and waiting for a husband to come home and reading about lives in biographies and writing about one in a child's Lifebook while her own passed by.

How had she accepted it for ten years?

When Conor – a few days later – got excited about how the smallest thing in the universe became the biggest, and said she was therefore the smallest thing in his world, Bernadette knew. She knew that she could not wait at home for Richard anymore. She wanted bigger things.

*

'Oh, Bernadette,' says Anne.

Bernadette doesn't speak for a moment because her throat is as sore as it was that morning. The windscreen wipers have been measuring the beat of her words, like a musician's metronome maintaining the tempo; swish, beat, swish, beat, swish, beat. She is glad they have passed the time and are now halfway to Conor's mum's house.

'Does he hit you a lot?' asks Anne.

'Oh, no,' says Bernadette. 'That's the thing – that's why it shocked me. He gets angry and rants – more frequently in recent years – but it passes and he says sorry. There have only been two or three times in ten years when he struck me. And there was always reason. Other times he simply didn't speak. Went into this quiet place where I couldn't reach him.'

'But has he always been so controlling?' asks Anne.

'I suppose someone is always what they are.' Bernadette pictures him in their early days, dressed more casually, in soft shades, and affectionate in his own moderate way. She talks because it is so easy with Anne. 'It's only when we don't like it that it becomes a problem, doesn't it? If you love someone fully at the start, you forever remember it when things decline, don't you? He was thoughtful back then. Never forgot a birthday or the anniversary of some little event only we knew about. We went to Scotland once before we were married – our only holiday. In January because it was cheaper. It was cold and the hotel was basic, but I've never forgotten it. We walked in the hills and talked and talked. Richard used to talk in such a way, you almost forgot where you were. I wish we'd taken some photos but we never bothered. I can still see the hills though; I can remember how he said the rain only made him want to hang around and see them again in the sun, like the day we met, in that café, during the downpour, how he wanted to see me again in better weather. That's my happiest memory with Richard – Loch Lomond in the rain. He first said he loved me there. Said he'd protect me from the dirty and brutal world.'

'Dirty and brutal is a harsh view of the world,' says Anne, sadly.

Bernadette nods; she's right. An upbringing in a strictly Catholic home by a mother obsessed with cleanliness and purity and discipline left Richard with some extreme views, ones that had at first been refreshing compared with those held by more worldly and outgoing men.

Bernadette once liked that she was only his second lover, that he believed sex was about love, and marriage was a bond in which two people sacrificed everything for one another. It sounded like the kind of marriage her parents shared, full of devotion and commitment. Such a union was all she'd ever hoped for. When it didn't quite turn out that way she refused to give up hope, and certainly refused to ever let on to her parents that she'd failed. But hope dies eventually, like a potted plant in an unused room.

'He took me to a beautiful restaurant once,' says Bernadette. 'He never likes to waste money so I was quite excited. It was the kind of place where people talk in low voices and the waiters hover close by to tend to anything you want. I chose fish in parsley sauce but it was awful and I could hardly eat it; I think it was off. Richard told me he'd be hurt if I wasted it so I made myself. I was sick later. That's how much I loved him.'

'Oh Bernadette,' says Anne again. A police car speeds past, chasing a yellow van. 'I'd say I'm surprised you stayed so long – but I'm not. People stick things out, hoping it will get better. I did with my first husband. I stayed for our children, but that wasn't enough reason in the end. They were unhappy as well. So I left. And it worked out for the best. I met Sean. I might have only had him briefly, but love like that lingers, keeps you nourished. You could still meet someone, Bernadette, you're only thirty-two. Could still have children.' Anne looks kindly at her. 'You'd make a lovely mum.'

Bernadette can't talk about children, about the one time she got pregnant. She won't think now about how they tried for a long time, how Richard believed sex was about love and creating life, how they almost gave up and he said she couldn't sleep in their marital bed if it didn't happen soon. She won't try and understand now why she just accepted this so wordlessly and slept on the sofa until conception occurred – by some miracle – following a violent act of love where Richard came upon her in the shower, and the water barely cooled his heat.

Bernadette won't dwell on the time she missed a period, and then two, and doctors confirmed their pregnancy. When Richard kissed her feet and said she would make the purest of mothers. When he insisted the water had had God bless their union and grant a child.

But Bernadette can't stop the thoughts. Rain zigzags down the windscreen as blood had down her leg. Anne looks at her with concern, just as the nurse had. Nothing could be done; nature had her way.

It was a boy; a tiny, too-early boy.

When they came home from the hospital Richard let Bernadette go to bed first for a change. He usually retired while she locked doors and windows, closed curtains and washed up. She'd get into bed carefully so as not to disturb him, glad at least that it was already warm. That night of going in first meant the bed was cold, as empty as her womb.

In the morning Richard said Bernadette couldn't have really wanted the baby, that God knew this and took it away. He never spoke of it again, and rarely instigated sex. When it did happen he made sure – despite his Catholic upbringing and a belief that conception is sacred – that no baby would follow. They never got the blood out of the rug in the lounge and he threw it away.

'Conor has been like my child,' says Bernadette.

'I know,' says Anne. 'He belongs to everyone and no one. That's why I've always fostered children, rather than adopting one. I don't want to make them mine, I just want to help them find where they really belong, I suppose. But you could have many children.'

'I sometimes wonder why, even though Frances can't have Conor, she won't let him be adopted either,' muses Bernadette. 'I suppose she can't let go. She's sticking it out like we have and I imagine you never give up hope where a child is concerned.'

'If she'd kept him,' says Anne, 'we'd never have known him. Everything happens the way it should.'

She's right; if she hadn't lost a baby, Bernadette wouldn't have volunteered at BFL and met Conor. The need to mother someone had built up like steam in a pressure cooker. She'd only needed one child; one friend had been enough in childhood; one husband. One lost baby.

Bernadette fingers the cheap gold band Richard placed on her finger, a ring she has never since removed. Imperfect after catching on a wall hook once, it has otherwise worn reasonably well for ten years. She tries to remove it now – twisting and pulling the deformed circle – but the more she tries the warmer her finger gets and the more impossible the task. It won't budge; she's still tied to Richard.

'So where do you think he is tonight?' asks Anne.

'Conor?' says Bernadette.

'Richard.'

'I have absolutely no idea.'

And Bernadette is not sure she wants to know.

17

Conor

When I got to the car, I looked in the open window at the strange mister and kept my face dead not bothered.

The man didn't ask about where the library was. He wore smart clothes. He smiled and it wasn't in a way that was to trick me. I'm sharp like that. I *know*. He asked if I was Conor and I was surprised he knew my name. So I said, *If you really know me tell me something about me.* He said I don't like to not finish things. I was really spooked. He was right.

It makes me mad when I can't finish something I've started. I get into trouble at school when I yell out loud. So I keep the black words in my throat. I stomp about at home if we have to go shopping before I finish an Xbox game. I slam my chair into the desk if dinnertime interrupts me drawing.

My favourite thing is drawing you see. It gets the blackness out. That's why I was mad when I didn't finish my THUNDERSTORM painting.

And that's what the strange mister said next. He said I loved drawing. And then he said he knew my mum. I was a bit shocked I admit. I think I stepped back from the car and he looked all worried. He said I should trust him. He would even take me to Mum's.

I realised I wouldn't have to pay for a train ticket if he took me and I wouldn't have to find her house when I got there – cos really I wasn't totally sure about that.

Where does she live then? I asked him.

And he said Doncaster.

He couldn't be a total stranger cos he was right. Plus his car was cool. Smart inside and it smelt all new. I can take care of myself. Make my own decisions. So I decided – I got in. He smiled at me.

We drove off.

And then Bernadette came into my head. I saw her on Saturday. My favourite days are when she takes me out. She's kind of like Sophie but older. Like an aunt but nicer. Like a mum. Anyway she came into my head cos the last time I saw her she said something real strange to me. Can't remember what I was going on about but she said bye when we got to my house and then she came back and hugged me and said, *You've saved me*.

We're not supposed to hug. It's about all that crap called boundaries. She's only meant to touch me if it's essential – that's what she said: essential. Boundaries is as stupid as supervision. But this time Bernadette hugged me. It was nice. She smelt kind of warm, like a duvet. She'd understand about me doing this. Out of everyone she'd understand most.

So now I'm in a car with a stranger.

Except he isn't. He knows Mum. And we're going there. We went past Sophie's house and Anne's a while back. We passed where Bernadette took me for a burger last week. We passed Stan Chiswick's house and I smiled cos he'll be well jel. He always tells me I'm weird cos I don't have a mum or dad. He's a coward. He wouldn't get in a car like me. I'm not scared.

Anyway this stranger knows me. Said his name's Paul. He isn't talking much now but he asked what music I want on and I said the radio. So we're listening to Tinchy Stryder. I think this is going to be a real adventure.

18

The Book

5th October 2003

COUNSELLING REFERRAL
SUBJECT – Conor Jordan   **D.O.B. – 10/11/2001**

Reason for Referral: The subject, a 23-month-old male, was referred for counselling by his doctor and social worker due to acute sleeplessness and a tendency to act out in a violent manner when in close proximity with others.

Notification of Purpose and Limits of Confidentiality: The subject's current carer was notified that the social worker referred him for counselling in order to help him sleep, to lessen anxiety and to help him follow directions in a more appropriate manner.

Evaluation Instruments and Sources of Information: These evaluation instruments were used: a standard age-appropriate test, known as play therapy, which is primarily used with children ages 2–11 years old; a test for anxiety; and a test for other basic psychological problems, many of which are often seen in children.

Background Information: The subject is a white male, of almost two years of age. The subject's birth was normal, no effects from mother's drug-taking were found, and he was taken into care due to his mother's on/off addiction to drugs and current behaviours, including depression. Age-appropriate milestones were met, with the exception of a current lack of willingness to play with or respond to others, and an inability to sleep through the night. There is no evidence of sexual or emotional trauma in early childhood, and the subject showed no other developmental issues in early childhood. He suffered second-degree burns on his legs at the age of 20 months. The subject lives with his current carers in a three-bed home within the city limits and has a sibling but doesn't see him. The subject is isolated when it comes to interaction with other family members as the mother is estranged from the subject and the father is unknown. The referral has been made for this specific reason: the subject pushed a girl in the home where he recently lived and pulled her hair so roughly it came out of her head. The subject then hit a boy with a pan so many times he suffered a broken wrist.

Treatment: The subject will receive six months of play therapy. The subject will be seen by a qualified counsellor in a fully equipped playroom with specially chosen toys that will allow the safe expression of feelings and support the development of healthier behaviours.

Play therapy sessions with the subject will generally last 45–50 minutes. Initially, the carer and the subject will come into the playroom together. When the subject feels comfortable with the carer leaving the playroom, the sessions will be conducted with only the subject and the counsellor in the playroom.

Elena Vella

19

Conor

I love being on the motorway cos you know you're going somewhere good and not just to town or boring Morrison's. Motorways mean you're going on holiday or Alton Towers for the day or to Mum's house. And that's where we're going now. To Mum's.

But I'm with just me and someone interesting.

Paul is interesting cos he's not saying much and he's just staring at me now and again with this look on his face like he's not happy or sad but kind of okay. I study him secretly. I'm good at that. At school I always know what mood Mrs McCartney's gonna be in cos I'm so good at seeing. You have to look at more than hair colour or eyes. You have to watch how they breathe and how they walk and talk. Paul is breathing slow. Of course I don't know how he walks yet but he talks different from me. Like someone on *EastEnders*. Slow – as if he's thinking about it.

I don't reckon he's a serial killer. I watched this film with Sophie when her mum wasn't there and the killer hid his face behind a white mask. I don't reckon that face would be anything like Paul. He's not trying to hide. And if he knows my mum and where she lives that's good enough for me.

His car clock says it's half past four. Anne will be all worried now. I don't want her to be. So I ask Paul if we can ring her or something and tell her I'm okay and that I'll back later.

Paul says there is no need to. He already told Anne and she was very happy we're going to see Mum.

That's good. I'm big style grinning now. If he knows Anne too that's even better. So I tell Paul I was going to my mum's house anyway and he says great minds think alike.

We keep passing big trucks and I wave at the drivers and they mostly wave back. On school trips when they don't wave back we stick two fingers up at them. Last year school went to Derbyshire for three days and me and Sophie couldn't share a room cos she's a girl but we sat on the coach together and waved at everyone. I love it when you stop at service stations on journeys. They're like outer space towns with all the shops and arcades and burger places. I hope we can stop soon cos I want a wee but I don't want to ask.

Tell me about why you're going to your mum's house, says Paul suddenly. *Tell me what she's like.*

If he knows her why is he asking me?

I reckon it's so he doesn't have to talk. When Anne's tired she asks me summat that'll take ages to tell so she can close her eyes for a bit in the chair. I don't mind though.

I think Paul will be dead impressed by my plan. I just wish I'd got to tell Sophie first. If we stop at a service station I'm gonna def try and ring her there.

So I tell Paul about my big plan. I've been saving up for it for like a year. Anne gives me two quid when I wash the car and I do it every time a bird craps on it. I got money at Easter instead of eggs and some for Christmas. I never spent a penny of it, just put it in my *Doctor Who* tin. It's cos I want to take my mum on holiday. Every time we go and see her she gets mad if my little sister Kayleigh plays up and says she wishes she could get away from it all some day. I bet she means somewhere like Bournemouth where we went this year. I loved it there. Mum might too. The beach was real nice and we were on it all day. You can see for miles from the end of the pier.

I've saved ninety-six pounds and forty-two pence. I know it's not enough for a big holiday. When Anne's friend went to Spain it cost like three hundred. I was listening to them talk the other night when they thought I was in bed. I went on the internet in the school library and there's this one website called National Holidays and they do short holidays to Bournemouth for like ninety-nine quid.

So I've got nearly enough for her. I reckon Mum could borrow the other three quid from someone. I can't book it cos I don't have a credit card or owt but Mum can go to the office with my money and do it herself. Someone will have to look after Kayleigh. Maybe Anne will. Yeah, she's nice like that.

I tell Paul all this. He just listens and listens. Even turns the radio down. Then he tells me it's a very nice thing to do and asks if my mum is worth it though. I'm annoyed that he's mean about her but I know other people don't like her. Stan Chiswick says she must be crap if she doesn't come to my house and forgets to get me a Christmas prezzy. I punched him in the head for that. Got a detention. Didn't care. She's my mum. She had me born. It's not her fault she's ill. I might still be able to live there one day my social worker Yvonne said. If I could I would, even though her house isn't as nice as Anne's and I do like Anne lots.

I ask Paul how he knows my mum and he just says from way back. I wonder if he knew her at school? Or maybe he's her brother or something? I haven't seen my brother in ages either. I tell Paul I bet he's nice to his mum too and he says yes she was wonderful. He frowns though and bites his lips.

I really want a wee now and ask Paul if I can go. He says there will be services in five minutes but we shouldn't stay long as we need to get to my mum's before—

Then he stops. I wonder before what? He doesn't talk for a bit and I don't neither. My tummy rumbles and I think about tea at Anne's. Sausage and mash is my best. At least she'll keep mine cos Paul has told her we'll be back later.

We go into a service station and Paul parks and turns and looks at me. He frowns like when you're thinking what to say exactly. Then he says people get suspicious when children aren't with their parents so if anyone asks, I'm his son.

I quite like that. I don't have a dad. Paul says I mustn't go off or anything. Doesn't he realise I don't want to? I *want* to go to Mum's. And anyway I wouldn't know how to get back home from here. He says we can go to the toilet and he'll buy me a burger if I'm hungry.

Then we go inside.

I try and walk the same as him so we look like a dad and son. His walk is kind of slow even though we get there fast and his trousers swish like my school ones. A lady smiles at me. Someone wins some money in the arcade and I hear all the coins clanking. We both go in the toilets and I feel a bit shy so I go in the cubicle. When we come out, he tells me to wait by the bubblegum machine and he queues up for a burger.

Now's my chance. There's a phone right at the door. Paul can't see me while he queues up. I ring Sophie. I know her number off by heart. Even know the area code you need. I'm good at remembering. I use some of my money but keep dropping it. Then I get it in and dial her number. She usually answers cos her mum is always with her baby sister.

First thing I do is swear Sophie to secrecy and of course she gets all excited then. I tell her I don't have long to talk but that a man who knows my mum picked me up and we're going there now. I tell her real quick about the big holiday plan. She's totally impressed. She has never said bad stuff about my mum like some idiots. I tell her I so wish she was here. She says she was so sick today she threw up chunks of black stuff and I go eeuurghhh.

Paul is at the front of the queue now and I don't think he'll like me ringing Sophie so I tell her I have to go and say I'll try and ring her from Mum's.

When I put the phone down I feel real sad all of a sudden. Like when you think you're not going to see someone for ages. I've felt like it before. Lots. When I was little and moved around lots before I lived with Anne. I'd get used to being in a house. Get used to the smell of the pillows on my bed and the people there. Then it was, off you go, Conor.

I feel that way now.

Maybe I wouldn't go and live with Mum if I could. I'd have to change schools and not be near Sophie. I'm more used to Sophie than any bed or sheets.

Paul hands me a bag with a burger and some chips in it and tells me I should eat it in the car so we can get going. I don't know what the rush is. Maybe he *is* a bad person and maybe he's on the run or something. I just know I'm suddenly not sure about going to Mum's. I don't know why. Maybe Anne deserves a nice holiday more than her.

Maybe Mum *is* crap. I feel crap. The burger stinks.

Paul is practically marching me, not like rough or anything but making sure. He opens the door and I get back in his car. When he gets in he watches me again. Now I'm wondering if he's one of those pervs people talk about. He asks me what my life has been like so far. How do I answer that? I want to swear but he's an adult. He'd tell Anne. I hate upsetting her. So I just start eating even though my hunger has gone away.

Paul says maybe things in the future will be different and he starts the car up. When we pull out he nearly hits a van that suddenly comes out of nowhere. The driver shouts and waves his hand but Paul ignores him and just says to me that he doesn't have time for fools.

We go back onto the motorway. I ask how long until we get there and he says only half an hour. When I've eaten all my food I close my eyes for a bit. The hum hum of the car gets me all drowsy. I don't fall asleep totally but go into that kind of sleep where you jerk out of it now and again. I always do it when we go anywhere. I love it cos I dream while I'm awake.

This time I dream that Bernadette has come with us. She can't drive so she's in the back seat. When we go anywhere together we go by bus or we walk. She's never, ever late when she comes for me.

After our burger last week we went for a walk on the foreshore. Cos of all the stupid boundary stuff I'm not allowed to know where she lives. But when we walked near the river she pointed towards some trees and said she lives behind there. It looked real old-fashioned and spooky in those woods. She laughed when I said that. Said maybe it was haunted. I said I wouldn't be scared of any ghost. I could spend a night in a scary house on my own.

She looked real sad then. Said she wished she could take me to her house but she would never be able to. She said it wasn't just the boundaries thing but she didn't say what it was. I wonder if it's the ghost?

We picked up some stones then and I chucked one in the water. She said she liked all the ripples they made. Said something about the ripples always being a surprise no matter how many times you do it. She told me once that she lost a baby boy. Did she mean she had him and he ran away? Not sure. She's not meant to tell me about herself. Stupid boundary stuff again. But I guess it just came out. Then she said seeing me made her happy again.

Seeing her makes me totally happy.

I wish she was here now. No matter what he says or who he knows Paul is a stranger and I'm sick of strangers. Soon we will be at Mum's house. Really she is the biggest stranger of all.

20

The Book

Hull Social Services
Assessment of Need

Name: Conor Jordan   **D.O.B.:** 10/11/2001
Date: 16/10/2003

Child: Conor is a twenty-three-month-old boy who has lived in a succession of homes, who has particular special needs resulting from a burn injury.

Family Composition: Mother has history of depression and drug use, father is unknown. One older sibling, Sam, also in care, another sibling not yet born.

Current Living Circumstances of Child: Until a more permanent residence is found, Conor lives at Redcliffe Children's Home.

Significant history of child and family: Depression, drug use.

Family concerns about their child: None given.

Summary of Assessment of Need: Having suffered second-degree burns at the age of twenty months, Conor has not settled well with a recent large family, responding violently to others, and having to be removed.

Recommendations: Conor urgently needs more specialist one-on-one care.

Likely implications of Recommendations not being put in place: Conor may continue to display violent tendencies and continue in failing to achieve expected milestones for his age.

Signed: *Jim Rogers* (Social Worker)
Date: *16/10/2003*

31st October 2003

Hello Conor.

Messy handwriting alert! This is Jim Rogers again.

Very sadly we have had to move you from your new home with Jayne after only a month. (It is our mistake.) Jayne loved having you but you were distressed by her big noisy family. She has five children of her own and is currently fostering two boys along with you.

With your injuries still being painful, you are reluctant to be touched in any way and get distressed when the children play rough. What is just a game probably appears intimidating to you and so you over-respond, being quite violent and using whatever instrument is on hand to hit out. We know this is just self-defence against what feels like an attack on you.

Jayne has been wonderful at taking proper care of your scars after poor Julia couldn't but it's hard for her to give you full one-on-one care. It was rash of us to place you with such a large family. Until we find a foster carer who can dedicate more one-on-one care for you you're staying in a care home. This will hopefully be for a short time. We don't like putting you with lots of other people again but we want to make sure you are matched with a perfect carer, and this can sometimes take a while.

On a positive note, Jayne told us you particularly like painting and that you're really good for such a small child. She used to let you go in the conservatory when all the kids were outside and give you big sheets of paper and a variety of colours. One day she came in and you had painted a person. It was very good she said. You said it was Mum. (It's a word you like saying.) And the funny thing is it looks like her. It's amazing because you haven't seen her since you were born. It makes me wonder if we store memories like photographs. I've stuck it on the next page.

There's also a photo of your mum that we recently got. You will see how much the painting resembles her. You will also see that in the picture she is pregnant. A few weeks ago she had a baby. It was a boy and she called him George. She is still unable to care for children and George is going to be taken care of by another family. When we have a picture of him I will give you one.

I've also stuck in a photo of you painting at Jayne's house. I'll make sure that future carers know how much you enjoy it and that they provide you with lots of paper and paint.

Jim

10th November 2003

Today is your second birthday! We wanted to take you to Little Monkeys PlayZone but you're still not up to it! My name is Kerry and my husband is Colin and we have a dog called Bennie. You have been with us a week. You are our first! We are very excited. We can't have children of our own. I was so excited when they told us about you. It happened very fast! It was a lucky coincidence because we just wanted one child and they said they had just been made aware of the perfect boy. You were so cute when we first met you! You were kind of shy but looking at everything. You wouldn't let go of your black and white cat. They told us how much you like to paint so we got you an easel and paper and stuff. You do it a lot. You're so quiet when you do it that I keep wondering if you're even breathing! You get scared of going in the bath. The first time you kicked and struggled so much. I know it's the water. You're always scared it will be too hot. So I get in with you! You like that. I have to wear my swimming costume and you do too, because I'm a girl and you're a boy, and it's what I'm supposed to do as your carer. I make sure the water is cool and we sit close with your back to my tummy and I wash your hair gently. You never giggle or play in the water. As soon as your hair is done you stand up to get out. You don't like being left in bed alone. I let you fall asleep on the sofa with us! Jim told us you used to be more of a chatterbox. He said you used to climb and get into all sorts. I hope that you go back to being your old self while you're with us. My husband Colin says you're a still water that runs deep, which is funny when you don't like water much. But today is your birthday so happy birthday! We are going to see my mum who loves you loads too and then we're going to watch a Winnie the Pooh DVD with her. I stuck in a birthday card that came from your birth mum. It is below.

Kerry xxx

Dear Conor,

Happy Birthday Son.

Lots of love,
Mum xxx

21

Bernadette

The rain continues as Bernadette and Anne travel through the dark, heading for Doncaster and hopefully Conor. It pounds hard on the roof as though insisting it be heard too.

'Do you think something *happened* to Richard?' asks Anne.

Bernadette has asked herself this many times in the last few hours. Even though he hasn't been missing as long as Conor, it's just as odd. Not as worrying though – not a priority now.

'I can't believe how angry I am that he ruined my plan to leave. I finally had the guts to do it and he has the audacity to not turn up.'

'It's curious them both going missing,' says Anne. 'Such an intense night for you. Does he have a mobile? Did you call him?'

'He does,' said Bernadette. 'But I didn't. It always goes to his answering service and I don't want to leave a message about this there. Do you think I should?'

'I don't know. He might answer and at least you'll know he's okay.'

Bernadette realises she has been quite cruel, more concerned with her own anger at him not turning up than about whether he's hurt or in trouble. Even though she's leaving, she should perhaps make sure he's okay first.

'You can use my phone,' says Anne. 'Do you know the number?'

Bernadette stares at the device in Anne's hand. She realises she's scared – scared of why Richard didn't come home, and yet she has no clue what has kept him away. The rain finally slows outside and the traffic picks up speed. Doncaster isn't far now. Suddenly the phone rings in Anne's hand – the name YVONNE flashes.

'Hi Yvonne,' she says quickly. Bernadette can't hear the social worker's words and tries to interpret Anne's 'yes's' and 'okay's' and 'oh God'.

She hangs up and says, 'PC French just rang Yvonne. A boy in Conor's class, Stan, told his mum he saw him getting into a black car with someone after school. Stan's mum just rang the police to let them know. Stan said Conor seemed to *know* him. God, I feel sick.'

'Do you want to pull over?' Bernadette puts a hand on Anne's arm.

'No, I'll be okay. I just want to get to Frances' house now.' She takes a deep breath. 'That's not all. They were checking on Frances and it seems her twin brother Andrew got out of prison last week.'

Andrew is the only sibling Frances has kept in touch with. Bernadette knows from Conor's Lifebook that Frances has seven brothers and two sisters, some living in the UK and others in Belfast. Andrew was angry he couldn't have Conor when his sister wouldn't have him. He's a drug user; has been in and out of prison for petty crimes and such.

'So they think *he* might have picked Conor up?'

'Yes,' says Anne. 'Which is good, isn't it?'

'Yes. It *has* to be. At least Conor is with family. Do you think they arranged it? That Conor knew? And that's why he took his money? Maybe they're all going somewhere and that's why we can't get hold of Frances?'

Anne looks doubtful. 'I don't know how Andrew would have got in touch with Conor – they only ever met at George's funeral, and barely spoke even then. Unless he's caught up with him on his way home from school some time. Maybe sworn Conor to secrecy?'

Bernadette nods; knowing something makes her feel better. She feels sure Frances has all the answers. A sign for Doncaster appears, offering more than just physical guidance; a beacon of hope. They turn off and head into the town.

As a child Bernadette always loved the adventure of arriving somewhere in the dark – it usually meant a holiday or trip to relatives, and she'd know that an alien bed and interesting people awaited her. She has missed travelling while being with Richard. The world is now waiting. All those travelogues she's collected over the years might soon guide her through other unlit places.

Suddenly Bernadette sees something clearly – her books, the shelf.

She suddenly remembers, absolutely. She *did* put Conor's Lifebook in its place.

'It *was* there,' she says abruptly, her words accompanying the recollection that lights up her night.

She remembers reading it on the bus on Saturday after seeing Conor. Top Taxis had three drivers off sick so she'd taken two buses home and read to pass the time. Maybe it was her mood after seeing Conor, but the book upset her. So much sadness and rejection in its much-fingered pages. She decided then that she would not read it again for a long time. Decided Conor's future was more important than his past. She didn't even write about their trip to Ferens Art Gallery or their stroll on the foreshore. She simply put the book back on the shelf and walked away from it.

'What was there?' asks Anne.

'Conor's Lifebook. On my bookshelf.'

'Of course. Then it's not lost,' smiles Anne. 'It's at home.'

'No,' says Bernadette, softly. 'It's more lost than ever.'

'What do you mean?'

'When I said I'd lost it, I meant it wasn't on my shelf *this evening*. That's the place I always put it so Richard doesn't find it. So I wondered if I maybe hadn't put it back there the other day. But I did. I absolutely *did*. And I didn't look at it after that. I was going to just give it back to you next week.'

'I know you told me –' says Anne, '– about keeping the book with all the others to hide it. But I did wonder if that was really such a good hiding place. Do you know what I thought?'

'No,' says Bernadette, not sure if she wants to know.

'That maybe at some level, deep down, you wanted it to be found.'

Bernadette lets the idea sink in, but it struggles – like air-filled cups trying to stay afloat in a washing up bowl. No. She knows how angry it would have made Richard. How he would object and stop her volunteering.

'So what does it mean?' asks Anne.

'What does what mean?'

'If the book isn't there but you definitely put it back.'

'Someone has to have taken it,' says Bernadette.

'But who would want it? And who knows it's even there?'

'No one,' says Bernadette.

Anne concentrates on looking for the right street. 'Could Richard have come across it?'

Bernadette pictures him at Tower Rise; he isn't a big reader and she's never seen him anywhere near her bookshelf. He prefers to watch films and documentaries or play around on his computer. 'I don't see how,' she says. 'But no one else has been to our flat.'

Anne parks near a row of small terraced houses, most with dirty net curtains at their windows and many with no front garden. 'What if he *does* have it?'

'Well, he would know about my volunteering.'

'And what would that mean?'

Bernadette doesn't speak. She looks at the houses, tries to guess which belongs to Frances. If Richard does have the Lifebook he'll be angry that she hid it and angry that she went behind his back. That she lied. And all of this would explain why he didn't come home. But where did he go instead? Perhaps he has left her, beaten her to it.

'It means he knows the truth,' says Bernadette softy. 'And I suppose you're right – I'm glad.'

'Do you want to try calling him before we go in?'

'No. Let's find Conor. My marriage being over can wait.'

They get out of the car. Just as she did when arriving in a new place as a child, and as she did upon first entering Tower Rise with Richard all those years ago, Bernadette closes her eyes and smells the air. You see so much more without your eyes. There's a karaoke going on some-where nearby and a woman is shrilly trying to sing a ballad. The smell of Indian food drifts up the street and merges sickeningly with the stench of rotten food from overturned wheelie bins.

'Number fifteen,' says Anne.

'Let's find Conor then,' says Bernadette.

22

The Book

24th May 2004

To Conor,

They told me I could right you a letter for your book to read when your older. Im not good at righting would rather text but your too young to have a fone. They said your two and a half now I do no but I forget sometimes. They said your family is nice people I am happy. When you was born I did get to look at you and told you I was letting you go cos its better for you. I didnt mean to fall pregnant again but it happens I wouldnt get rid of you my dad said thats wrong. I am not sure who your dad is but maybe I might no who he is. Yes I might do. I dont think he gave me his real name probably faked me out cos they do sometimes so theres no point telling you it but I do remember him cos he was a bit diffrent to the rest. Your just a kid I wont tell you all that stuff just say that he did treat me ok. He was dressed nice and there not usually. He talked nice and he said we could just walk by the water and chat and stuff. He wanted to know about my house and me mum and dad. None of them ask that stuff normally. He said he was on a kind of mission and I said what like in the Blues Brothers film? You wont know that movie but my dad always had it on. He said he would like to help me but I dont need it. Thats your dad not mine. So anyways I remember him. Im sure its him thats your dad cos after him I was ill a while and there wasnt nobody else. So you come from a nice man. Im sorry Im not a nice woman. My dad always told me I never would be. Ive got seven brothers and two sisters but now I only see my twin brother Andrew sometimes. I was the naughty one. I try hard not to be but it never works out. Do you get like that? I read that you like drawing. I used to like that when I was little too. I hope your having a great time and when I get myself sorted they said I can start seein you and then we can maybe be friends. I called you after my first boyfriend. That was a long time ago when I was like about fourteen. I was good then. He loved me loads and loads. We only split up cos my family moved from Belfast to England. I cried and cried and never got over it. Maybe if wed stayed there and Id married him it would be diffrent. But its this and I wish it wasnt. Be happy little boy. Im sorry.

Your Mum xxx

10th November 2004

Hi Conor,

This is Jim Rogers again.

Gosh, you probably know my messy writing by now. Sadly two things are about to change. First, I will be retiring. I'll miss this work very much and all the children and adults I've met and got to know along the way. I was hoping to work a few more years and would have liked to see you settled with a forever family but my health is in decline.

I have loved knowing you for the last three years (today is your third birthday) and I hope I made all the right decisions for you. While social workers have the pleasure of making a difference, sometimes we also feel guilty that we perhaps didn't do the right thing even though we can never know it at the time. I'll miss you very much and hope that one day, when you're an adult, we can meet, and that you have a safe and successful life.

The other thing that's sadly changing is that Kerry and Colin have had to leave the Hull area and move to Australia. It's something they never thought would happen when they took you on, a sad but unavoidable circumstance.

Because they can't adopt you (they really wanted to) they can't take you with them. So you are living in a temporary care home until we find a new placement. You loved being with Kerry and Colin and have come on so much and progressed well. You have started a local nursery and mix well with other children now. (We hope to keep you in there but it depends where your next home is.)

You continue to draw and paint beautifully. The play therapy helped a great deal. Your counsellor said you've found your own healing process in creative expression. Hopefully it's something you'll always enjoy.

A lovely social worker called Tracy Fenton will replace me. She has lots of experience and has what we often call a sixth sense about who belongs where. You'll like her and I know she'll like you. She'll find you a good home. I have asked Tracy to include reports she thinks will be important to you in the future, even if some of them might make difficult reading.

Have a happy birthday, Conor. The care home staff always make sure birthdays are special and you'll have a small party. (I have stuck a few of your birthday cards in over the page and a recent photo.) Kerry said you had the kind of smile that spreads across your whole face.

Gosh, I hope it stays that way.

Jim

23

Conor

Paul says we're only ten minutes from Mum's house. Ten minutes can feel like longer than ten hours. Like when Mrs McCartney says we've got ten minutes till the bell goes and it takes forever. You watch the second hand on the clock and it goes dead slow. So I know we're still real far from Mum's house.

I'm glad cos I'm kind of nervous now. Not sure why. Maybe cos really I don't know my mum that well and a social worker or Len is always with me when I see her.

I know Paul much less even if he does seem to know me.

The sun is getting quite low in the sky now and it makes the road all orangey like Christmas sweets. Paul turns the radio off in the middle of Beyoncé. He says he understands what it's like not having a dad. No one even knows who my dad is. Sounds like a knobhead to me. I never understood how Mum can't know who he is. You have to do the sex stuff and how could you not notice doing that? So I think she just isn't telling me.

Sometimes I pretend who it might be. I told Stan Chiswick it's probably someone real famous and that's why I can't know. He has to keep his identity secret. Could totally be David Beckham or someone from *EastEnders*. Might even be a secret agent like that *Bourne Identity* mister.

Paul tells me this story about his dad. I listen good cos I know it'll pass the last ten minutes in the car. It goes a bit like this: Paul's dad was quite a somebody. He came from a wealthy family and they wanted him to do something great with his life. I think like a psychiatrist.

They're the ones who look at your head. I saw one but my head was okay. Anyway Paul's dad fell in love with a girl they didn't like. She was poor but dead pretty. When she got pregnant Paul's dad realised she wasn't right for him after all and the family were glad.

So Paul's mum brought him up all by herself. I guess the rich somebodies can be as bad mums and dads as the poor nobodies. They can all be knobs. Even if you have money you don't always do what you should.

We're driving down thin streets now with rows of houses and I recognise it. I've walked down here from the train station with Len. Paul is looking for something. Even if he knows my mum it's like totally obvious he hasn't been here before. But he did say he knew her from way back.

I ask if I can talk to Mum by myself first and tell her about my holiday plan. But Paul says no dead firm. He parks the car and turns to look at me and says he has to have a word with her so it's best I wait in the car while he does. He says it's been a long time and it's best they catch up and say hello and stuff first.

I know all about those first hellos. I've done it so many times. Going into a house and it's all new people. Hello hello hello new people. Hello new toys and rules. Boring and annoying and they might be idiots. But Mum isn't new to Paul. Just a half stranger.

Stay here, says Paul. *Don't go anywhere.*

Where would I go?

He gets out of the car and knocks on the green door I recognise. Last time I saw it I was with Len. He's from this Action for Kids thing and does stuff with me quite a bit. I took some flowers he let me buy at the corner shop.

Now Paul looks up the street and then at me and sort of smiles. It's a smile that does something real weird to me. I kind of feel like you do when someone whispers you a secret and it's the kind you don't quite understand but you know you might one day. After a bit Mum opens the door. She doesn't smile. She looks real shocked. All wide-eyed and open-mouthy. Then she steps back and puts a hand on the door like she's gonna close it but Paul goes in and slams it.

I'm not sure what to do. Are they okay?

Anne always tells me if ever I come home and for some reason she isn't there I should go to the neighbour and raise the alarm. But I'm not sure I need to raise any alarms. Maybe I'll just wait a bit. Maybe Mum is nervous like I was when I saw her for the first time.

Yes I'll wait a bit.

I tap my feet and shuffle about in the seat. Wish I had some paper and could draw for a bit. Drawing makes time go real fast. I remember I used to do it before I was at Anne's when I lived in this crappy care home where they never had time to bother with you and we always had cold chips for tea and there was only one telly that the older kids watched and didn't let us pick a programme. When I'm drawing, every line I do slows me down somehow. When the lines become something I breathe real calm. I don't have to think words like fuck and wank. Then when I shade, my body warms up.

Maybe Paul has some paper in the car. Wonder if he'll mind if I look? They're still in the house. I look in the flap thing but there's no paper just some sunglasses and a bag of mint chocolates (I get one) and some wires and one pen.

Maybe I should go and knock on the door?

I'm still trying to decide what to do when they come out of the house. My mum is first, holding Kayleigh's hand. Mum's face is red and wet. Kayleigh is pulling and crying. I do like my little sister but every time I've been to the house she cries and makes loads of noise. Makes me mad cos she's lucky enough to live with our mum but she always messes about.

Paul comes out of the house now and gets in the car. He says we're going somewhere together. All three of us.

I ask, *what about Kayleigh?*

She won't be coming, he says.

Mum knocks on the neighbour's door. A man with a tattoo answers and they talk for a bit and he nods and looks a bit worried and touches her hair and then takes Kayleigh inside.

Then Mum gets in the back of the car.

I haven't seen her for a month. Last time when me and Len went she got all upset at my flowers. She sniffed loads and took them in the kitchen and put them in a mug with Simon Cowell on it. There were too many and they wouldn't all fit in. She cut some shorter and put them in the sink. Mum's house is always messy. I want to tidy it all for her. I want to pick it all up and get rid of the food wrappers and stuff. Can't stand it not being finished.

Last time she sat on the same sofa as me for once. Mostly she sits on the floor and I sit with Len or Yvonne. But that time she got nearer and I liked it. She has freckles. Like me. I never noticed until then. Her hair has some bits of red in it too but I reckon she don't like it cos most of it's dyed blonde. She smelt odd, like the school PE changing rooms. But I didn't mind.

Now she is too far away for me to smell her. She asks me if I'm okay and I say yes cos I am. I ask her if it's good to see her old friend Paul and she says that he isn't Paul, he's Andy.

I'm all confused now.

She looks at Paul – no *Andy* – and asks him if I know. Paul – no *Andy* – says very firmly that I don't and now isn't the time. He says I am traumatised and she has put me through enough already and they will go to their old place and figure it all out.

I just want to cry. But I don't. I never do. I squeeze my eyes like you do your legs when you want the toilet bad. The scars on my legs tingle when I get like this. Right now it feels like someone is rubbing gravel on them.

I wish I knew what to call Paul. I wish I knew what this is all about. I want to go back to Anne's now. I want her nice sugary tea and some cake.

That's what I say to them – *I want to go home now*.

Paul – no *Andy* – looks at Mum like it's her fault and she says, *Well, you took him, they'll be after you*.

I say that I don't mind, I just want to know what to call people and then I want to go back home. Once I know what to call people I can try and fit in.

Paul says I can still call him Paul since I'm used to it. Not sure why he has so many names but I'll stick with Paul. He says I can't go back yet but I can afterwards. I'm not sure about afterwards. After what?

He tells me not to worry real kind.

I'll try not to, I say. *Where are we going?*

Paul looks at Mum then like she has the answers. She says it's up to him. Paul says to me that we're going to a special place and when we get there he will tell me everything. He says I deserve to know everything. Everything is such a lot and I'm not totally sure I want to know it all.

Paul starts the car. I look back at Mum but she's turned away towards the window. I bet she's squeezing her eyes tight so she doesn't cry. I want to tell her about my holiday surprise to make her happier but right now I don't know if it would work. Paul drives off.

I wonder how long it'll be until we get to this special place. I wish I could ring Sophie. Or Anne. Wish I had Bernadette's number.

Mum and Paul don't talk and I reckon it's just cos I'm here. Adults always go real hushed and quiet when kids come in and you just know they were either talking about sex stuff or things they're going to do that you won't like. I want to ask how they know each other and what it has to do with me.

We leave the town and go back onto the motorway.

Wish I could draw right now. I like doing people best. Anne says my people are as good as ones in photographs. Don't know how I do it just know that I do it best when they're not there and I can't see them. Anne says it's maybe to keep all those people with me.

I drew Muhammad Ali for my Art project last term and they hung it in the school corridor. Wanted to bring it home but they wouldn't let me. Did my head in. It was *my* picture. I won this big art competition once but I didn't get to go to the awards thingy cos my brother died.

I ask if Paul has any paper and a pen. He tells Mum to go in his laptop case on the backseat and get out the big notepad. Then he gets the pen from the flap and gives it to me too.

Now I can shut out the motorway and the slow passing time and escape. It might not be as good as usual because of the car moving, but

I'm relaxed now. I hardly even look at the paper. Sophie once asked how I don't go over the edge. I laughed and said, *What, over the cliff edge*?

I draw her now. I do wavy hair and the mole on her neck and the top lip a bit thinner than the bottom one. I shade her eyelashes and eyebrows cos I don't have no colours. My legs don't hurt anymore.

Who's that? asks Paul.

I tell him it's my best friend and quickly say that I do have boys as mates too cos people always think you're a weirdo for having a girl for a best friend. Mum is interested now. She says I'm real good. She asks if I can draw her and I say I did once at home.

Then I draw Anne. Makes me smile to do her short and easy hairstyle with jagged points and to sketch her laughy lines and her gold earrings. It's getting darker now but I don't need the light only the pictures in my head. I tell them this is Anne my foster carer. Mum looks at her for a long time. They met once or twice already. She says she looks kind in the picture. Paul says that it's a good job and looks at Mum in the mirror.

I think about drawing my brothers but it might upset Mum when George isn't alive no more. Anyway I just don't want to.

It's almost totally dark when I get to draw Bernadette but it doesn't matter because for some reason she's the one that sticks most in my head. The lights at the edge of the road flash past us and make the paper look like it's on fire. That makes Bernadette's hair the right colour. I just wish I had some colours for her eyes. They are real green like those sweets in a Quality Street tin. I never have any sort of crayon or pencil to get that right. I always make her smile in my drawings. She doesn't do it loads but I prefer her that way.

Mum has her eyes shut in the back but I'm not sure if she is definitely asleep. Paul looks at my picture when I hold it up. He has to stare for a while cos it's dark. He says she's pretty. Then after a while he asks who she is. I tell him she's Bernadette and that she is like an aunt but even better. I don't say that she's like a mum should be cos I don't want to hurt my mum's feelings if she's listening.

Now I'm tired. Now I want to close my eyes too.

Paul asks if he can keep the pictures and I say he can. I ask if it will be long until we get where we're going and he says no. I guess soon I'm going to know everything. Anne says you learn a new thing every day.

What a day this is going to be then.

24

Bernadette

The house where Frances lives is dark; there's no evidence of lamplight between curtains to give hope of anyone being home and no sound from a TV soap opera or clattering pots disturbs the night. The front grass needs cutting and the bins are stained with food. With a little care it could be lovely.

Anne knocks on the dark-green door, and they wait.

Bernadette likes the small house. Tower Rise is a huge creature in comparison – in their flat she often feels it's digesting her. But in a house like this she might feel safe, calm, complete. She might hang Conor's paintings and drawings on walls. She might travel and return to a place that is hers alone.

'What should we do now?' wonders Anne when further knocking is met with silence. 'I'm *sure* Conor's been here. What do you think?"

Bernadette agrees. She is about to suggest they try knocking on other doors in the street when the one next door opens and a middle-aged man looks out. Behind him, the sounds of children and dogs and a washing machine form a chaotic background music.

'You looking for Fran?' he asks, gruffly. His T-shirt is stained with something dark brown and his muscled arms are tanned and tattooed. A blonde woman, whose lower body is a snake, spirals seductively about his left bicep.

'Yes.' Hope is shrill in Anne's voice. 'Do you know where she is?'

'Who are you?' he asks, suspicious.

Anne goes to the fence that divides the gardens. 'I'm her son's foster carer.'

The man lights a cigarette. An Alsatian thrusts its dirty head out between him and the doorway and barks at them; the man's immediate response is to lash out with his foot and kick the animal back inside, growling, 'Get in, you bastard!'

Bernadette fears how he must treat the children she can hear arguing over a games console.

'Fran said coppers might come looking,' he says. 'Not talking to no cops.'

'We're not police,' says Bernadette. 'We're looking for her son. We just want to take him home.'

'When did she talk to you?' asks Anne. 'Why would she think the police might come?'

'I saw her about an hour or so ago, maybe longer. She went with the kid you was just talking about.'

'Conor?' Anne smiles, looks at Bernadette. 'What did she say?'

'She asked me to look after Kayls.' He flicks ash onto the street. 'All she said was that Andy had turned up and they had to sort something out. Don't know who the fuck Andy is. Might be a punter, might be a boyfriend. So she goes. No idea where. The kid was in the car.' A child starts crying in the house and the dog barks again. 'For Christ's sake!'

Before Anne or Bernadette can ask any more questions he goes in and slams the door.

'Andy,' says Anne. 'Frances' twin brother is Andrew.'

'I remember reading that Frances lived with him briefly,' says Bernadette. 'That it wasn't a suitable place for a child. I think that was when Conor first met her and it didn't work out.'

'What shall we do?' asks Anne.

'Surely we need to go to wherever Andrew lives now,' says Bernadette.

'PC French said he just got out of prison so that could be anywhere. I should let her know Conor isn't at his mum's. She'll be able to tell us where Andrew lives, won't she? Let's get in the car and call her.'

In the car Anne turns the heater on full. Bernadette realises how cold and hungry she is. The last thing she ate was a ham sandwich at about one; how long ago that seems.

She hopes Conor isn't hungry; that someone has thought to feed him. His huge appetite never fails to surprise her. They have eaten burgers at some fast-food place for a treat and he asks for more fries, saying his belly is telling him it needs them. She always gives in – knowing he's playing her a little. Who could not?

But Bernadette's hunger can wait. They have a good lead now.

Anne finds the card with PC French's number on and dials. Bernadette watches a too-thin dog search through overturned rubbish on the street and listens to Anne tell the police officer what they've discovered. She can tell that PC French has said again that they really could use the Lifebook, because Anne lowers her voice and says, 'Well, that can't be helped. It will turn up, I'm sure. And if you need to ask us what's in it, anything at all, we can tell you.'

Bernadette realises how useful the book would be. It paints such a full portrait of Conor. It could certainly give his life so far to the police. But what can she do? She is sure Richard must have it, and until she finds him, no book.

When she hangs up Anne says, 'PC French is going to get Andrew's current address and call us back. They have to provide one when leaving prison. She thinks it's close to here so it'll be a lot quicker for us to go there than them. Shall we find a café until she rings back? There's not much we can do until then.'

Anne drives slowly up and down the unfamiliar streets until they spot a corner pub with parking at the back. Inside they pick a table by a small fire that does not warm or brighten quite like the one at Anne's house did. Despite being past eight-thirty the place is almost empty; the only other customer is an old man reading his paper at the bar. Anne orders sandwiches and brings back crisps and lemonade.

For a while the two women sit in silence.

'Thank you for being my friend,' says Bernadette quietly.

'There's no need to thank me for that,' says Anne. 'I've hardly been any sort of friend, have I? We see each other briefly twice a month. Talk occasionally on the phone. Circumstances have just thrown us together, haven't they – and I'm glad. I should thank *you* for being Conor's friend.'

The barman brings two plates of cheese sandwiches, each decorated with limp lettuce.

'I need to do it,' says Bernadette, nibbling some of the crust.

'Do what?'

'Ring Richard before we find Conor.' Bernadette swallows a gulp of pain with her bread. 'We have no idea what … well, what state the poor little lad might be in. So I should call Richard before we leave and see if he's home. If not, try his mobile. Tell him everything. Well, some of it. That I've left at least. And tell him we really need the Lifebook if he has it. That he's going to have to get over being annoyed about me and hand it over.'

Anne nods and passes her phone. The grated cheese feels like worms in Bernadette's throat. She struggles to swallow, to think of her home number. When she manages, the sound of ringing mimics her heart's beat. Bernadette imagines the sound at Tower Rise, rudely disturbing the dark silence. Then there's the click and her own voice saying, *We're sorry we can't take your call, but if you leave a message we'll ring as soon as we return.*

As soon as we return – Richard hasn't returned. If he had he would certainly answer before the machine. Now, almost three hours after his usual arrival time, Bernadette feels sick. Something must have happened to him and, if it has, is the Lifebook okay? People are irreplaceable but so is that book. Documents and letters and photos that exist nowhere else might be gone forever. Conor's history might be erased, creating a question mark for his future.

'No answer?' asks Anne.

'He can't be at home,' says Bernadette. 'I'm concerned now.'

She dials the long-memorised mobile number, waits for it to connect and listens again to a ring tone.

After a while he answers. Bernadette's heart contracts, with relief and with panic. Richard doesn't speak but she hears a gentle background hum.

'Richard? Are you okay?'

'He's not here,' says someone who isn't Richard; a female someone.

Bernadette moves the phone away from her ear as though it will change everything. Like it might cancel the words. Cut off the strange woman saying them. Is this the 'sister' Richard took to Bob Fracklehurst's home?

'Who are *you*?' she demands.

'What's it to you?' asks the woman.

'Why do you have Richard's phone?' demands Bernadette.

'He left it here on Saturday.' After a pause the woman asks, 'Are you Bernadette?'

'How do you know me? Or Richard? Who *are* you?'

The woman sounds tired – or maybe the connection is bad. 'I'm Ruth. I've had his phone all week. I've been waiting for him to call.'

Has Richard really not had his phone all week? Bernadette tries to think back to each morning. Warm realisation surfaces like excess acid; he hunted for something when packing his laptop bag on Monday. Bernadette had asked what was wrong. 'Nothing,' he said. 'I'm sure it's at work.'

And she'd thought nothing more about it, presumed he'd found the lost item in his office.

'How do you know Richard?' she demands now.

'*He* should maybe tell you that,' says Ruth, not unkindly.

'Well, I have no idea where he is. Do *you*? Why were you with him last Saturday?'

'I have to go.' The woman called Ruth pauses. 'When Richard comes back, get him to call me for the phone.'

'No, you have t—' But Bernadette realises the woman has gone. She redials but it goes straight to messages. What point is there in leaving one? What point is there in dialling again?

'What's happened?' asks Anne, pushing her empty plate into the middle of the table.

'I have no idea,' says Bernadette. 'Absolutely no idea.'

Until this night her life has been simple, routine, monotonous. Only the two days when she sees Conor highlight her months with joy. But now a mystery; a woman.

'Someone called Ruth has Richard's phone,' she says.

"Do you know her?"

'No.'

'A work colleague, maybe?'

'He's never mentioned a Ruth. And she was too vague. And he doesn't have a sister, like he told Bob Fracklehurst; neither of us does. It's one of the things we had in common when we met – no siblings. Maybe *she's* this Ruth. The woman with him on Saturday. Maybe he's having an affair with her.' Bernadette waits for feelings of jealousy to surface and is sad when they don't. She hardly cares. 'Whoever she is, Richard isn't with her now. He's still missing and I've no idea where.'

On the table Anne's phone vibrates and tinkles. She picks it up quickly, and nods and says yes, then asks Bernadette for a pen, and writes down some directions.

'Andrew's address?' asks Bernadette when she hangs up.

'Yes, and it isn't far. We need to go back to Frances' house and continue up and then go left at the top and straight along, and his street is the third on the right. I just hope Conor's there.'

As they rush back out to the car, Bernadette remembers last Saturday with him. In his own inimitable style, he explained how the narrator in the science show said that because every part of the universe was one during the Big Bang and because every point has been expanding away from this since, the centre of the universe is everywhere.

He tugged on Bernadette's arm before she left, and said, 'The narrator is wrong though, isn't he? The centre of the universe is me. Cos I'm looking at it.'

Bernadette realises that this night, she is the centre.

And she's looking for everything.

25

The Book

Hull Social Services   **Child Protection Service Assessment Report**

| Date: 23/11/05 | Case #: 876004644 | Social Worker: Tracy Fenton |

Child	D.O.B./Age	Gender	Race
Conor Jordan	4 yrs.	Male	White

Parents(s)/Caregiver(s)

Name:	Toni Wilkinson
D.O.B.	28/10/1975
Address:	34 Creston Garth, Hull
Phone:	No phone
Employment:	Unemployed
Marital Status:	Single
Relationship:	Foster Carer

Reason for Assessment

Conor was found by police to be outside of the carer's home in the street late at night. Neighbours report that this often happens.

Date	Name	Role	Method of contact
18/11/05	Tracy Fenton	Social Worker	Consultation
18/11/05	PC Mark Cogg	Police Officer on scene	Phone call

Date	Name	Role	Method of contact
21/11/05	Conor Jordan	Child	Observation at foster home
21/11/05	Toni Wilkinson	Foster Carer	Home visit
21/11/05	Tom Lord	Landlord	Phone call
22/11/05	Frances Jordan	Mother	Phone call
23/11/05	Police Officer	PC Mark Cogg	Phone call

Risk Assessment

1. Child's ability to protect or care for self.

Conor is a four-year-old boy who seems to be growing and developing normally. He is of normal size and weight, with good coordination and a good vocabulary. He was able to answer the police officer's questions with his name, and his foster carer's name, but was unable to provide information about where she had gone. Although Tracy Fenton describes him as 'bright', at his present stage of development he is not capable of performing self-care tasks. Physically, Conor is coordinated enough to perform such tasks as opening doors, climbing over a gate, turning on an oven, and other activities, which could place him in danger. He is not capable of summoning adult help or of understanding the danger of leaving the home late at night.

2. Child's mental health.

Conor is described by Tracy Fenton as being shy at first with new people but warms up quickly and then gets very clingy. His foster mother describes him as a helpful child but very needy and demanding. Information from the police officer at the scene indicates that Conor exhibited signs of severe distress. Mild symptoms of stress were observed when the foster home was visited.

3. Child's behaviour.

Conor's foster mother described him as a handful and stated she did ask her own mother a few times for help following the placement. He is her second foster child. He is the only one at the residence currently.

4. Severity and/or frequency of neglect.

Conor was discovered by police in the street in a rough neighbourhood late at night. Information from the landlord and locals indicates Conor has been left home alone on at least one other occasion.

Additionally, the foster carer said she doesn't like cooking and sometimes Conor just eats a banana for his breakfast. She stated, 'we eat', but gave no description of what foods are available, who prepares Conor's meals or how regular meal times are for him. The foster carer's mother said she worried about whether adequate food was provided for Conor.

5. Location of injury.

There were no injuries reported or observed.

6. Condition of home.

PC Cogg said the house was messy, with clothing strewn about and pots in the sink, but did not have any rubbish lying around, etc. He said the child's room had toys on the floor but there were sheets on the bed and only a slight odour of urine. Overall, he was not concerned about the living conditions in the house. However, PC Cogg indicates there is more than minimal drug-related activity in the area, which may present additional dangers to Conor when he is home alone.

Tom Lord, landlord, said that Ms Wilkinson (foster carer) moved into the house in early 2004 and he did not know her very well. He said he had received numerous complaints from other renters about the number of men coming in and out of her home at all hours, making noise and frightening other residents. He said he reported a party to the police and then 'things settled down for a while'. Mr Lord said he was worried about the boy living in a home with rough-looking people hanging around.

Police took Conor into protective custody and he was placed in a care home at 1:00 a.m. Foster carer Toni Wilkinson was interviewed.

7. Caregiver's alcohol and drug use.

Toni states she drinks only 'a little bit' and describes this as 'socially'. She admits drinking wine when Conor is present, approximately once per week. She said this drinking occurs with 'a few friends' but denies there are parties. When told that the police had been called to her home because of a loud party where Conor was present, Toni replied, 'coppers have a cocky attitude' and stated, 'Conor was fine'.

8. Caregiver's parenting skills.

Toni's parenting skills appeared sufficient that she was able to foster children. When assessed she presented well, background checks were clear, home suitable. Toni describes leaving Conor home alone as a mistake but expresses no empathy for him waking up alone in the house or concern about what could have happened to him. She showed no understanding of the child's limited capabilities.

9. Caregiver's supervision of children under age ten.

PC Mark Cogg stated that Conor was located outside in the street. Cogg said the boy was crying and said he was looking for Toni. He had a black-and-white stuffed cat in his arms. The child did not know where she was, when she left or when she was coming back. He was unable to give any information about how to locate Toni.

Toni said her mother was on her way to care for the child, 'as soon as she finished doing her fake tan'. Toni said she had counted on her mother to stop over within a short time after she had left. Toni provided her mother's phone number. Toni said she left between 11:00 p.m. and midnight. Toni said Conor was asleep when she left and admitted her mother had not yet arrived. Toni said she went to 'pick up some people'. She said she had not planned to be gone long and estimated she had been gone less than one hour. The call to police was received at 11:15 p.m. Toni said that leaving Conor home alone was not something she does routinely but she did not deny that she has done it before.

Mr Lord, the landlord, said two weeks ago he discovered the door to Toni's house was open and he went inside to see if everything was all right and found Conor sitting on the floor watching cartoons. He called out for someone who might be with the boy, but no one answered. Just as he was about to call the police Toni came home carrying a bag of food and said she had run out for milk. Mr Lord said he did not report the incident because he felt sorry for the young woman.

Brief Summary of Risk and Supporting Information

At the time of the reported incident Conor was in significant danger, having been left home alone late at night and discovered in a dangerous situation on a busy street. Conor has been left home alone before and Toni takes no responsibility for leaving the child unsupervised. No information was provided by Toni that indicates Conor will be appropriately supervised in the future if returned to her care.

Despite Toni's initial strength as a foster carer she has few positive supports for her role as a carer now. While she says she has friends, she is resistant to giving much information about these friendships and the facts do not confirm her claims of support from these friends.

Toni's recent association with a known drug dealer also causes concern and needs to be explored fully. It is Tracy Fenton's opinion that, even with improvement in terms of the concerns listed above, it won't be possible for Conor to remain with Toni. He will remain in a temporary care home until a new foster carer is found.

Child Protection Team Staffing   Date: 28/11/2005

Case Decision
Services Required

Note – Conor's father's identity is unknown.

26

Bernadette

During the short drive through the deserted Doncaster streets Bernadette and Anne try to recall what they know of Andrew from Conor's
Lifebook. It isn't much. Just that he's the only sibling Frances still sees
and that neither of the twins has found adult life easy. Both have surrendered to bad behaviours, behaviours that perhaps have provided
escape. Bernadette recalls a letter to Conor from his Aunt Rhona,
in which she describes Frances as a sweet, sweet girl, and says Conor
should keep that in his heart when thinking of her.

They pass Frances' darkened house. Bernadette wonders if she has
ever woken one morning and wanted to pack her favourite things in
two bags and escape. She wonders whether Frances likes to read and
dreams of travel and sniffs the air in a new place; if she still thinks she
might make something of her life.

Andrew's house is its twin: dark, uninviting, unkempt, with bulging
bins and dirty windows. Like Frances', his grass needs cutting.

'Please God let them be here.' Anne doesn't sound optimistic as she
parks the car and they get out.

The house glares, its top two windows frowning eyes that dare
them to approach. Bernadette does, more boldly than she intends. She
knocks. Hope sinks with each unanswered rap, like dropped conkers
lost during a schoolyard game.

Then suddenly the door opens.

'What?' demands a black-haired, topless man, who blinks like
they've just woken him. There is a resemblance to Conor – something
in the eyebrow shape, the eye slant.

'Andrew?' asks Anne, nervous.

'Who wants to know?' Like Frances, his voice hasn't lost the Belfast twang; the t comes out more like a d.

'We're looking for Conor,' explains Anne. 'Is he here?'

'Conor? Our Frances' boy?' The antagonistic attitude evaporates a little. 'Why would he be here? I'm not allowed to have him, am I? Never even met the bugger properly.'

Bernadette steps back and Anne puts a steadying hand out. *We're not going to find him.* The thought comes hard, like the Ali punches Conor mimics when they're at the park and there's a sports club or soft play area. Cheese threatens to resurface.

Anne asks Andrew if they can come in a moment so Bernadette can sit down. Reluctantly he steps back to let them through.

'It's a mess,' he says. 'It's not my pad – it's Bill's. Just ignore him. He won't be conscious till tomorrow.'

The place smells of strong cigarettes and old beer. A cider-yellow hallway leads into a barely furnished lounge, where someone sleeps beneath two coats on a floral sofa. Bernadette sits on the only other chair. The stench is all that exists. Someone hands her a chipped glass with brown liquid in and encourages her to drink, which she does. Whisky; it reminds her of after-dinner Christmas drinks as a child when she'd smell it around the table and smile up at her father.

She wishes there was more.

'Why the hell would you think Conor's here?' asks Andrew, lighting a tab end from the overflowing ashtray.

'He's been missing for about five hours,' says Anne. 'It seems someone picked him up from school and took him to Frances'. Her neighbour says a man called Andy went there and took her and the child.'

'Frances has never called me Andy,' says Andrew.

'Maybe the neighbour got it wrong.' Anne takes the empty glass from Bernadette.

'Maybe. But if Frances told him she went with Andy, she wasn't talking about me. And as you see, Conor ain't here. Search the place. I'd love to have the kid over but they won't let me. I've never even met him, at least not to talk to. Not properly. Not met none of her lads. Only Kayleigh. Little George died and I'd never even set eyes on him. Went to the funeral of a kid I'd not seen. Even wrote in some damned book thing after we buried him. Conor and Sam were there but I never got close to them. Them bloody nosy social workers didn't think I should. I'm not suitable apparently. Criminal record and all that. What's worse – kids living with strangers or a family who love them but made a few mistakes?'

'I'm Conor's foster mum,' says Anne, her voice low but firm. 'I *was* a stranger at first but I assure you I'm not now. He's loved at my house. He's been with me five years.'

Andrew studies her, dragging deeply on the cigarette. 'Maybe so, but it's a known fact that kids is best with family.'

'Look then, we have a common purpose,' she says. 'To find Conor.'

'Well, *you* lost him,' snaps Andrew. 'Not me.'

He has a curious tick where he blinks three times in quick succession at the end of a sentence. His long eyelashes remind Bernadette of butterfly wings flapping in a panic. Is he nervous? Emotional? She hasn't met Frances and wonders if they look alike. She has seen photos in Conor's Lifebook but of course that isn't like meeting someone in the flesh – expressions and ticks and mannerisms make a person. These are the things Conor somehow captures when he draws.

The outsides of Frances and Andrew's houses are alike. Do twins naturally look for the same traits in people, places, and things? Why are Andrew and Frances so close to one another but seemingly far apart?

'Look,' says Bernadette, feeling a bit stronger now. 'No one lost Conor. He didn't come home after school and we just want to find him. Where would Frances go? Who might this Andy be? Has she mentioned him before?'

Andrew laughs, but not like he finds it genuinely funny. The person under coats on the sofa snorts and turns over.

'Well, what do *you* think?' asks Andrew. 'He's likely a punter. A trick. You know what I'm talking about.'

'I don't,' says Bernadette. She notices Anne looks as though she does.

'You don't?' Andrew's butterfly eyelashes flap again as though caught in a storm. 'I'm surprised. *She* obviously knows.' He points to Anne. 'That interfering social worker – what's her name? – *she* probably does. Frances is a prostitute. A hooker. A woman of the night. Whatever you want to call it.'

'Oh,' says Bernadette. There doesn't seem much else to add.

'I always wondered,' says Anne. 'I mean, I maybe knew. No one told me. It's not written anywhere. But some of the things Yvonne said over the years ... and some of Frances' entries...' Anne pauses. 'It's very sad.'

'It's just life,' says Andrew. He stubs out his cigarette. 'It's not right if she's taken the kid off with some punter though. He might have forced her – maybe she owed him something. Wish I could tell you who he is or where they went, but I can't. Did anyone call her mobile? Her work one.'

'I doubt that's the number the police have,' says Anne. 'Have you got it?'

'No.' Andrew sits on the arm of the sofa. In the grim light his pale face appears moonlike. The place is unusually quiet; no heating clicking on and off, no fridge humming, no life.

'How did Frances get into it?' asks Bernadette, gently.

'Our father,' says Andrew.

Bernadette looks at Anne, and sees in her face that they both heard correctly.

'Your *father*?' Bernadette repeats, perhaps to delay the inevitable horrible truth.

'Back in Belfast,' says Andrew. 'He used to take her down the pub with him. She was thirteen but looked a whole lot older. Real pretty too back then. Had a sweetness that not many lasses where we lived did. He'd make some money letting his mates have a bit of a fumble with her in the toilets. She didn't mind. Our Frances was quite wild anyway, liked the lads. Dad would give her pocket money out of it. Our two sisters, Janey and Margaret, were always a bit jealous that she got extra. Don't think they ever knew why. When we all moved over here to live with me dad's lot I suppose it carried on. Frances took charge though.

Dad lost his job so to speak. She realised she could make more on her own. Got with some guy called Snake – really, that was his name, and trust me he was – and he got her hooked on all sorts. I mean, I can't judge. But she's my sister. My twin.'

Andrew suddenly looks half the age he did when they arrived, like a boy – like Conor, only with darker hair and sadder eyes.

'She's not into it like she was, but I think there's a lot she hides from them nosy lot at social services, though. None of their fucking business. Stick with your paperwork and leave real living to the rest of us. It's hard to break habits. Especially habits started in childhood.'

Bernadette knows how true this is. Richard is obsessed with purity, having watched his mother fervently praying to the Holy Mother every evening. Her own mother taught her to surrender all for the one you love. The dogmas of childhood stick, whether you believe in God or sacrifice or Muhammad Ali.

'Poor Frances,' says Anne. 'Hardly had a chance in life. But she's still young. Still got a chance to find happiness."

'What, round here?' Andrew flings his arm out. 'Yeah, right, with two kids she doesn't have, one gone and one who likely won't be with her much longer.'

'Is your dad still alive?' asks Bernadette.

'Yeah. Somewhere.' Andrew looks in the ashtray for another tab end. 'Not seen him in a long time. Don't want to. He disowned me first time I was inside. Bloody hypocrite.'

'Does he see Frances?' asks Anne.

'No.'

Noise now invades the quiet; a phone rings in the hallway, shrill in the unfurnished shell. Andrew goes to answer it, closing the door after him.

'We can't stay here,' says Anne. 'We'll have to let PC French know that he doesn't know where Frances is. I really thought Conor would be here. This is terrible. It's so late now – past nine. He's never out at this time of night. I can't bear not knowing if he's okay.'

'I know.' Bernadette hates that there are so few words to convey properly what this pain feels like. Torn and broken and shattered hearts are just clichés; really the heart quietly aches in such moments.

She follows Anne into the hallway, where Andrew talks on the phone in a hushed voice, bent over as though to disguise further who it is. He covers the mouthpiece, says, 'Will you at least let me know that you found the kid?'

'Of course,' says Anne, opening the door.

'Is there anything at all you know that might help?' Bernadette asks him.

Andrew sighs. Thinks. Shrugs. 'What can *I* tell you?' He pauses. 'Frances said he's a little fighter. Not that he's bad and fights, but that he's tough. Never let that fool you. The fighters are crying inside.' Andrew goes back to his phone call as though they were never there.

Doncaster has been a dead end. There's no knowing if Frances and Conor are still here or whether they've taken flight. No clues, no trail, no answers. They close the front door on the smell and emptiness.

The night waits.

In the car Anne calls PC French and updates her. While listening, Bernadette feels she's flying above her own body. Up there, she watches herself and Anne, and feels sad for them. Sees Anne listen to whatever PC French is telling her, the lines on her tired face ones Conor might draw with love. Sees her hang up and close her eyes for a moment. Sees both of them sigh and then discuss the new information, as the night gets closer.

The Doncaster police are searching the area, since it's where the last sighting of Conor was, but a search will continue in Hull. So PC French has told Anne they should just come back so Yvonne can go home.

In truth, Bernadette is relieved. There will be peace at Anne's house. It's the refuge Conor will return to when he can. He *has* to.

Anne starts the car. 'I'm going to do something I haven't done for years,' she says. 'I'm going to pray.'

'It can't hurt,' says Bernadette.

Richard's childhood means he often prays – not kneeling with rosary beads, but privately when he thinks Bernadette is asleep, words she can never make out.

When she and Anne arrived in Doncaster – only an hour ago – she was as hopeful as when she was a kid enjoying the adventure of arriving somewhere in the dark. Now the night is full of monsters again. Fathers teach daughters that life is about giving yourself to them. Strange women lurk in the shadows. Men take children. Husbands disappear.

'Please God, bring Conor home,' says Anne.

'Amen,' whispers Bernadette.

It's a word she knows well; one Richard uses to bless a line of thought, one he got from his mother. As the car pulls away, Bernadette remembers a time he used it after saying he loved her, as though to cement the words further.

Two years after they'd moved into Tower Rise – when she still thought there might be children one day and that Richard protected her from the outside world the way a burglar alarm protects a house – a couple moved into the flat next door. They were young, not married, and happy to chat in passing on the stairs. They engaged in loud sex, which, since their bedroom neighboured Bernadette and Richard's, meant many a disturbed evening.

Though Bernadette smiled while trying to sleep through the moans, saying they were just youthful and full of vigour, Richard pulled the covers over his head and said that no one respected the sanctity of marriage anymore, and that some acts were private, meant only for the ears of those involved.

In the morning he pushed their bed against the opposite wall.

'That surely won't make much difference,' said Bernadette.

'It will,' insisted Richard, and Bernadette should have left the matter there.

Instead she said that the bed wouldn't look right on the fireplace wall as it would have to go in front of it, or next to it, which would be too close to the window's icy draught.

'Do you *want* to listen to their sex acts?' asked Richard, pausing by the bedhead.

'Well, no,' said Bernadette. 'Of course not. But I just think the bed will look stupid there.'

'Stupid?' Richard repeated the word in a way that made all others insignificant. 'What I'm doing is stupid?'

'No, not *you*.' Bernadette would soon learn to not use such words, that Richard had been bullied by classmates for years and was particularly sensitive to them. 'I meant ... look, it doesn't matter. I'll help you with the bed.'

Bernadette moved to help Richard but he took hold of her arm and said, 'Why must you question me? Use words like stupid? Why can't you just be *with* me?'

'I am,' insisted Bernadette.

Later Richard would insist through tears that it was the angle of her arm and the nearness of the thick, oak bed frame and the moment and not knowing his own strength. Bernadette would agree, would say it had been a clean break, thankfully, that the pain had been bearable and she knew it was an accident. To the doctor she simply said she had fallen. A plaster cast for six weeks meant no bathing or showering or washing pots, and a husband who tended to her every need.

When it was removed life went back to normal as though the injury had never happened. Sometimes, when she looked at her once again perfect arm, it was as though it never had.

'I love you,' Richard said when he first saw the white plaster cast. 'I love you. Amen.'

Anne says it now too: 'Amen.'

Amen to the night.

Amen to bringing Conor home.

27

The Book

SCHOOL REPORT

Year Group: Year 1   Teacher: Mrs Sowden

Child's Name: Conor Jordan   Date of Birth: 10/11/2001

Literacy

Conor needs to be reminded to listen during group discussions. When concentrating he makes valuable contributions. He has a tendency to veer away from the issue and bring alternative information into the conversation, which is his 'news'. Conor's writing has improved and it displays greater control. Letter formation is coming on.

Numeracy

Conor can grasp new concepts. He can add and subtract within 10, though he needs reminding to look more carefully at the signs. He has difficulty with time and money, but we will work further on this. He can describe properties and positions using everyday language. He needs to be reminded not to shout out. He is restless at times.

Science

Conor has trouble using simple scientific language to explain his findings. He finds it difficult communicating his results in simple graphs and charts. He is keen to talk but not about the subject in question. However, in our work about light and dark he named a number of light sources, including the sun, and recognised that dark is the absence of light. He enjoyed this topic particularly.

Art and Design

Conor has made superb progress in this area. He enjoys using a variety of materials and techniques. He always has interesting ideas. Most of all he likes to draw or paint. When he has access to paints or pencils he sits still and never interrupts or chats over others. It is often hard to speak to him at these times since he is so absorbed. His artwork is exceptional for his age. He is definitely gifted.

History

Conor has enjoyed listening to and discussing stories from the past, such as that of Guy Fawkes. He is starting to display a sense of chronology by placing events and objects in order and using everyday language about the passing of time. He has a very good understanding of how and why people's lives have changed. He often talks about his own life in such a way.

General Comments

Conor is bright and likeable but has struggled at times to adapt to life at school. He has trouble with group work and wants to do things his own way rather than the way that works for everyone. When mixing with others he is very keen but at times overbearing. A few early incidents, where the scars on the backs of his legs were revealed during play, resulted in his being picked on. The school counsellor, Kate Sharpe, will have a few sessions with him next term.

Targets for Next Year

Conor needs to listen better in class.
Conor needs to make sure he does his homework.
Conor needs to consider others when working in a group.

Teacher: Mrs Sowden   **Headteacher:** Mr Grimshaw
Date: 21/12/2006

*Please see attached letter from Art teacher, Mrs Connelly.

I felt it important that I draw your attention to Conor's superb artistic skills. As a new pupil, he is a joy to witness. Whatever materials we use, he fashions something outstanding. But most wonderful of all is his drawing ability. I understand he has lived in a variety of places and I wonder if this escape in his art is a way of coping. In which case, as a lover of art, too, I urge you to make sure Conor has plenty of materials at his disposal and plenty of quiet time to develop his talent. In my fifteen years as a teacher he is, without question, the most gifted artist for his humble five years that I've had the pleasure of teaching.

Sincerely,
Mrs Connelly

Something strange wakes me up. It's a song. Is it the radio? It goes Nah Nah Nah Nah Nah Hey Hey. I know it. Then Mum talks and I remember where I am. I fell asleep in Paul's car.

It's dark still and I don't know how long I've been out. Hate that. So many times I've woken up in a different place and had to figure out why I'm there. I've learned to wake up real fast when I need to. I do now. I look at Paul driving and then at Mum talking on the phone. She's saying she will be back later and then she hangs up.

The song that woke me was her ringtone. It's a song by this girl band and Sophie loves it, but I can't remember the name.

Mum shuffles around like she wants to get out or something and says real angry to Paul that she should really call the police and say he's abducted us. He'll go to prison then and what will he do about that? It's not a very nice thing to say. He didn't force me in the car and he's been dead nice to me. Nicer than lots of people I've known. She's probably just annoyed cos she wants to be back home. Maybe she's missing one of her favourite TV shows. I know I hate missing *Doctor Who*.

Paul smiles and says in his calm slow voice that once they hear that she left Kayleigh with a neighbour she'll lose the only child she's managed to keep so far. That's mean too. I don't like him dissing Mum. I've punched Stan Chiswick before for saying that kind of stuff. But there's no point me even trying to hit Paul. He's like a great big mountain and I'm just a tiny pebble. I reckon even Muhammad Ali would back down from a man twice as big.

Mum doesn't argue anymore and I'm glad. She sits back with her arms crossed and looks out the window. Paul just drives. I want them to get along. Hate arguing. Get a real twisty feeling in my belly when people do.

I see the Humber Bridge and realise we're heading back towards where I live. I love seeing the rows of lights. They're like lines of tiny spaceships. If we go out for the day Anne always says we're nearly home when we see them. But I don't reckon we're going home now. I don't think Paul would pick Mum up and then take us to Anne's.

Should I ask? Will they start disagreeing again?

Before I can, Mum says she hasn't been here since then. She doesn't say what then was but Paul looks like he knows. I think they keep forgetting I'm here. I'm used to it. People always do.

Paul says, *Well, I have – I've been up this end lots, but not to the place we're going*.

I wonder if I've been? I wonder where it is?

I need the toilet again and don't know if there will be any when we get where we're going. Should I ask if we can stop somewhere before? Paul was nice earlier and got me a burger too. Mum should be nice cos she's my mum. I touch the ninety-six pounds and forty-two pence I've got in my pocket and think of the holiday I want her to have. If Paul wasn't here I'd definitely tell her about Bournemouth, but I want it to be just us. So she notices me.

Then I remember ringing Sophie earlier. How much did I spend? Forty pence? So I guess I've only got ninety-six pounds and ... two pence now.

I *do* need the toilet.

Paul says there are some where we're going.

Good.

Wonder if there's food too. My belly is rumbling big style. I always think of Bernadette when it happens cos she never minds if I have two desserts or more when we're out. One time I had burger and chips and ice-cream and milk-shake *and* a cookie. She's ace.

We're driving through the city now. It's cool to be out at this time.

Hull Fair will be coming soon. That's what I think of when I see the lights from the pubs and shops. I go on all the scary rides at the fair and never get sick or scream. Last year they said Mum might be able to go with me but then she couldn't and I never found out why. Maybe this year I'll go with her.

I might ask her later.

Wish I could ring Sophie one more time. Tell her where I've been and everything. It feels like loads of stuff has happened since I spoke to her. Plus she will totally keep it all secret. If I knew where we were going I'd tell her and she could sneak out the window and share this adventure. I bet tonight will end up being the latest I've ever gone to bed. Maybe I won't even get to bed.

At the big gold statue of the man on the horse, Paul turns towards the water. I know where we're going. I love this place. The Marina.

Me and Anne come here sometimes to watch the boats. I love the tinkling sound the ropes make against the masts. It looks mega at night. The water is like a black mirror and the lights in it go all wobbly. They're red and blue like a flag.

Now we drive past the water though and go along a cobbled street and park outside the Minerva pub. It says so on a huge sign thing. It's one of those olden days kinds, not the ones that have flashing lights and spinning balls.

Paul turns the car off and we just sit there.

I can see all the way up the river. I wonder how far away the other shore is. How long would it take to swim to it?

Mum says, *Well, now what? We're here. Is that it?*

Paul turns and asks what she means. He tells her she should think about it. Think about how she had no right not to tell him afterwards. To somehow find him and tell him.

They're talking like people do in those serious dramas on telly. Anne likes them. The characters all talk real weird. Say stuff about dignity and equality and what's right. I sigh super loud and Paul seems to remember me. He ruffles my hair and says to Mum that I never asked to be born. More serious drama talk. How can you ask to be born? Paul says he will see if they'll let me go to the toilet in the pub and tells Mum to wait there for us.

We get out and it feels really cold after the car. The pub is cosy though. Paul says something to the man at the bar and he lets me go to the toilet. When I come out Paul is sitting at a table looking all sad or something. Like Anne does when she sits in the kitchen and works out her money. He doesn't look up for a bit. I wait. When he sees me he says I can't stay in here cos I'm just a kid but I should look at the place cos once upon a time my mum and him liked it. It's got really tiny rooms and fishing pictures everywhere. Guess they love all that kind of crap.

Back at the car Mum is still sitting there. She's like a black shadow with all the lights behind her. Paul doesn't seem to know what to do now. He tells me to get into the back of the car this time. Through the open door he tells Mum to stay with me for a bit, cos he needs to think. Then he walks off up this narrow pier with water splashing on all the sides, his legs all slow and swingy.

This is the first time in my whole life I've sat on my own with Mum. Like without social workers or Len or some knobhead with a folder. None of that crappy supervision stuff. I've waited so long for it to be just us two. When I imagined it though it definitely wasn't like this. I thought maybe we'd be at her house and I'd be like fifteen or something.

I used to pretend that one morning I'd get up and she'd be in Anne's lounge having a cup of tea with her. And she'd say, *I've come for you. I'm better. I've bought this really nice house by the sea. And your dad is going to be there too. He's this really nice mister and he wants to make it up to you.*

Now I try and think of all the stuff I've ever wanted to say to her. All the questions I think of at school and then forget to write down cos Stan does my head in. All the things I get chuffed about, like doing good in Art.

But none of it's in my head. My head is just totally empty. I try and think of how Sophie is with her mum. She's just natural. They act normal. Sophie's mum doesn't sit real stiff. Sophie's mum has lots of words. They argue but in the way you do when you love each other. Sophie's mum is just there. Wish I could ring Sophie and talk to her right now. She'd know exactly what to do.

All I can think to ask Mum is why she didn't come with me to Hull Fair last year. She shrugs and says she doesn't remember. You'd think she'd know how to be. She's got Kayleigh. It's not like she hasn't been around kids. I ask if she'll take me this year and she looks at me then. She says they probably won't let her. I tell her she could try harder. I don't mean to talk so bad to her but I can't help it. I've got all this thick black stuff churning around inside me.

Mum still has her arms crossed. I read this book about being a detective once and it said body language is important. I always watch it anyway. I see everything. She is either mad or she's hiding something.

Then she says, *I don't know why he came tonight.*

She's talking about Paul. She says, *All these years and now he shows up.* So I ask how they know each other.

A firework suddenly lights up all the sky in red and yellow. It's far away across the river I reckon. I wonder if it's a party or a really early Bonfire Night thing. It's reflected in the river. Like twins.

Mum starts to cry. Now I feel real bad. I tell her I didn't mean to be unkind and sort of pat her arm. The sleeve is all fluffy and soft. I don't know how to hug her though. Mum shakes her head and sniffs and says it isn't me. I bet it is. Adults lie. I want to tell her that I'm real glad we got to be on our own together. Tell her I've saved up so she can go on holiday next year.

But she says that she's sorry for not being there. Sorry she never told me anything about my dad when she could have.

Now I want to cry. But I don't. I have to be the man.

She says she needs to talk to Paul for a bit on their own and then they will talk to me.

When she opens the car door, cold wind comes in. She kind of gasps and then she slams the door. I watch her walk along the pier to where Paul went until she disappears.

It seems really quiet now. Not sure what to do.

What time is it? Five past nine. I wonder what time Paul told Anne I'd be back? Will she be worried now? I hope she still kept my tea. My belly's really rumbling now. The best time of day is just after tea when we sit and watch *Deal or No Deal* together. Anne always says deal because eight thousand is a load of money but I always say no deal cos I'm braver.

Muhammad Ali would never deal.

There's an ice-cream-coloured phone box just up the road. Got change in my pocket but it's just notes and one quid and two pence. Could only call one person probably. Have to be Sophie. Wouldn't take long. Could just run and do it quick now. Adults always take forever talking about serious stuff.

Real nervous, I get out the car. Don't want Paul being cross at me.

The phone box stinks of piss. I push my quid into the slot and dial Sophie's number. It rings for a long time and I wonder suddenly if she's gone to bed. Does she go at nine? I have to on a school night. Anne says the stuff on TV after nine isn't for my eyes.

Then someone picks up. Sophie's mum.

Not sure whether to speak.

She says hello and hello. Then she pauses and says, *Conor, is that you*? I feel kind of guilty for standing there in the dark and not answering. She's nice Sophie's mum. She says, *Conor, if that's you just tell us where you are. You won't be in trouble. They just want you to come home. Please talk to me.*

Why would I be in trouble anyway? Paul told Anne where I am. Paul knows Anne cos he talked to her. He knows Mum. Did he lie? Real quick I put the phone down. Feel sick now. Like you do when you've nicked goodies from the corner shop and you're walking away thinking they're gonna get you any minute.

I go back to the car and sit in the front this time. The fireworks have stopped and the sky's all black again like the paper we use in Art. Sophie's mum said they just want me to go home. Does that mean Anne's worried then? I don't have no more change to ring and tell her I'm okay.

Could I find my way from here? It might be totally miles. Maybe I should just sit tight and when Paul and Mum come back I'll tell them I absolutely have to go now. I can't wait for them to tell me *everything* anymore.

It's nine twenty-five now. They've been gone a long time. Especially Paul. Wish I could see them out on that pier but it's too dark. Don't like it when people don't come back. It's just not fair to promise a person you will and then you don't. I'll never do that to anyone.

The car isn't warm anymore. Getting bloody cold now. Only got my thin jacket on. Anne said on October the first I have to start wearing my big coat for school. How long should I wait here before I do anything? What will I do if they just don't come back?

I remember one time when I lived with this woman called Toni and I woke up one night and I was all on my own. Dunno how old I was. Maybe four. Had this toy cat called Blackie. I was a big weed then and had to have it with me all the time. Don't need it now of course. Anyway I went looking for Toni I remember, up and down the street. Some policeman got me. I never went back to Toni's. It was all big drama and stuff.

But no one ever asked me what it's like when someone never comes back. I can tell you exactly what it's like. It makes you put half your feelings in this made-up box and lock it up. So I do like Anne loads but not totals. Cos if I do she won't come back. I know it. But I wouldn't ever tell her this cos she's nice and she's been so kind to me.

The only person I've ever given the whole box to is Bernadette and that's cos every single time she goes away in that taxi she comes back two weeks later. She's like one of those Frisbee things me and Sophie play with in the field near her house. Even if I don't always catch it, it always comes my way.

Bernadette always comes back.

And I know in my heart that she always will.

I decide I'll draw for a bit and if no one comes in that time I'm gonna have to go and look for Paul and Mum. I find another sheet of paper in Paul's laptop bag and close my eyes and sketch. It's always amazing how quickly I feel better with a pen in my hand. The whole world goes away.

Now he's gone I can draw Paul. The sound of the pen on the paper makes me shiver a bit. Always does. Sometimes it's like I don't even do the drawing myself. It's like someone gets hold of my hand and does it for me. Never takes long. Shade dark and light. Sketch lines and contours. Put the special marks and stuff in the right place.

Paul's face looks back at me. I think I got the hair just right but maybe his eyes are wider. I put it on the back seat with the ones of Bernadette and Anne and Sophie. Maybe he'll want to keep it too.

Okay, now it's nearly ten and they're not back. Something's happened. Something real bad. Story of my bloody life. And if I don't go and find them I'll have to raise the alarm like Anne always tells me to, and then I reckon we're all going to be in big trouble.

I wish everyone would just go and find themselves for a change.

29

The Book

Hull Social Services Report   **Tracy Fenton (Social Worker)**
Home visit: *to assess recent change of placement*
Name: Conor Jordan   **Date: 09/01/2007**

I visited Conor at foster carer Georgina Caine's home. Conor appeared to have grown in height and had a healthy appearance with clear skin and eyes. Mrs Caine said he is eating and sleeping better now, and gets on with her older teen son Mark.

I spoke to Conor alone in his bedroom while playing several games, and then to Conor and Mrs Caine together in the lounge. The following is what was discussed. Conor was happy to share his feelings but got agitated when his mum was discussed.

Access

Mrs Caine reported that Conor's first supervised access with his mother, Frances, had occurred the week before, on 3rd January, but had not gone well. The access supervisor Craig collected Conor from school and then supervised access at the social services office in Doncaster, where Frances was waiting. Frances does not have a secure home – she is staying with her brother Andrew. Due to Andrew's circumstances the place is not suitable for a child. Conor stated that he was excited to see his mother and maybe one day, in the future, his two brothers, Sam and George. Once together, Conor was reluctant to engage with his mother and showed signs of stress. Frances failed to engage in any way either, despite Craig trying to mediate. Conor tore up the drawing paper in the room and ignored both Craig and his mother for the remainder of the hour. Frances cried, which distressed him further. When the session was over Conor didn't want to talk about it. Back home Mrs Caine reports that he didn't sleep and refused his evening meal. This is rare, she said. After discussion with Frances and Mrs Caine it has been decided to postpone further access until Conor is ready.

Schooling

Conor said he doesn't like schoolwork, and finds reading and maths hard, but enjoys art and playing with his friends at lunchtime. His 'main' friend is a girl called Sophie, though he stressed that he has 'lots and lots' of other mates too. Mrs Caine reported that Conor's teacher informed her last week that he won't concentrate in class and has been moved to a desk nearer the front. Mrs Caine will follow this up to see whether this improves the situation. There was an incident during school break where some older boys pulled Conor's trousers down to show everyone the scars on his legs. This was dealt with; the parents of those concerned were invited into school, and Conor appears not to have let the incident ruin his playtime.

Home

Mrs Caine reported that they have not had any particular issues with Conor and he has settled into their family well, thriving off the routine and enjoying particularly the company of their teen son Mark. It took a while for him to allow anyone to touch him in an affectionate way but he permits it now. He still needs his black-and-white stuffed cat (he calls it Blackie) at night. We discussed the possibility that this may be a 'honeymoon' period and Mrs Caine said she had given thought to this.

When I spoke with Conor alone he reiterated that he is happy living with the Caine family and especially likes Mark, their teen son. He joyfully spoke of time with him, watching sports videos and taking the pet dog Shana for walks. The teen boy appears to be fond of Conor, too.

In response to a letter from Conor's art teacher, Mrs Caine tries to make sure Conor has plenty of art materials. She reports that now and again Conor wets the bed and is embarrassed. He tends to get clingy at night and likes someone to sit with him until he goes to sleep. Mark often does this, watching DVDs with him.

Assessment

Conor appears to have settled into his new placement well and was able to identify positive aspects about living with the Caine family. Conor and Mrs Caine were observed to have a warm relationship, where Mrs Caine put her arm around Conor on one occasion. Physically Conor looked very well. Some difficulties with his concentration at school have been identified and the occasional bedwetting has been discussed with a doctor, who suggested a star chart. Conor is settled and thriving.

*Note from Frances Jordan (birth mum) after first access meeting with Conor

04/01/07
To Conor,
I am glad we was aloud to meet but am sad it didnt go very well. It was hard cos I dont know you. When you know someone properly you know what to do when they are feeling upset and that. I think you are mad at me and I understand. Id be mad at me if I was you. I have let you down. I was hopin we could be friends. I had got a teddy bear for you but I will maybe give you it another time or let your social workers have it. Your such a cute boy and you look lots like my brother Andrew did way back when he was little. That made me want to cry. I hope there is a next time and you can forgive me.

Your Mum xxx

*Letter from Mark Caine, seventeen-year-old son of current foster carer.

18th March 2007

Hi Conor,

They said I can write a letter for your Lifebook. I looked through it too. Wow you have been through some stuff. Makes me sad kinda. Cos your my little mate. You deserve a lot better. You deserve to have a proper mum and to know your dad. I admit at first I was annoyed when Mum said she was going to start fostering again. She did it a few years ago and we got some right brats. I mean I know they had it rough and I feel bad saying this but you shudda seen some of them. Then Mum stopped cos it wore her out. She said her heart broke a bit every time they came and went. So when she said a few months ago she was doing it again I got all ready for the rollercoaster. But your okay. Your the youngest we've had but your definitely the coolest. I mean I know you got issues but your interesting too and talk much older than five sometimes. Your an ace drawer. Didn't we laugh when I said you should draw curtains and you said it's easier than drawing breath! And your just so cool for watching all my Muhammad Ali DVDs with me. Ali is the greatest! I'm smiling now cos you sound so funny when you repeat it after me. And when we watched his fight with Sonny Liston and you said it was black and white so how would we know what side they're on. Theres only one side in boxing Conor and thats your own. My dad told me that. He got me into it. I'm gonna join a club soon and gonna be as great as Ali. You can come and watch me train when your bigger. Ali said he hated every minute of training but also he said don't quit suffer now and live the rest of your life as a champion. Your gonna be a champion too Conor! I reckon your early days that werent too good mean it'll happen. I hope so. I guess your like the brother I've never had. Anyway I don't know how long you'll be with us cos they never know but I hope it's a long time. Really do.

From,
Mark Caine

30

Bernadette

In the car returning to Hull, Bernadette thinks about the other time Richard was late home. The memory forces its way into her head; a child pushing roughly to the front of the school-dinner queue. It's as though now she has begun to cut Richard out of her life, his ghost is trying to reclaim her.

One of the first questions PC French asked them earlier was whether Conor had ever gone missing before. Does the fact that Richard came home late once before make his non-appearance now more or *less* meaningful? Whether or not she wants to remember, the car's motion and the occasional swish of passing vehicle encourage the recollection.

Like then, she is closed in a dark place.

'He came home late once last year,' says Bernadette.

Anne starts as though she'd fallen asleep at the wheel. 'Richard?'

'Yes. I think it has to mean something. When something out of the ordinary happens.'

'Maybe,' says Anne.

'I'm sorry to keep going on,' says Bernadette. 'But it's like how people say your life flashes before you when you die, except it's my marriage I'm seeing.'

'Tell me about it,' says Anne.

Bernadette does.

*

Autumn is always prettiest at Tower Rise. While the evergreen trees smugly retain their colour, the oaks and beeches slowly die. But in their demise they are most captivating, as though wanting to leave a lasting impression. Burnt oranges and plum reds dominate the landscape, a scorched desert under blue sky.

That evening the trees seduced Bernadette.

Instead of beginning her five-thirty ritual of laying the table and checking the chicken, she forgot the time. From the lounge window she counted falling leaves, and smiled. The leaves were leaving. She said the ditty aloud: *The leaves are leaving.* Pretty. She might write it down. Tell Conor. He'd likely have to paint leaves at school, a theme they'd often covered when she was a kid, observing the lines and creases as you might in a hand's palm.

Bernadette had been reading all afternoon. Halfway through a new paperback she'd put the chicken in the oven and peeled some vegetables. Then, when her eyes got tired, she shut the novel and put it on the shelf by Conor's Lifebook. The view beckoned. Low in the sky, a wan sun struggled to compete with the dazzling leaves. She watched it sink.

When Bernadette turned to the clock it was five-forty. The carrots and potatoes were still cold in their pans, the table not set. She had barely twenty minutes until Richard returned. Running to the kitchen, she turned the hob rings on full; he'd grumble if the food was undercooked, but something was better than nothing at all. She poked the chicken with a fork – white, thank goodness – and knew the gravy would only take a moment. She grabbed the cloth and napkins and cutlery and set the table – crisp, symmetrical, perfect. If the vegetables cooked quickly he need never know she had forgotten.

Five-fifty. Soon his car would sound on the gravel, followed by slow footsteps that misled with their languid pace and soft sound. Time to stir the carrots and warm his plate, to put out a glass of ice-cold water.

The leaves are leaving. Bernadette smiled.

Everything was in place.

At six she hovered by the door, the eternal hostess in her own home. Soon it would open and he'd stroll in – no thank you for her efforts – and fold his jacket, put it over the back of the sofa and kiss her cheek without touching it. She sometimes wondered what it would take to get a word out of him at that moment, and was sure that only if something lacked would he notice.

By six-ten he still hadn't arrived. This had never happened in nine years of marriage. Bernadette often thought he had some control over traffic so that none got in his way. He always took the back streets, he said. Never got caught up in rush hour like other fools. Tonight he must have done.

Bernadette went to the vegetables – they were ready but would go cold if served now and he didn't turn up within minutes. What to do? Leave them on low and turn the chicken off so it wouldn't dry out. Yes, she would do that.

Back in the lounge, Bernadette peered anxiously down at the drive, anticipating Richard's car emerging from the archway of trees. Surely if she willed it he'd come? Was she more concerned that the meal would be ruined or that something terrible had happened to him? It was hard to know.

Push away the anxiety and think calm solutions – her mother's words. Bernadette would whisper them often, but tonight they had little effect. She tried to picture her mum in the kitchen, flowered apron tied about her thick waist, but just couldn't see her.

The leaves are leaving. She went to Richard's desk as though it might present answers. Tonight the damp patch by the wall shelves looked like floating leaves. She heard his voice – *You see too much in things.*

Was she seeing too much tonight?

At six-thirty she decided to call his mobile phone, something that usually led to a message service. Tonight was no exception. What was the point, she wondered, in having a phone you never answered? At six forty-five she wondered if it was too soon to call the police. Would they laugh at her concern, say they had bigger things to deal with? Of course they would.

At seven Bernadette threw away the burnt carrots and wrapped the chicken in foil. She emptied the warm glass of water and sat in Richard's chair at the table and considered that he might have left her

altogether. Perhaps he had tired of their marriage, changed his mind
about loving her.

Over the years his gentle hunger for her had waned, their love
becoming more like that between sister and brother, punctuated by
rare moments of touch, a pat on the hand when shopping, a shove
if she made him laugh. Perhaps he knew if he withdrew his affection
entirely she'd die, just as animals do when abandoned, or babies when
neglected in those Romanian orphanages.

Eventually at eight-thirty a car engine sounded outside followed by
footsteps on the stairs. It was like nothing had changed. Bernadette
glanced at the clock as though it was she who had made a mistake.
Richard came into the lounge, put his coat over the sofa and looked at
the empty table. No almost kiss.

'Where's my tea?' he asked.

Bernadette looked at the table surface as though it might appear. 'I
... well, it...'

'What's the matter with you?' Richard frowned. 'Can't you adapt to
me being a bit late? Can't I expect to come home to a welcoming meal?'

'I did. I mean, there was.' *The leaves are leaving.* 'It got ruined. I tried
to keep it.'

'So there's nothing? I haven't eaten since one.'

Bernadette couldn't finalise it with a no. She wanted, really, to ask
where he'd been but that might be like insisting the bed should remain
on the wall next to a younger, happier couple.

'Come here, darling,' he said, taking her hand and leading her into
the kitchen, voice and fingers gentle like he wanted to play. They stood
by the now cold oven. 'No matter what time I got in from college or
work, my mother had something hot ready. She said we could cope
with just about anything in this world if we came home to nourish-
ment, served by hands that love.'

'I'm sorry you're hungry,' said Bernadette. 'I can make something
now.'

'But it isn't ready *now*, is it? It'll take an hour and by then I'll be past
caring.'

Richard opened the pantry door; chill air escaped in silent relief.

'When I was small and I messed up,' said Richard, 'my mother told me I just needed time to think about what I'd done. In silence, God would come and help me see the right path. She'd send me to sit in her wardrobe. Of course, she was right – the solitude did me good. Calmed me.' Richard looked at Bernadette, kindly. 'You need some, just for a while.' He motioned to the pantry.

Bernadette looked into the dark space. As a child she had hated them. Once, aged nine, she got stuck in an abandoned fridge freezer they found in the woods behind her house. She climbed in and the door shut and locked after her. For what felt like hours she struggled to breathe. It had only been minutes her mother later insisted, but time lasts longer in the dark.

'You expect me to go in there?' Bernadette said.

Richard nodded.

'But I don't want to,' she said.

'You think you don't,' he said, 'but it's really helpful. You just need to know what it's like for me to come home and remain calm when I'm hungry and I have a wife who's here all day and is supposed to love me.'

Sometimes Richard's words made no sense; yes, he spoke them and they were in the correct order, but it was as though he quoted someone else.

'In there you'll be able to see better,' he said now.

'I don't want to,' Bernadette repeated, childlike.

'If you don't, I can't believe you love me. It's only for a while and then we'll watch some TV and have some supper.'

She had once eaten spoiled fish for Richard – was this worse? If she just got it over and done with the evening might settle into normality. They could watch a film, talk about his day.

How bad could it be?

So she walked into the cool space. Richard closed the door and darkness ate her up. Scraping sounds came from the other side and then a clunk. Had he pushed the table up against the door?

How long did he mean by a while?

'Richard,' Bernadette called. 'I don't like this. I'm really sorry about the food. I am. Just let me come out.'

No answer

Bernadette half sat on a low shelf and her eyes got accustomed to the dimness. She could do this. He'd come for her soon.

What did he want her to think about? That she was an awful wife? That she didn't love him. But she did – didn't she?

A scratching sound; had she imagined it? She stood and wrapped her arms about her body. In the small space she felt big, too big. More scratching. Richard was her husband, a man who sometimes doled out curious punishments for seemingly small mistakes, but then brought home a single rose or told her he'd thought about her all day. He'd let her out if she were scared.

'Richard!' she cried. 'I said I'm sorry and I am! Let me out. I feel sick.'

He didn't come.

Bernadette remembered his mother telling a story one Sunday of how Richard had looked after an injured hedgehog they found in the garden. He'd kept it in a cardboard box in the shed and patiently fed it and given it water. When he got up one morning and it had gone, he cried for a week. Richard admitted that he was angry he'd given the creature everything he thought it needed, only to be rewarded with abandonment. Bernadette had kissed him and said that somewhere a very happy hedgehog remembered him. Richard said he hoped she'd never do that to him – that he only liked to have her home all the time so he could give her all she needed.

Bernadette needed him to open the door. She called his name again and then curled up in a ball on the hard floor and imagined Conor there, snuggled up to her, smelling of chalk and chewing gum.

Was he really there?

Yes – she could see him, a silhouette in the dark, feel his sweet breath in her ear and spikes of hair against her cheek.

He said, *There's a mountain in your shoe, but I'll exchange it for a pebble.*

So she took off one of her shoes and held it out, and he took off one of his trainers and did the same. When she took it from him he faded away.

Fluorescent light savaged her. Richard had opened the door.

'What are you doing down there?' he asked. 'Your shoe came off, darling.'

Bernadette got up and looked behind her. Nobody there now, and in her hand a dirty washcloth.

Just like her mother after the fridge freezer incident, Richard said, 'It wasn't as long as you think. It was only twenty minutes. Do you think I'm some kind of monster?'

No, he wasn't the monster. Her inability to leave him was.

*

Reliving the experience has Bernadette curled up in a ball, and Anne has pulled into a lay-by. Cars whizz past like carriages on the Twister at Hull Fair. Anne unclicks her seatbelt and strokes Bernadette's back to stop her trembling.

'It's only because I've never talked about it before,' says Bernadette, embarrassed.

'Of course,' says Anne.

'I'm okay, really I am.'

'You must have been so scared, especially after your experience as a child. Did he know about that?'

Bernadette tries to think. No, she never told him. Did she think he might use it as a weapon one day? No, Richard was not so calculated. 'He never knew,' she says.

'Has he done that since? The pantry thing, I mean.'

Bernadette shakes her head vigorously. 'No, it was the only time. There have been strange things over the years. Things he did just one time and never again. Things he was often sorry for, and that made it even harder to hold it against him. He comes out with odd beliefs all the time; things I never even knew he thought and I wonder if they've always been inside him, hidden away. He had such a strict childhood.

Bound to affect him. I try and keep that in mind.' She looks at Anne. 'I do wonder how Conor's early years will affect him, you know.'

Anne nods. 'I worry all the time what's simmering below the surface. Tonight even more so.' She pauses. 'Did Richard ever tell you where he was that night?'

'No, he never mentioned it again.' Bernadette sits up, looks at her face in the mirror and tidies her unruly hair. 'He often did that – things happened and he simply forgot them.'

'Wherever he was, do you think he's there now?'

Bernadette shrugs. 'If he is ... well, he's probably back at Tower Rise now. He'll know I've gone.'

'How do you feel?' asks Anne.

'Ready,' says Bernadette.

31

The Book

*Note to Social Worker, Tracy Fenton

2nd May 2007

I had to write a little note to say how sorry I am that it came to this. I feel
very sad about it all, really I do. I'm fully aware that Conor had no intention
of bringing harm to Shana, but my mum left the dog to me, and so her
death has hit me hard. I stopped fostering some time ago because I found
it tough, but I craved it again. It was perhaps too soon after my mother
dying, and other private things I've been through. I feel terribly bad for the
boy, and hope all goes well for him. My son Mark would like to keep writing
to him if that's possible? He got very attached to Conor. I did too. I'm glad
we had him. I think I just did it for the wrong reasons. Thank you for your
understanding and the kindness of your team.

Very best,
Georgina Caine

Statement of Tracy Fenton   Dated: 15/04/2007   Case No – 6879967788
RECENT CHRONOLOGY – CONOR JORDAN (D.O.B. 10/11/2001)

30/03/2007 – Mrs Caine (foster carer) contacted social services asking
for support after her family pet dog, Shana, died while with Conor on an
unsupervised walk. She told me Conor was told he must always go with
Mark (Mrs Caine's teen son) when walking the dog. He disobeyed on a

number of occasions, and on 27/03/2007 at 8 p.m. he escaped out of the back door with Shana. While out, the dog got off the lead and was hit by a car. Shana's injuries were such that she was put down the following day.

31/03/2007 – Assessment visit. I found Mrs Caine to be distressed about the dog's death and angry with Conor. She agreed to receive support and grief counselling. Conor appeared in good health and very sorry for the pain he had caused. My concern for Conor feeling guilty about the events is why I arranged further assessment.

01/04/2007 – Request made to Befriend for Life voluntary organisation. Conor is now five so he can have a volunteer friend. I feel he would benefit enormously from such one-on-one friendship. A recent supervised visit with Conor's mum Frances went sufficiently well that it was planned to arrange another. Frances Jordan expressed a wish to see her son, but said she wasn't ready for it to be a regular event.

02/04/2007 – Return visit to Mrs Caine's home, where I spoke with her alone. She is depressed about the death of the dog. While she has grown fond of Conor, she does not feel strong enough for the day-to-day care of a young child anymore. She doesn't want Conor to feel rejected, but sees no other option than to cease fostering.

04/04/2007 – Application made for new placement.

05/04/2007 – I returned to Mrs Caine's home and held a meeting with Conor, Mrs Caine and her son Mark, where it was explained to Conor that his move has nothing to do with the dog's death. He understands he did not cause the events and that Mrs Caine is dealing with some personal issues that mean . she can't care for him anymore. Mrs Caine and Conor hugged. Son Mark hugged Conor for a long time.

06/04/2007 – Conor moved temporarily to Redcliffe Children's Home.

08/04/2007 – Mrs Richmond from Redcliffe contacted me about Conor's behaviour. He smashed numerous glasses and plates in the kitchen and would not go to bed.

09/04/2007 – I visited Conor at Redcliffe. He was sorry about smashing the plates and said he could not remember doing so. He was scared he wouldn't be allowed to see his mum the following day but I assured him he would.

10/04/2007 – Len Coupland (Action for Children volunteer) took Conor on a supervised visit to Doncaster social services where they met his mum Frances for an hour. The session did not go well. Conor swore at his mother and said he would kill her like a dog. She was very distressed. The session was cut short.

11/04/2007 – Assessment determined that visits with Conor's mum would cease for now. I discussed this with Frances Jordan and she agreed that she could not cope.

ASSESSMENT
Conor's recent display of anger and violence means he needs one-on-one care from a more specialist foster carer. Until then he is at Redcliffe Children's Home. Further counselling sessions have been arranged. His school is monitoring his behaviour and have arranged for him to see their counsellor, Kate Sharpe. He has seen his birth mother, Frances Jordan, three times this year, but these supervised visits have been temporarily suspended. The court will decide when these should resume.

Signed: *Tracy Fenton*   **Dated:** *15/04/2007*

*Please include this note from Georgina Caine's son Mark

To Conor,
I'm really glad they said I can write to you. I know your not really able to write back to me cos your writing isn't that amazing and your only five but

at least I know you got this and even if you can't really read it now you can one day. I guess it'll go in your book thing. I'm real annoyed to be honest. Not at you God no not at my little mate. At my mum and stuff. She shoulda never gone back to doing the fostering stuff if she wasn't sure. Just so you know she did like you. We all did. But she shouldn't of got you here and then got so upset over the friggin dog. I loved Shana but dogs aren't people are they. You mattered more. And I know you never meant for her to get off the lead. I mean she does it all the time. She did it for me a couple of times and I just stopped her running out on the road in time. I know why you went out that night when you shouldn't of. I tried telling mum you had a crap day. You told me the kids at school was annoying you. One called you Freddy Krueger cos of your burns. So of course you took Shana. She loved you. But she was old anyway. I hope your allowed to watch them Muhammad Ali DVDs wherever you are. I couldn't give em all to you cos some my dad got me. Maybe one day you'll get to know who your dad is and he'll give you cool stuff too. Remember, your the greatest! Shout it out! You left your little Blackie cat here. Did you mean to? It was on my pillow when I came in from college so I guess you did. Made me get such a lump in my throat little mate. I'll keep it always even if I hide it when my mates come. I kept that picture you did of Ali too. No one would believe a five year old done it. I hope you have a good life little mate. Maybe one day when I'm a world famous boxer (middleweight) you can come and watch me. Shout out I'm the greatest and I'll know its you! Do you remember when we was sitting on my bed when mum thought you were asleep and we were reading my Ali book and the bit where he said something about the mountains not being the big test or something but it's the little pebble in your shoe that does your head in. And you said so cute 'I've got the mountain in my shoe.' You always said such ace stuff. I really wish you could of stayed longer. I won't ever forget you. I hope you get that mountain out of your shoe little mate I really do.

From,
Mark

32

Bernadette

'Perhaps you should try calling Richard again, at home,' says Anne. Traffic swooshes past their still-parked car.

Bernadette considers it, shrugs. 'You must wonder what kind of woman I am to go into a dark pantry like that, just because he ordered me to. You must think me weak, stupid.'

'I don't think anything of the kind,' says Anne. 'We all do things others might say they wouldn't. I think back to my first marriage and it's like looking at another me. For love we'll probably do just about anything.'

'It wasn't for love,' says Bernadette, quietly. 'It was because I was afraid. Not of him, but of being alone. I went into a dark place on my own because I don't want to *be* alone – makes no sense. I wish I could be less cowardly.'

'You've been brave tonight,' says Anne, fastening her seatbelt again. She pauses, looks at Bernadette. 'Where were you going to go tonight, if I hadn't rung you?'

Bernadette looks out across the fields, at the distant house lights. 'I had no clear plan. I'd planned what I would take and what I'd say to Richard. Beyond that ... maybe a hotel.' She looks at Anne. 'I'd never have gone far from Conor.'

'If you're stuck tonight, I have the spare room.'

Bernadette nods, grateful. 'Can I use your phone one more time?'

Anne passes it over. She starts the car and pulls back onto the carriageway while Bernadette dials the Tower Rise number, once again reaching the answering machine. Still no Richard.

What time is it now? Nine-forty. It's like the effect of time passing slowly in a dark cupboard is reversed here and the night is slipping by too quickly. What will they do if it ends and they still don't have Conor?

As though reading her thoughts again, Anne asks, 'Who the devil do you think this Andy is?'

Bernadette knows she's changing the subject from Richard to Conor to take her out of the black pantry.

'He must be someone that could easily get Conor into a car,' says Bernadette. 'I know he's young, and he can be too trusting at times, but there's a steel in him too. He won't do something unless he wants to.'

'If it's one of Frances' … you know, clients … he must have some sort of link to them both. Or he's using Conor to get something out of her?'

'Maybe.' Bernadette's window mists with her breath. She wipes it and remembers a time on the bus when Conor wrote his name and hers in the window's condensation.

'If this Andy got any info about Conor from Frances then he could have used that,' says Anne. 'If he mentioned Muhammad Ali or something about drawing, Conor would have gone anywhere in the world with him.'

'You don't think…' Bernadette can't finish the sentence.

'That he'd hurt him? No. We can't think that. We mustn't. We have to just think about finding him.'

'But what are we doing?' snaps Bernadette. 'Just driving. We should be calling people. We should be doing more! Shouldn't we?'

'We are,' insists Anne. 'We've been where he was last seen and we spoke to the neighbour and to Andrew. We're doing what we should be, Bernadette. At my house we'll be where we need to be. We can continue ringing people from there and one of us can go out and physically look in the area. Okay?'

'If only I had the Lifebook,' says Bernadette.

'What difference would it make?' asks Anne. 'You and I probably know the words in there by heart.'

'But there might be a clue,' says Bernadette. 'Something we've overlooked.'

'I don't think we've overlooked anything. We've thought about nothing else for the last few hours.'

'Last Saturday I hugged Conor so tight,' she says to Anne. Had she somehow foreseen this night and hugged him for the first time because it might be the last?

'He told me,' says Anne.

'He did?'

'Yes. He was happy about it.'

'I'm not supposed to,' says Bernadette.

She knows she overstepped BFL's boundaries to hug Conor. Touch can only occur where necessary – picking up a fallen child, wiping a tear. Richard might say this was now her punishment – that God had taken Conor.

'Those boundaries are there to protect,' says Anne. 'And they should be. But when you've been with your child for five years I think it's safe to assume that you know him better than anyone. You know what might frighten or disturb him. You know his background.'

'It was still selfish of me,' says Bernadette. 'I needed the hug. I didn't think of him.'

Anne shakes her head. 'Of course you thought of him.'

The boy occupies Bernadette's thoughts a good deal of the day and most of the night, when she tries to imagine how it must have felt to have been abandoned so many times. She supposes that being in a dark pantry or abandoned fridge for a brief time would be nothing to a boy let down by adults, by his own family, over and over and over.

Anne's phone rings. She looks at Bernadette before answering. News? Face alight with surprise, she hands it to Bernadette and says, 'It's that Ruth woman again.'

Bernadette takes the phone like it might detonate and cautiously says hello.

'Has he come back yet?'

'No,' says Bernadette. 'But I'm not sure what it has to do with you. You won't even tell me who you are.'

'Is he okay, do you think?'

'I've no idea.' Bernadette isn't angry. The poor woman sounds worried, but she's no threat. 'What's your relationship to my husband, anyway?'

There is a short pause. Bernadette holds her breath.

'Can we meet?' asks Ruth finally.

'You want to *meet*?' Bernadette can't conceal her surprise.

Anne looks wide-eyed at Bernadette, and then nods firmly.

'I might be able to help you find Richard,' says Ruth. 'But not over the phone.'

'Why would you help me?' Bernadette is suspicious now.

'I think you deserve it.'

'I *deserve* it?'

'Look,' says Ruth, 'I know where you live. I could come over later if Richard still isn't back. We can talk. I'll explain. What do you think?'

Bernadette isn't sure what she thinks. This woman knows Richard and knows where she lives. But if she can help find him then Bernadette can concentrate on Conor.

'I'm not at home right now,' she says. 'I've something more urgent to do. But I may call you if Richard still hasn't turned up later.'

Ruth doesn't speak. Eventually she says quietly, 'Ring me if you need me then,' and hangs up.

'She wants to come to the flat,' says Bernadette.

'Goodness,' says Anne. 'Do you think she—'

'Is his mistress?' Bernadette has considered it, and now it seems likely. 'Maybe. But I'll think about all that later. Let's concentrate on Conor.'

Like two sparkling skipping ropes, the lights of the Humber Bridge twinkle ahead. They're not far from Anne's now. Maybe fifteen minutes. Bernadette feels guilty that she's looking forward to a cup of tea and the warm fire. How can she when Conor won't be there to enjoy it? He always scoops extra sugar into his and asks Anne for a biscuit. She says no if he hasn't had his dinner yet, and yes if he has. Such simple rules make childhood feel safe.

Bernadette remembers such guidelines: no dessert if you don't eat all your greens, bed early if you haven't done your homework, ten minutes less playing out time if you come home late. Bernadette might have hidden soggy broccoli in her pocket so she'd get Angel Delight, and rushed her maths so she could stay up, but she never came in late. Not once.

Now everyone is late. Conor and Richard and Bernadette herself. She is late to her own life.

'Won't it be wonderful if he's just *there*,' says Anne. 'We walk into my living room and Conor is with Yvonne.'

'God, if only,' says Bernadette.

The phone rings again and the women glance at one another.

'You'd better answer,' says Anne. 'I shouldn't really keep picking it up while I'm driving.'

It's PC French. She explains calmly that it's good they're on their way back to Hull because the police had a call from a Mrs Macarthur – Sophie's mum – twenty minutes ago. Apparently, at approximately nine-fifteen, she received a phone call in which no one spoke. Sure it must be Conor, she dialled 1471 and got a local number, which she gave them. PC French says that whoever called was in a phone box on the Marina, by the Minerva pub. Police are on their way to investigate.

'We'll go straight there,' says Bernadette. 'We're five minutes away.'

'Perhaps it's best you go back to Mrs Williams' house and wait there for our news,' says PC French. 'It could be a false trail, and we don't know what to expect yet.'

'Surely you don't expect us to just sit at Anne's house?'

'For now, it might be best.'

When she's hung up, Bernadette looks at Anne. 'Sophie's mum had a random call where the person didn't speak. It had to have been Conor! It came from the Marina and PC French is heading there now. But she said we should just go to yours.'

'We can't,' says Anne, adamant. 'And that's that. He's my boy, and we're going wherever he might be.'

'Absolutely,' agrees Bernadette.

As they speed along the final stretch of dual carriageway, and the lights on the river bounce in anticipation, Bernadette remembers how she told Conor the pretty leaf ditty that came to her that autumn evening at the window. *The leaves are leaving*. He chanted it then while kicking crunchy leaves in the street. He ran and jumped into the golden piles and sang it out loud. *The leaves are leaving*.

Hopefully, they will say it together again soon. They will sing it with abandon and she'll let him have his favourite fruit pastels even if he doesn't eat Anne's broccoli and no one is going to deduct ten minutes playing time because he came home late.

33

The Book

New Placement Assessment Form – Conor Jordan (D.O.B. 10/11/2001)
Foster Carer – Anne Williams (D.O.B. 18/05/1954)

1. Details of social services department or agency.
Hull Social Services Department, Hull, East Yorkshire.

2. Basic details of proposed foster carer.
Language – English
Religion – Church of England
Ethnic Descent – White British
Occupation – Retired (ex dinner lady)
Health – Non-smoker
Permanent UK home – Yes
Compulsory Checks – All up-to-date

3. Recent photograph.
Attached.

4. Outline of children in household.
Children, two daughters: are grown and have left home. Grandchildren
(three granddaughters) occasionally visit.

5. State what type of care is being offered.
Long-term fostering is being offered. Anne Williams is an experienced foster
carer, having previously looked after seven children long term, over the last
fifteen years. She is looking to foster just one child with greater needs.

6. Type of child or children that will be suitable to foster.
Age range – no specification
Gender – no specification
Carer is capable of looking after a child from a different ethnic or religious background. She will consider children with severe learning difficulties or who have severe physical disabilities. Carer will accept children who may have been physically abused or neglected. She especially wants to look after a child who is unlikely to make relationships easily. We feel she will be ideal for Conor Jordan.

7. Describe foster carer's family.
Proposed foster carer has a secure home, and enjoys great relationships with her grown-up children (two daughters) and grandchildren (three granddaughters). She has been a foster carer for fifteen years, and cared for a wide variety of children. She was widowed some years ago. Anne enjoys a warm relationship with her neighbour's children and is liked in the area. She was a popular dinner lady for twenty years.

8. Details of home.
The home is a well-maintained and safe three-bedroom semi-detached house. Child will enjoy an enclosed garden and his/her own bedroom. This privacy and independence, and the attention of one person, will be ideal for Conor Jordan.

9. Details of other adult members who are part of household.
There is only Anne in her home – daughters and grandchildren occasionally stay over.

10. Proposed school
The school Conor currently attends is close enough to the residence for him to continue to attending.

10. Family lifestyle
Anne enjoys a simple life – likes walking, crocheting, cooking, and the theatre.

1st July 2007

Dear Conor,

Welcome to my home, Conor. I'm blessed and also very excited to be writing for the first time in your Lifebook and I hope we're going to become good friends. When you arrived this week, you looked as though you were quite exhausted. Like you had travelled for a long, long time. You stood in my kitchen with one case and a plastic bag with Muhammad Ali DVDs in it and you didn't move. You didn't want me to come too close, and I understand that. You didn't look me in the eye, and I understand that too. Lack of trust is visible in every movement and in your quiet voice, and I understand. I promise I'll do everything I can to make this home a good one and there is nothing you will do or say here that means I'll send you away. I imagine I seem old to you. I don't have all the gadgets here that I know kids like but there's Lego and I've been told I'm a great cook. Kids seem to eat all my cakes! I read that drawing is your passion and so I put lots of paper and packs of pens in your room, but so far you haven't touched any of them. You don't eat cake either. So I know how sad you are. But I'm patient. I was good at helping my mum knit when I was small because I'd hold the wool for her for hours and I like things that take a long time. You have to wait when you bake and if you get impatient and open the oven door too early on a cake it sinks. So I'm not going to try and open any doors too early. I understand you need patience and so I'll sit and watch your Muhammad Ali fights with you, even though boxing makes me cringe a little. And I'll wait until you talk to me.

Love,
Anne

Befriend for Life,
234–5 James Street, Hull
15th August 2007
Dear Tracy,
We are pleased to inform you that a suitable volunteer has been found for Conor Jordan. Bernadette Shaw can begin seeing him as soon as is suitable

for you and Conor's current carer, Anne Williams, whom we have also contacted. Please find enclosed some forms to complete regarding funding and a profile of said volunteer, Ms Shaw. Please don't hesitate to contact me should you require more information.

Yours sincerely, *Carole Johnson*

Name – Bernadette Kathleen Shaw
Date of Birth – 01/08/1980 (aged 27)
Address – Flat 4, Tower Rise, Foreshore, Hessle.
Email – N/A
Mobile – N/A
Home Number – 01482 334321 (Only call during the day, weekdays)
Police checked – YES
Background – Married, non-smoker, housewife, no children.
Qualifications (where relevant) – Diploma in Health and Social Care
Experience – N/A
Reason for Volunteering – 'I watched a BBC documentary about children who are in care and I felt compelled to look into how I might do some sort of voluntary work with them. I found the Befriend for Life website and decided they were what I was looking for. I contacted them and went through all the necessary checks, and did the intensive ten-week training course. Emotionally and age-wise I'm ready for whatever challenge awaits me. I've been unable to have children and feel I have a lot to give to a child who might need a good friend. When asked what "kind" of child I would like I didn't want to state a preference, since I didn't want to be prejudiced against one. I asked that Carol and the team decide which child seemed right for me. An experienced BFL volunteer came and talked to us during our training course. She said the team were very instinctive in matching a volunteer with a child, and that she had enjoyed a long relationship with hers as a result. So I was happy to let them decide. I am looking forward to meeting Conor. I have read his file. In truth, it made me cry. I really hope that I can make a difference to his life.' – Bernadette Shaw

34

Conor

It's totally freezing. Why does it get this cold near water? Once, when me and Anne went for a walk in Bridlington it had been dead hot all day but as soon as the sun went it was like winter. I reckon family are like the sun and when they leave you get so cold your teeth chatter. When I say stuff like that out loud adults hug me or go *Awww, you're so sweet.*

How can I be sweet when I feel so sour most of the time?

I'm sour now. Sour and cold.

There's a big square pier thing past the cobbles but I have to climb over a wall to get to it cos the gate thing's locked. There's water on all sides. I can't see it cos it's dark but I can hear it splashing away underneath. Kind of scary to think of it down there. Wonder how deep it is. Bet it's mega-freezing.

There's a white railing on both sides. I bet it's to stop people jumping over. They're not very high. Wouldn't stop me.

The Deep – that's this museum with sharks and stuff in it – is all lit up on one side. On the other side real far away is the Humber Bridge.

The water looks black like when the workmen at school were putting tar on the path. There's this light that's as green as a pea hanging at the end of the pier and I make my way towards it. I go up some wooden steps to a thin platform. There are gaps in the wood. It's like the water could reach up through them with icy fingers and get me. And more metal railings to stop anyone crazy climbing over.

There they are, Mum and Paul. Standing right at the end of the platform like I'm not even waiting for them in the boring car. I could jump in the water and they'd not notice. Just think it was a big stone and carry on talking.

Except they're not talking, more arguing. Paul's voice isn't soft but quite loud now. He's saying something about how she's abandoned me and how he knows what that feels like cos his dad did it to him. Mum sobs a bit. And he says if she'd just told him he could have helped. Mum sobs some more and says he has no idea at all.

They both look green cos they're near that light, like they feel sick or something. Or they're gonna turn into the Incredible Hulk. I don't like him getting cross with Mum. I don't like Paul making her cry.

So I go up to them and I tell Mum about the holiday to cheer her up.

I tell her about the luxury coach and the toilet they have on it and how you can choose your seats and if you're at the front next to the driver you can pretend you're the one driving the coach. And that there's lots of stops at the service stations – Anne told me all this cos she went a few times with her friend Carla – and if you've got a friendly driver he does games and tells you stuff about the place you're going to and everyone passes sweets around and sometimes they all sing. I tell mum she will love it and I've saved almost all the money for her to do the one to Bournemouth but she just has to lend three quid off someone. I say maybe Paul will even give her it.

Then they both go quiet and look at me. Eventually Paul says to Mum, *This is what you've done*. And I don't know what he means. She didn't do it all – *I* did. I looked up the holiday. I thought of it. I memorised all the coach seat numbers. I saved and saved and *saved*.

And then Paul says to her, *You should be the one taking your son on holiday*. Mum says that he has no idea about it and goes back towards where the car is. Should I follow her and make her feel better? Maybe tell her that the seats on the holiday coach recline too.

Is she even bothered about my surprise?

Paul asks me to wait with him a minute. There's a bunch of rotten flowers stuck in the railings and a letter. All the words have got wet and faded off. The water swishes and splashes. I remember my last lesson in art when we had to make words into the image that matched them. Splash would have been cool to do.

I suddenly feel real tired thinking of school and stuff. That was such a long time ago. Wish I could just get into my bed at Anne's. She got me a *Doctor Who* duvet and it's mega snug. I used to wake up loads at night and lie there thinking and thinking stuff. But at Anne's I sleep real good.

Listen, Conor, Paul says to me. *Maybe I shouldn't have picked you up. Maybe I shouldn't have done it like this. But when you find something out like this you don't really think straight. You don't plan. I don't know what I was thinking, keeping you out until this time.*

He comes closer to me and I'm not sure what he'll do. Then he puts an arm on my shoulder like real light and says that it's cold and we should go and get warm in the car with Mum.

I say, *I thought you were going to tell me everything when we got to the special place. And we're here and it's not that special.*

I tell him I don't want to go back to the car until he tells me it all. I start off with a real cross voice cos I'm tired and then get nervous and say it more nice cos when he tells me everything I reckon I'll be able to go home to bed.

Paul says we should find somewhere out of the wind and we walk back down the steps and on to the big concrete pier. There are benches on both sides and one of those orange and white rings you save people with. It's still cold here.

Paul takes his jacket off and puts it around me and we sit on one of the benches. The jacket smells like men always do. I remember when Santa Claus came to visit me at Anne's house and I was eight so of course I didn't even believe anyway. But he smelled just like Anne's neighbour Roy, all man and gardening and stuff. So I'd have known anyway he was a fake Santa.

I like sitting on the bench with Paul's jacket around me. It doesn't totally stop the cold but it feels good.

I bet it's dead late now. I bet everyone in my class is in bed. Paul starts to talk and then stops. It's like when our headmaster Mr Grimshaw had an assembly once cos a girl at a school near ours died in a car crash and he kept starting and stopping and then he had to get Mrs McCartney to finish for him. Mum isn't here to finish for Paul and I can't cos I don't know what the words are.

Paul says he's really, really sorry. And then his mouth trembles. I've never seen a man cry except on telly and that was somebody on *Jeremy Kyle* when I had tonsillitis and was on the sofa off school. Paul isn't exactly crying like that but he is sniffing and I don't think it's just the sea air.

He asks me if I can feel it and I reckon he means the cold.

I say, *Of course, your coat is nearly as thin as mine.*

He smiles a bit then and says, *Don't you know who I am?*

To be honest I don't. He was Paul and then Mum called him Andy but he stuck as Paul. I don't think he's either of those names. So I say, *No, not really.*

And Paul says, *Don't you know though? Can't you feel it?*

And I sort of get that feeling like there's the start of a memory coming. Like when I once saw this black cat on a girl's T-shirt and I wanted to go and rub my face against it. Of course I didn't. I'm not a total knobhead. But Anne reminded me about the black toy cat I loved, that I left it with Mark. I remember Mark. He got me into Muhammad Ali. He was my mate. But I hadn't thought of Blackie then until Anne reminded me. This is what I feel like now. Like Paul's going to tell me something I sort of know but have forgotten.

So Paul tells me about how when he was little he used to sit at the window and wait for his dad to come. Says he never did. That he'd never even met him but he used to think that a dad can't stay away forever; he has to come one day.

And then Paul says, *Conor, I'm your dad.*

35

The Book

*Please stick in this leaflet so Conor will know what BFL are all about – thanks.

BFL – Befriend for Life

What we do
We aim to give children in care a friend for life. We believe that, with support, all children have the capacity to change their lives for the better. For many all that's needed to help them get their lives back on track is support and friendship.

Befriending a child improves their lives immensely. Our volunteers help young people stay out of trouble and enable them to rebuild family relationships, which gives them stability and gives them self-confidence and ultimately independence.

Mission
Our mission is to offer personal support and practical guidance so children grow up confidently and happily, thus enabling them to eventually make better choices and to improve the quality of their adult lives.

Our values
We believe:
Every child should be treated equally, with respect and kindness.
Our volunteers make a huge difference.
Working together we can change the lives of children in care.
We offer a valuable and free service.

We are committed to:
Delivering the best service to the children we work with.
Contributing to local policy regarding children in care.
Building Befriend for Life to ensure the best delivery of services.

BFL people
We believe our volunteers make all the difference. Our success depends on the adults we accept as volunteers. We work together to embrace diversity and we draw upon the abilities, empathy and experiences of all our team.

We strive to give everyone a voice and ensure all opinions are valued. We accept volunteers of all ages over eighteen. We commit to children over the age of five until they are able to live independently. Around thirty staff work with approximately one hundred trained volunteers to deliver our support services.

We believe that when we come together with hard work, commitment and the enthusiasm of our people we can achieve something very special. We have found that when people are given the chance to learn, work and volunteer, great things happen. Volunteers thrive as much as the children they are befriending.

Volunteers
If you live in the local area – for constant contact with your child you should live within twenty miles of Hull – and are over eighteen years of age and have no criminal record you can apply to be a BFL volunteer. No previous experience is needed. Our extensive and free ten-week training courses are run on a variety of days to suit anyone working full-time or with family priorities.

Quote from one of our children
'When Malcolm came into my life I knew there was one person who would listen to me and not mind how much I talked. He helped me learn how to ride my bike. We laugh lots' – Elsie, aged nine.

Conor

Just like that. Paul says it.

Conor, I'm your dad.

The words sort of sit there in the air like they're clouds or some-thing. I try and imagine how I'd write them in art. Kind of maybe all jumpy like a surprise. But then heavy and made of brick too.

Then I think of when I was drawing Paul in the car and how I got a bit stuck cos I've only known him like four hours. And so I cheated a bit and drew my own eyes. And now I guess my eyes are his, aren't they? Like when Len took me to my mum's once and said I had her ears. It was a real weird thing to notice. But I looked and checked and he was right. We both have flat ears. Loads of crazy thoughts are coming to me at once and so I don't speak.

Paul – except he isn't Paul now – looks at me. He asks if I'm okay. I want to ask if he's fibbing. Ask if this is a trick like when Stan Chiswick said he was going to Florida and maybe I'd be able to go with them but he was lying.

So I ask, *Is it real?* And Paul nods.

I always imagined my dad would be some kind of secret agent or a famous person. I never thought he'd just be normal. Definitely never thought I'd find out right near The Deep. But this is actually better. If David Beckham was my dad I'd have to share him anyway cos he's got like ten kids. Wish I could tell Sophie. She'll be mega excited. And Bernadette. She's got a dad. He's nice she said. So she'll be pleased. Cos Paul seems nice too. Maybe I can let him off shouting at Mum cos he's my dad now.

I have to be on his side as much as hers.

I know you must be shocked, says Paul. *I am too. I only just found out. It's all sinking in for me as well. We'll have to figure it out together, won't we?*

My teeth start chattering. Now I know what to call him. But I've never said Dad so it's hard. Can't talk anyway. Teeth are too chattery. Paul says maybe we should go and get warm in the car with my mum and then he should get me home and tomorrow we can work everything out. That sounds so good.

We walk back down the pier and climb over the wall and head to the car. I can see Mum in the back like a dark shadow. Wonder if she loves Paul? She must do. They made me. Wonder if he loves her? Maybe they will get married now. Will I go and live with them or stay with Anne? Sometimes when you find out everything it just means more questions.

In the car I sit in the back cos I don't want Mum to feel left out.

Paul says to her, *I told him.* Then he says, *Like you should have done.*

She screams out, *What would have been the point when you fucked off?*

Paul (I should call him Dad really) shouts at her for swearing in front of me and says it's probably better she wasn't around for me. He says it's cos of her that little George died.

I hate this. They're supposed to like each other now.

But they carry on like they've forgotten me again.

I try not to listen but it's hard. Mum gets so mad she says she wishes he was dead. Paul tells her she's a dirty whore. So Mum scrunches up the drawing I did of Paul and that makes me mad. I know that years ago when I first met her I tore all the paper up in the room – but that didn't have any pictures on it.

So I call her a twat like I did years ago at one of our sessions. I felt so bad about that, but now she deserves it. She *is* a twat. I call her it again and grab another one of my pictures and jump out of the car and climb the wall and run back up the pier. In the distance I hear them get out the car too and Mum telling Paul she loves me more than he knows and Paul saying, *Well, go and tell him then.*

As I run the wind grabs the picture out of my hand. It's the one of Bernadette. Her face spins and spins and then the paper gets stuck in a bin. No time to get it now. No time to stop.

I run back up the thin wooden pier to the end. There's a locked metal gate. I bet it's locked cos the pier on the other side doesn't have railings and all the crazy people could jump off. I'm not a crazy though. I'm just gonna show them I *might* be. Scare them. That might shut them up.

So I get over the gate and go carefully along the platform. Here I'm real close to the water. It even splashes me a bit. Looks all thick and churny, like if you touched it, it would stick. I go all the way to the end. The green light is spooky. Reckon it's one of them ones that guides you or warns you or something. It's so quiet except for the water. And I'm not really even cold anymore.

Wonder what it would be like to stick a toe in the water?

Mum's voice makes me jump. She's at the gate and her face is glowing in the green light. She shakes the handle and realises she can't open it.

Conor, she says. It's the first time I've heard her use my name. *Conor*, she says again, and I smile. So then she smiles at me and tells me to just come back and she's sorry.

People are always sorry when they *have* to be. For a reason. Like getting someone over a gate.

Why can't they be sorry anyway?

Then I see this one leaf. It's crinkly and leather-brown and floats past me in a circle. Where did it come from? There aren't any trees. One social worker – can't even remember who now – said I liked being under the trees in my pram. Bernadette likes trees. Said she's got loads near her house. Right now her pretty face is stuck in the bin. We used to sing this thing – it went, *The leaves are leaving, the leaves are leaving*. She said it's kind of clever cos leaves can mean two things. Leaves that are on trees and when people leave.

The leather-brown leaf is leaving. It can't go. Bad luck if it leaves. So I lean over to get it for Bernadette.

My mum yells, *Conor*.

When I turn to look at her my foot slips. It's like when you miss a step going upstairs and your heart goes mad as you feel around for it. Except this time there isn't one. There's nothing.

And so I fall.

Everyone says that those bits in films where it goes slow are done by special effect. But I think they happen in real life too. Cos when I go over the edge it takes forever. I see Mum's face go all round-mouthed and wide-eyed. I see the sky above me. The clouds move past and a half moon comes out like the side of a face. The wind rushes past my face even though I'm falling slow.

And then suddenly I'm colder than I've ever been in my life. And wet. And it's dark. And I can't breathe. When I try water gushes into my mouth. Tastes thick and salty like bad chips. It's Mum I shout first but it kind of gurgles and stays inside my head, all bubbly.

Then I'm above the water and I cough and cough and cough. I flap my arms and legs. I'm not really a very good swimmer. We had some lessons last year at school but I missed half of them cos me and Stan pulled Jonathon Pinnock's trousers down in the changing rooms and weren't allowed to go anymore. Was glad. The kids laugh at my burns.

My shoes feel dead heavy now, like two bricks. And it's so cold.

Then I go under again so when I yell for Bernadette her name sinks.

When I come up, the pillars under the pier are a bit farther away. Mum is standing on the edge screaming but I can't hear what she's saying. Her hair is blowing all crazy like she's got her finger in a socket. Where did Paul go? I yell for Anne but it makes me cough and cough and cough. I want to yell for Paul too but that's not his name now.

What should I yell? Dad?

But he might not answer cos he might not be used to it yet.

I'm scared if I sink again I won't come back up cos it's so cold my heart is stiff, and my legs can't move much longer, and my arms can hardly lift. I wonder if George felt like this when he died. Was it hard to breathe? Mum will be sad if I go too. Don't want to. But I'm going. I'm going. Sinking. Don't want to. Want to get out and get warm and watch my boxing DVDs and have sausages and jam tart and go to bed.

Under the water it's not so bad this time. Not so cold now. Don't have to move at all cos I'm floating like a fish. It's dark but I don't need to see.

Someone tickles me. When I laugh loads of bubbles come out. Even though I can't see, I hear them – pop, pop, pop. Tickle, tickle, tickle. It's Bernadette. She's got my shoe in her hand. How come I can see her but nothing else? How come she's here, all silvery, and floats like a mermaid? She says, take the pebble out of your shoe and then you'll rise to the top. She shakes my shoe but nothing comes out. I say, *But there's a whole mountain in my shoe so I'll never swim up*.

Then she grabs me real rough. She drags me back to the surface.

But it isn't her. It's Paul.

Except he's not Paul is he? He's my dad. That's who he is. And he's here in the water. His teeth are chattering real bad, like mine were before. He's got hold of one of those white and orange ring things. And his other arm is round me, under my arm so I'm on my back in the water, and all I can see again is the sky.

He says all shivery, *It's okay, hold on*.

But he's holding me so I don't need to.

He's grunting and swimming. I can hear Mum now and she's screaming, *Head for the steps, head for the steps*. That's where Paul must be going. It takes forever. Splash, splash, splash. We must be so far away. Lost at sea like the men in action stories. Water swills into my mouth and I cough and cough.

Paul says, *We're nearly there*, and he's really out of breath now.

But he's not Paul. I want to yell it out – this is Dad.

And then I twist and see Mum real close, just above us with big big eyes. And Paul lets go of me. No, not Paul. My *dad* lets go of me. I kick out cos all my energy suddenly comes back. There must be water in my ears cos when I yell out I can't even hardly hear my own words. But even though I can't hear it I know exactly what I'm saying.

I yell, *Don't let me go, Dad, don't let me go, Dad*.

But he lets me go.

Like everyone always does.

37

The Book

*Letter from volunteer, Bernadette Shaw.
3rd October 2007

Hi Conor,

I've taken you out four times. I wanted to wait before writing in your book because I felt it was better to have a few things to record. I know you won't be reading it until you're eighteen so I'm taking this into account. I'll tell you everything I think you'll want to know.

Volunteering for Befriend for Life is the biggest thing I've ever done. On the course we read real social work files on children to prepare us, but really it doesn't. We had sessions on boundaries and talked about confidentiality. There was so much to take in but it was worth it.

Especially when I met you.

The first time was supervised. You'll know what that means. I came to your house with my team leader Carole. I was so sick she had to stop the car and let me out. I kept telling myself you must be more scared. I read your Lifebook before meeting you but it didn't prepare me for the realness. When we came in Anne had made bread and the house smelt good. You were in an armchair with a pile of Muhammad Ali DVDs and your hair was wet like you'd just had a bath. You looked tiny. You didn't look at me. I said hi but you ignored me. I wanted to squeeze you but of course I couldn't. I tried to imagine how you must feel, how big and strange I must look to you.

I said I'd heard that Muhammad Ali was the greatest. You still didn't look at me. I knew that you couldn't until you felt sure I wasn't a monster. Anne asked you to say goodbye when we left and you wouldn't. She didn't push you, and I didn't mind. I said if you wanted me to I'd come back. Some children say yes to a volunteer but then change their minds. I was scared you'd say no. But two days later you told Anne you wanted to come out with me. I was so happy.

The following Saturday we went to the park by your house. For the whole afternoon you didn't speak. You had a purple rucksack on your back with your Ali DVDs in it. Anne said you take them everywhere. The Saturday after that I took you to the same park. You still didn't speak but you let me push you on the swing instead of struggling to do it yourself. Two weeks later I returned and you were waiting on the stairs with your rucksack.

Last week I came a fourth time. Anne said you were picking which top to wear, which meant you thought I was important. But you still ignored me all afternoon. At the end of the day you handed me one of your DVDs and said, 'If you look after it, you can have a lend of it.'

We're meeting next Saturday. You may not talk, but that doesn't matter because you will eventually. I know that after all you've been through, you have to get used to me. Make sure I mean well and won't disappear. I can't wait until you do.

Love, Bernadette

Hull Social Services Report – Yvonne Jones (Social Worker)
Home visit to Conor Jordan to assess recent change of placement
Date: 10/10/2007

I saw Conor this afternoon at foster carer Anne Williams' home, where he has lived for three months. I spoke with Anne and Conor at length. He was not as chatty as he can be and Anne did much of the talking. But he appears healthy and to have grown a few inches again. She said he eats well (here Conor said this is because she makes nice stuff) and that he sleeps much better than he did when he first arrived.

It took a few weeks for Conor to adapt to his new environment, but it appears that the one-on-one care from Anne means he has settled well. I spoke with Conor for ten minutes. He didn't make much eye contact but

said he likes Anne. He got agitated when his mother was mentioned. Until
this week it had been six months since a supervised visit. On 7th October
Conor saw Frances at the Doncaster office, with Len Coupland from Action
for Children. Conor said he would like to see his mum again; this will be
reviewed. His agitation when she's mentioned is likely due to past incidents.

Access with mother
On 7th October access supervisor Craig collected Conor from school and
took him to the office in Doncaster, where Frances was waiting. Frances
is currently sharing a flat with a friend, Gill, and agreed that this was not
the best place to meet Conor. Craig reported that, like the previous time,
Conor was reluctant to engage with his mother and showed signs of stress.
He eventually talked to her after fifteen minutes. Frances encouraged
this by asking about school and his current home. When the session
was over Conor didn't say much but didn't seem upset. Back home Mrs
Williams reported that he was quiet but slept well and ate his tea. During a
discussion with Frances, Conor and Mrs Williams we decided that Conor and
Frances should meet again in three months.

Schooling
Conor still finds schoolwork a challenge but continues to enjoy art. He
is having extra after-school tuition with art teacher, Mrs Connelly, which
he looks forward to. His best friend is still Sophie. Conor's past difficulty
concentrating in class has improved. Foster carer Anne Williams liaises
regularly with the school.

Social life
Conor has been seeing Befriend for Life volunteer Bernadette Shaw for
six weeks. She reported that it was going well, that he was 'delightful and
well-behaved'. When asked about her, Conor didn't say much and seemed
guarded, but foster carer Mrs Williams reported that he sleeps and eats
particularly well after seeing Bernadette. Currently she takes him out every
other Saturday and this will continue.

Home

Mrs Williams reported that she has not had any issues with Conor since he arrived and said he has settled in well after being very shy at first. It has taken a few weeks for him to engage in any way but now she says he sits next to her on the sofa and talks animatedly. Though he has moments when he sits in his room alone for long periods, this is often just to draw.

When I spoke with Conor alone he reiterated that though he likes being at Anne's he does miss Mark, the son at his last placement. Mark has written to him twice since he moved. Unfortunately, due to circumstances with Mark's mum, it's not possible for Conor to see Mark. This distresses Conor. I will encourage further communication from Mark, if he is willing.

Mrs Williams provides Conor with plenty of art materials. He has quite a collection of stunning artwork now, mainly portraits. Mrs Williams reports that occasionally Conor wets the bed, though it's very rare. Naturally he is embarrassed about it. He likes her to sit with him until he goes to sleep. Mrs Williams assures me she wants to continue the placement indefinitely.

Assessment

Conor appears to have settled into his new placement very well. He often takes a while to get accustomed to a new environment, which is understandable, especially having just left one where he was very happy. Conor and Mrs Williams are well matched. She is patient and kind, just what Conor needs. He responds well to her attentions. Physically Conor looked well nourished. The occasional bedwetting is no problem for Mrs Williams, who deals with it with little fuss.

38

Bernadette

The illuminations on the Marina are not pretty ones, not welcoming amber boat and pub lights that mean a romantic stroll along the water followed by a glass of chilled wine. They are angry blue whirls and flashes.

Bernadette and Anne slow down by the water; the night is silent for now, only the colours are loud. Bernadette imagines the bad-news-filled noise waiting outside for them. An ambulance is parked near the boats and farther along – but hard to see fully – a police car blocks the entrance to the pier. Anne stops behind the ambulance, switches the engine off and looks at Bernadette.

'I'm afraid,' she says.

'Me too.' Bernadette shivers despite the car heater's warmth.

They get out and approach the ambulance. The open rear doors permit a full view of the inside; there's a white stretcher with an orange bag on top, padded grey pull-down chairs, an oxygen unit and rows of cabinets containing medical paraphernalia. Bernadette logs every item mentally and is relieved none of them is Conor.

But is that necessarily good news?

In the front, a paramedic talks on a phone, says something about the coastguard.

The coastguard?

Bernadette thinks of the many nights lying in bed at Tower Rise, listening to the foghorn on the water. It feels like all those mournful warnings led to this night. As an emergency helicopter's whirring blades disturbed their sleep Richard would say, 'poor beggar', and turn over.

Why do they need a coastguard now? Who's in the water?

The paramedic says on his phone that he must have been out there more than ten minutes now. *He*?

'Someone fell in the river,' says Anne, eyes glowing like headlights in the dark.

'A *he*.' Bernadette's thoughts race on in spite of the mental wall she builds.

They run; past the empty police car, climbing over the wall to the concrete pier, and then along the square, heels scraping and clicking on the hard surface.

They race up uneven steps to a thin wooden platform. Here the water is close, frothing beneath them. And at the far end of the pier a group is gathered.

Frances is the first one Bernadette recognises – the photographs in Conor's Lifebook did her no justice. Life suits her better. She stands huddled against the cold, moaning into a fist. Her blonde hair bobs and bounces in the wind, and with red cheeks from the cold and eyes bright with concern she looks bold. Hers is a kind of raw beauty.

PC French is with Frances, writing something in a notepad. On the other side of a locked gate another police officer, burly and bald, paces the perilously thin platform.

On the ground two paramedics tend to someone Bernadette can't see, their fluorescent jackets gaudy next to the black police uniforms.

Anne moves closer to the scene first, slowly, obviously afraid. Bernadette is still glued to the spot, can't follow. Frances squints for a moment as though to recall who Anne is, and then begins to cry. Bernadette can't hear Anne's words but they appear to comfort her. PC French joins them, patting Anne's arm.

From the ground, a chalk-haired paramedic says, 'Tell us your name, son.'

Anne turns.

He says, 'Do you know where you are?'

A mixed bunch of dying flowers has been attached to the railings with its red, half-price sticker still attached.

'How many fingers can you see?' asks the paramedic.

Anne is upon them; she bends down and her face says it all. But still Bernadette can't move.

'I'm his foster mum,' Anne tells the men. 'Is he going to be okay?'

'He's conscious and breathing well; a bit dazed, though,' explains the paramedic. 'His body temperature is our main concern.'

Anne bends down and whispers something into the ear of the child wrapped in a silver thermal blanket.

'So why do they need the coastguard?' she asks.

'The man who rescued the boy is missing.'

'He was so brave,' says Frances, her Belfast twang similar to Andrew's. 'He managed to drag Conor back to the steps and I pulled him out. But then he was gone! I yelled and yelled for him!'

Her urgent words compel Bernadette forward at last. Conor's pasty face sticks out of a too-big blanket. He looks like one of those dolls made entirely of cloth, apart from the porcelain head. His red hair is wet, black and oily.

He smiles, says, 'Bernadette, he saved me. I wanted to get you the big leaf. Remember the leaves? Mum said he saved me. You'll never guess who he is. Try and guess.'

'He may be a little delirious,' says the chalk-haired paramedic.

Bernadette leans down and kisses Conor's forehead for the first time; she hugged him last Saturday, and now a stolen kiss. Does this again overstep the Befriend for Life boundaries? Should she touch his cold face this way, her hands trying to warm his cheek? Does this physical act come under 'appropriate intervention' as her course leader defined it?

Why are all the rules coming to her now?

In the surge of water and swell of wind Bernadette hears other volunteers' voices, asking is this appropriate, is that appropriate? *What if my child's crying? What if he asks me for a hug? What if she jumps on me?* Appropriate, appropriate, appropriate. All Bernadette knows is that now isn't time for rules. It's time for instinct.

'It's okay, Conor,' she says. 'These men are going to get you warm and make sure you feel better.'

'But what about Paul?' He looks panicked now. 'Why don't they jump in and get him? He was just there.'

'Paul?' Bernadette looks at the paramedics and then PC French.

'He's the man who picked them up this afternoon,' says PC French. 'Paul's what Conor called him. It appears that when Conor fell into the river, Paul got a life-ring and jumped in after him.'

'His name's actually Andy,' says Frances. She looks like she has a lot more to say, but doesn't. Close up Bernadette sees a red love-bite on her neck. As though sensing she has been caught out, Frances pulls up the lapels of her coat.

'Why did he give a different name to the boy?' asks PC French.

Frances shrugs but avoids the officer's eyes.

'Why don't you jump in after Paul?' asks Conor, his voice thin and tired now.

'Because we can't see him,' says PC French, gently. 'So it's too dangerous. But the coastguard has been alerted and they'll get the big chopper out and launch the lifeboat. They'll find him.'

It occurs to Bernadette that this is a cruel promise to make Conor – don't they know how many promises have been made and broken over his short lifetime?

'We need to get him to the hospital,' says the paramedic, standing with Conor in his arms. 'Who's going with him?'

The three women look at one another. Who should go? Frances, the woman who gave birth to him; Anne, the one who has been his true mother for the last five years; or Bernadette, the woman somewhere in between?

'You should go,' Anne says to Frances.

The young woman shakes her head vigorously. 'No, he'll want you.'

From within the blanket Conor's one word surfaces like a cartoon bubble: *Bernadette*. Despite the long name, no one has ever shortened it. Not her mother, not a friend, not Richard. When they first met, Conor pronounced it Bern-dette, saying it in a solemn voice. Now he says it right.

No one ever said it so right.

But the flash of happiness is tempered by the thought that Anne and Frances might be hurt.

'I'd love to come with you,' she says softly to him. 'But I bet you'd rather I stay and help find Paul? I'll make sure we look really hard for him. Do you want me to do that?'

He nods and closes his eyes.

'You should go with him,' Frances insists, looking at Anne. 'When he's gets out he'll be going home with you. You're his mum, really. And I reckon I can do more here – I know what Andy looks like.'

PC French agrees. 'You're the one who'll be able to answer best any questions the nurses have about Conor,' she says to Anne.

'Will you be okay?' Anne asks Bernadette.

They have come so far together; this is the kind of experience that creates lifelong friends.

Bernadette hugs Anne tightly. 'Yes. Go look after our boy. Please call me later and let me know how he is.'

'Where will you be?' asks Anne.

Bernadette realises she doesn't know. 'I'll ring you,' she says.

She watches the small group depart and has never felt so lonely. This is her monster: loneliness. She fears it, avoids it, and yet she is the lone-liest person she knows, living in a huge, empty house with a husband who is a ghost, with her parents miles away and no friends to call on. As a child she often sought solitude in her room, closing the door and putting a chair against it so she could get lost in her books. But she always knew her mum and dad were just downstairs – that she was never *really* alone. In their quiet way, they were there.

And at Tower Rise she always knew Richard would come home. Whatever he could be, there was comfort in his being there and that's what made her stay so long, what made her try so hard to make it work despite her feelings having all but died.

Now, seeing Anne and Conor go with the paramedics, Bernadette realises there is a difference between being alone and loneliness: the former you choose; the latter you feel when you're not happy inside.

Anne hurries after the paramedics. Selfishly, Bernadette wants to call her back, wants to say she'll go with Conor in the ambulance, say he chose her, it should be her. But Conor has the right person with him. He's safe now and that's what matters.

39

The Book

25th July 2008

Hi Conor,

I enjoyed lots seen you again last week. Hope you liked the pyjamas I brung you and that they fit. They was from the market in town and the woman did your name on the front. I just found out I got my own house. Well its not mine like I didn't buy it but Ill rent it. What I mean is that Im the only one gonna be living in it. So they said that soon you can come there and visit me instead of at the office. Thatll be real good wont it? I think youll have to come with someone like a social worker but still its better than been in that stuffy room. You wouldnt of been able to tell when we met cos its early but Im pregnant again and this time cos my depresion is under control and Ive got my own place I can keep the baby. Im two months gone. So youll have another brother or sister in February. Youll be able to see him or her every time you come to my house. Its nice got two bedrooms and a little garden. The sociall worker told me your going to meet Sam and George soon. Bet your excited. I see a bit of them sometimes. Sam looks a bit like you but George doesnt. Hes like my dad. You are like the man I think is your dad. Anyway I just wanted to right another little note for your book thing. Bet theres loads in it now. Cant believe your six and a half little boy. Dont know where the time goes. Were your pyjamas for bed and think of me and I will you.

Your Mum xxx

Hull Social Services Report – Yvonne Jones
Record of Meeting with Siblings   Date: 01/09/08
Child: Conor Jordan   Date of Birth: 10/11/2001

Siblings Fostered Apart (Explanation for Lifebook) –

Placing siblings together is not straightforward for social workers and there
are many factors we have to take into account. In practice we do try and
keep them together but for many different reasons it's not always possible.
Because Sam, who was born a year before you, had already been placed
with a family who did not want to foster further children it was decided you
would go elsewhere. Sam also has extra special needs and needs a different
type of care. When George came along two years after you, and your mum
was still struggling, he stayed with her for a week and then also went to
another family. It is easier to place siblings in the same home when they
have already been living together, either with their parents or a carer.

Being placed in care with siblings is found by some studies to have more
successful outcomes for the children concerned. In other cases it appears to
make no difference. I think it depends on whether those siblings were close
to start with.

Unavoidable circumstances meant you didn't meet your brothers until
now. Sam has had a lot of problems that meant we felt him seeing you and
George might set him back rather than bring him on. We also felt you might
not handle it, with your own vulnerabilities. But you are thriving with your
current foster carer, Anne, whom you've been with for more than a year now,
and where we see you staying for the indefinite future. You have also been
seeing Bernadette for twelve months, two Saturdays of every month, and
have expressed to us and to Anne how much you enjoy this.

**Meeting with Siblings, Sam Jordan (19/11/00) and George Jordan
(13/10/03)**
Doncaster Social Services
31st August 2008

Review
Len Coupland (Action for Children) took Conor to the Doncaster office
where he has previously met his mother, Frances Jordan. Conor took
two drawings he had done of his carer, Anne, to let his brothers know
what she looks like. Sam, who is seven and has mild autism and ADHD,
came with his foster carer and social worker. George came with his social
worker. The two boys were already there when Conor arrived. George
and Sam have met once before, as they live quite near one another. They
were playing with Lego when Conor arrived and he was happy to join
in. Though shy at first, Conor engaged quite well. He seemed to enjoy
the company of Sam, perhaps because they are close in age, but also
because Len felt Conor had an innate sympathy with Sam's disabilities.
Conor was naturally able to communicate with Sam in such a way that
Sam responded positively. His carer said not many people can do this.
The boys built a spaceship out of Lego. They helped George too with the
smaller pieces. George was distressed when the meeting ended but Conor
comforted him.

Decision re. further meeting
01/09/2008
Since the meeting went well and was a positive experience for the three
siblings, we aim to schedule another within six months.

Signed:
Yvonne Jones

10th November 2008

Dear Conor,

I'm glad you had a great seventh birthday and that I was there. I enjoyed meeting your best friend Sophie – I can see why you're such good friends. She's funny. You two get up to all sorts, I bet.

I'm delighted that you liked my gift. At BFL we have a budget of £10 for our children but mine only needed the price of a stamp. However, it needed time. So I wrote in July and hoped I'd hear back. And I did, in October! A picture of Muhammad Ali arrived in Anne's post – and he'd signed it for you. Your face when you opened it – I'll keep the image with me forever.

You said it was a good year because you met your brothers and because Muhammad Ali wrote to you. Your mum even sent you a box of Lego.

Anne made a cake with boxing gloves made of icing. When you blew out the candles you whispered that you wished you knew who your dad was. I wanted to say that dads aren't everything, but that would have been wrong, especially when I'm fortunate enough to know mine. What do I know about how you feel?

I can't believe we've been seeing each other more than a year. I'm so proud to have seen how you have grown and pleased you've grown to trust me. It took time and you still have moments where you close up, like a shutter comes down. I don't mind. We all like to close the shutter sometimes.

Love,
Bernadette

Bernadette

Bernadette pulls her coat tightly about her body. She did not dress for a night by the cold river. She had no clue she'd end up here – on the Marina, Conor having been pulled from the water and another person missing – and even if she had, the cold down here always surprises.

Now Anne has gone to the hospital with Conor, PC French says, 'There's not much we can do here.' The other police officer has returned to the car. 'The lifeboat and coastguard helicopter will take over.'

As though to back up her statement, the whir-whir-whir of chopper blades fills the night and a yellow helicopter flies over them towards the river, like a metal wasp.

'How long has he been in the water?' asks Bernadette.

Frances shakes her head and sobs, 'It must be twenty minutes.' She goes to the locked gate and shakes it violently. 'We can't just fucking walk away! He's out there!'

'It's too dangerous,' says PC French. 'We have to let the right people find him now. Come on. Let's go back to the car, get warm. You need to tell us every detail of what happened this evening.'

The police officer guides Frances away from the gate and leads her back along the pier. Bernadette follows, like a forgotten child. On the concrete again Frances stops and puts her face in her hands.

'You just don't get it,' she says. 'It don't matter if his name is Andy or Paul. I don't even know his surname anyway. Don't even know where he lives, not now, not then. Didn't care. But you need to know what *does* matter.' Frances takes her hands away from her face and looks at PC French, who opens her notepad. 'No, you won't need to write it down. You won't forget it, I promise you. Andy is Conor's father. His dad. That's who he is!'

Bernadette wishes she could sit down. Of *course* he is. It's the only thing that makes sense, and yet it's still a shock. It still feels like the time she slipped on the ice while at the park with Conor and the fall winded her, took her voice.

Does Conor know? Did this Andy tell him?

What was it Conor said just now – *You'll never guess who he is. Try and guess*. So he *does* know. And she should have guessed. Wasn't a father the only person the police ruled out? The one they should have considered most as the person who had taken Conor? Maybe she and Anne knew but never watered the thought and let it bloom. Now it grows, fills her head.

How must Conor feel? The father he often talked about, wondered about, now here and real after all this time.

Bernadette imagines Conor's Lifebook, turns the pages in her head, finds a fresh one and writes in it that a man called Andy is his dad. A man called Andy rescued him and is now lost in the river.

'And he turns up today, totally out of the blue!' continues Frances. 'And I've no idea how he knew or how he found me. I never told him I had a baine. Never saw him again after that one week here.' She flings her arms towards the Minerva pub. 'This is where we met eleven years ago. If you think this was some perv stealing a kid, you're all wrong. He was good to the kid tonight. He jumped in the water after him! It was both our faults. We was arguing in front of Conor. Said all kinds of awful stuff we shouldn't of. And that's when he ran off. But I didn't go in the river after him cos I were fucking scared. And I'm supposed to be his mother!' Frances shakes her head, says more softly, 'I'm supposed to be his *mum*.'

She pauses a moment. 'So that's who you're looking for – Conor's dad. If you want a description I can try, but your best hope is Conor.'

'I don't think he'll be up to that until tomorrow,' says PC French gently.

'No, I mean the picture he did.'

'The picture?'

Bernadette understands immediately. 'Conor draws really well,' she says.

'Like that,' says PC French.

They follow PC French's gaze: a white sheet of paper flutters in the opening to a bin, like a flag of surrender. Even from where they stand they can see a face drawn on it in black pencil. They approach the sketch and PC French carefully removes it from the metal opening. It's Bernadette. Even she recognises herself – thin eyebrows, fine eyelashes, small smile. The details are what bring Conor's art to life. What he sees and makes you see.

'Conor ran off with it,' says Frances. 'I ... I scrunched up the one he did of Andy.' She pauses, says quietly, 'It's always been right that the kid don't live with me.'

'We need to see the picture of Andy,' says PC French. 'Where is it?'

'In his car, near the Minerva.'

'I'll join you in a minute,' says Bernadette, holding the picture to her chest.

Bernadette watches them climb over the wall and round the corner. Then she goes to the railings and looks out at the river. What a horrible place to be – so cold, dark and isolated. What are the chances of survival after all this time? Bernadette read once that the River Humber is one of the most dangerous rivers in the world, with shifting sands and seven-knot currents. The Humber Rescue team save lives on the estuary, launching from a boathouse at the foot of the Humber Bridge's north tower. They are out there now.

What must it have been like for Conor in the freezing water, thinking he might die? And then his own dad jumped in and got him out.

But sometimes the rescuer is the one who first puts you in danger. Richard locked Bernadette in the pantry. So he was the one to open the door and let her out. This man – this Paul or Andy – put Conor's life in jeopardy by missing it altogether and then unlocked the pantry door when he jumped in the river after him.

Bernadette studies again the drawing of her face. It's like looking in a gentle mirror, one that ignores frown lines and tired eyes. This is how Conor sees her. She wonders how he saw his dad, what that drawing is like. It's time to go and join the others and be wherever she is needed.

The ambulance has gone. Conor is likely at the hospital now, safe, warm and taken care of. PC French and the bald officer sit in the front of the police car, Frances in the back. Bernadette gets in next to her. The warmth soothes her cold skin.

'Could be anyone,' says PC French, holding a smoothed-out piece of paper up to the light. 'I don't recognise him. We could scan it into the PNC back at the station. Might get a hit. Have a look, Bernadette, see if he means anything to you.'

She takes the paper from her. They have clearly tried hard to straighten it out and the damage is minimal, just extra lines and criss-crosses across the male face. Bernadette looks at it.

She frowns.

She looks up again to make sure her eyes are not blurring in the waft of car heater air. No, PC French's face is clear, its youthful skin like an advert for an expensive cream. The bald officer's face is moonlike, dark where chin hair needs shaving, grey under bloodshot eyes. And Frances' feathery thread veins and tiny blackheads are signs of her self-destructive behaviour.

Yes, Bernadette's eyes are working perfectly. She looks back at the drawing.

She knows him.

'Where's the car?' she asks, each word sounded carefully.

'Andy's?' asks PC French.

'Near the Minerva, on the other side,' says Frances. 'Why?'

'Is it open?'

'Yes. He must have had the keys in his pocket when he...' Frances' words die.

'You have to call the coastguard *now*.' Bernadette squeezes PC French's arm but speaks calmly. 'Check if they've found him – they might have him now. Make sure they look harder if not.'

'We will, we are.' PC French twists in her seat. 'What's wrong? Do you know him?'

Bernadette opens the door, taking both drawings with her. She slams it on PC French's questions and hurries through the dark, feet twisting awkwardly on the cobbles.

Where's the car? She will know it when she sees it.

And then, in a badly lit spot near a tree she sees it – the black Audi. She recognises the registration plate, the two letters that are coincidentally the same as her first initial and his. She's been in this vehicle so many times, been in the leather seat and stared out of the window, listened to the music of his choice.

Anticipating the smell of lemon air freshener, Bernadette opens the back door. It's there like she knew it would be; the laptop bag. All this proof and yet her mind still pushes the truth away. Pursuing the evidence, she opens the bag, finds notepaper, pens, business cards (no need to read one, she knows the name and number embossed in gold), laptop, and a guide to some computer system.

But there is something else Bernadette recognises. Something she didn't expect, that doesn't belong among these items and stands out like a baby in a yellow blanket on a ward of all blues and pinks.

It is Conor's Lifebook.

She opens it at the first page, sees Jim Roger's messy handwriting and his simple *This book is a gift*. She turns the page, and another and another and another. So many words, so many stories. Bernadette finds that first letter from Frances; it's easy to spot as she always wrote in red like she'd dipped the pen in blood. Where's the part where she mentioned Conor's father? Bernadette touches the red sentences and reads aloud.

He was dressed nice and there not usually. He talked nice and he said we could just walk by the water and chat and stuff. He wanted to know about my house and me mum and dad. None of them ask that stuff normally. He said he was on a kind of mission and I said what like in the Blues Brothers film? Im sure its him thats your dad cos after him I was ill a while and there wasnt nobody else. So you come from a nice man.

Bernadette closes the book. She knows the truth and how Conor's father discovered it.

PC French comes around the corner, approaches the car.

'Do you want to tell me who he is?' she asks.

Bernadette looks at the two pictures, hers smooth and his rough. Side by side, it's like she smiles enigmatically and he watches her. It occurs to Bernadette that just as she has recognised him now, he must have looked at her picture when Conor drew it and pretended innocence.

Or did he admit to Conor that he knew her?

'Just tell us,' urges PC French, 'and then we know who we're looking for.'

'You're looking for my husband,' says Bernadette.

41

The Book

Conor's first (and only) entry in his Lifebook.
16/08/09
I will be 8 in November.

I like these things
Number 1 Berndete
Number 2 Ann and Sophie
Number 3 Muhammad Ali
Number 4 drawing stuff
Number 5 cake
Number 6 Saturdays
Number 7 Mum
Number 8 cake

I don't like this stuff much
Number 1 sprowts
Number 2 not nowing Dad
Number 3 get up early
Number 4 not been abel to finish stuff
Number 5 teachers
Number 6 Stan Chisick but just today
Number 7 wen Berndete goes
Number 8 wen Mum gets upset
PS I done 8 of each cos I am nearly 8.

42

Bernadette

PC French's mouth hangs open and Bernadette almost feels sad for her. Then – so suddenly that she actually enunciates a sharp little *oh* – Bernadette realises what it is that has always felt so right and so familiar about Conor.

He *looks* like Richard. God, he looks like him. He has the same soft hair; the same tone in his young voice. It's only now, with knowledge, that the similarities present.

Bernadette suddenly recalls with exquisite sharpness the moment she realised she loved Richard; *really* loved him. It wasn't when she first saw him on their curious 'wrong' date in the Cup and Saucer café. It wasn't when they married. It wasn't even when he first said he loved her during the rain in Loch Lomond.

It was a month after they'd wed when he found her reading alone in their bedroom. He asked why she went away to read, rather than sitting with him in the living room. Not wanting to hurt his feelings, Bernadette said she concentrated better when reading alone. It was true but she didn't want him to think it was something he'd done. Richard said he understood, that sometimes you had to go away from a person to really know they were there; like that corny saying about setting something free to make sure it's truly yours. Said he could face anything knowing she was at Tower Rise waiting for him, and that he would always be on the other side of the door while she read.

'But how did your husband find out Conor existed?' asks PC French, pulling Bernadette back to the present.

'This,' says Bernadette, holding out the lemon Lifebook. 'This is the book I couldn't find earlier today, the one about Conor. Richard must have come across it at home and read it and recognised himself and put all the pieces together. It was with him all this time.'

The sound of a helicopter has them looking up into the night sky, at the yellow lights and spinning blades.

'Are they coming back?' asks Bernadette. 'What does it mean?'

'Let's go back to the car and we'll find out,' says PC French. 'This is all quite a shock for you.'

'Where am I supposed to go now?' Bernadette asks, not sure whom she's addressing.

'Let's go back to the car and if there's no news we can take you home or get someone you know to collect you. I'll call the moment we know anything. Is there anyone we can contact to be with you?'

Bernadette shakes her head. Her parents live too far away and she wouldn't trouble them anyway. She has never troubled them with her worries, never wanted to upset them. There's no one else. This is her life now she's left Richard. Just her.

They walk back to the car, Bernadette with the two pictures and Conor's Lifebook under her arm. She asks if PC French will explain to Frances about Richard, as she doesn't think she has the energy, and the police officer assures her she will.

At the car Bernadette views Frances with new eyes; this woman slept with her husband. There is no anger. It's unlikely Frances knew there was a wife.

A date jumps into Bernadette's head as though from the pages of a book. One she'd always taken as a curious coincidence. Way back when she first read Conor's date of birth in the Lifebook she had touched the numbers, felt it was some sort of sign that their relationship would be significant – it was the day she'd met Richard. And now it helps her realise that Frances knew Richard *before* she did. It was no affair. It was before they met.

But what about this Ruth woman? Who is *she*? Does that have anything to do with this new situation?

PC French chats with the other officer and tells Bernadette there's no news yet; they are still searching. She should go home. But Bernadette doesn't know if she wants to return to her two packed bags at Tower Rise. It would feel as though she's lost a fight. Like she's returning a failure.

But there's nowhere else she can go. 'I'll go home then,' she says eventually.

'Can we drop you off?' asks PC French.

'No,' says Bernadette. She knows who to call, who should take her home.

PC French takes Bernadette's phone number. 'We'll be in touch with any news,' she says.

Bernadette walks away from the car, along where white boats line up as though being judged in a beauty contest. She glances back only once; Frances is looking out the back window and her eyes remind Bernadette of Conor's when he watches her leave each Saturday, bright with hopeless optimism, trusting her to come back but resigned to the fact that she might not. While Richard could be brusque – and he did some harsh things over the years – his eyes never looked at her with anything but hopeless optimism.

Bernadette starts to run.

Conor is safe, and so is his Lifebook, but the night isn't over until they find Richard.

43

Bernadette

Bob Fracklehurst took Bernadette from Tower Rise into the night five hours ago and she decides to ask him to take her back home now. This is what she calls it when she rings Top Taxis from the phone box near Queen's Gardens: home. After five years of booking this trip twice a month they know where it is, so she asks the receptionist if Bob can take her there.

'Home, love. Where's home?' asks the woman, and Bernadette realises she doesn't recognise the voice. This isn't Barbara, the gravel-voiced woman she's never seen but visualises as robust and ruddy-cheeked, the one who always says 'Eh pet' after every sentence. Of course – Bernadette has never rung the firm at this late hour. She recalls how her request earlier surprised Barbara, had her asking if Bernadette was running away with the bloke next door.

'Is Bob still working?' Bernadette asks now.

'Yes,' says the woman, 'but he's on his last job.'

'Would you be good enough to ask him if he can pick me up from Queen's Gardens? Tell him it's Bernadette Shaw. He said earlier he wouldn't mind if I needed a lift.'

'Just hold please.' The woman disappears; Bernadette waits.

The frothy fountains across the road are lit up blue, as though charged with electricity. When was the last time she saw them at night? Perhaps returning from some rare office party with Richard, neither of them having had a drink, him driving and grumbling about the fools he has to work with.

Bernadette's arm aches. She looks at her elbow. Remembers she has

Conor's Lifebook and two drawings tucked there. Pulling out the wrinkled one, she opens it and looks again at Richard's face, at her husband, at Conor's father. Richard who right now is missing; lost at sea.

'Bob says he'll be there in about ten minutes.' The voice pulls Bernadette out of the water. 'He's just on North Road.'

Bernadette waits on the corner by the bus stop. She doesn't want to be alone for too long. Company will prevent her thoughts from opening cupboard doors that she'd rather not, stop her seeing pictures in her favourite survival stories of emaciated men pulled from the sea after weeks in a lifeboat. *Be safe*, Bob said when she got out of his cab earlier. She still doesn't feel it though. When his familiar car pulls up she is grateful to climb inside and escape the dark.

'I'm glad you called,' he says, turning the music down.

More than ever he reminds Bernadette of her father. Something in the way his grey hair curls about his ear as though stroking it. Something about how he says he's glad she called like he really is. She wonders how she didn't notice such similarities between Richard and Conor.

She suddenly misses the dad who never said much in the way of praise or love when Bernadette was growing up, but whose absolute there-ness could be depended upon. She could look into the greenhouse and he'd be there, always, tending his plants and tomatoes. She doesn't often talk to him now – her phone calls home usually mean conversation with her mother – but she knows that should she ever need anything, he'll be there.

'I worried about you all evening,' says Bob.

'You're kind.' She doesn't know what else to say.

'Are you okay, love?' Bob frowns at her.

Bernadette nods. 'Yes. Sorry, this has been a long night. And it isn't even over yet.'

'Where do you want to go?'

'Tower Rise,' she says.

'To pick up your bags?'

Bernadette pictures them by the door. 'My bags?'

'You told me earlier you were leaving your husband,' says Bob, heading towards the BBC building. 'Tell me to keep me bloody nose out but I was actually quite relieved when you said it. I've sensed it isn't the best marriage. All you haven't said on our journeys put it in me mind. I don't really like taking you back there. See – I've said it all and it's none of my business.'

'Richard isn't at Tower Rise,' says Bernadette. They pause at the lights and she watches red turn amber, like a dying leaf, and then green as though reborn. 'He's gone missing – in the River Humber.'

'Jesus.' Bob reaches for a cigarette and opens his window a crack. 'What was he doing there?'

'Rescuing someone,' says Bernadette softly.

'I'm sorry. Did he manage to save them?'

Bernadette nods.

'I saw the helicopter earlier,' says Bob. 'I always think, poor sod, when I see one. They'll find him. They know what they're doing, don't they?'

His taxi joins the A63 and the river appears, a fat black snake that squirms and slides. It parallels them on the opposite side to where Bob picked Bernadette up. Lights that normally enchant have her tonight thinking of candles at a funeral, so she doesn't look at them. If Richard is still out in those thick, churning currents his chances of survival must be remote now. Maybe there will be a message on the machine when she gets back to Tower Rise – your husband is safe, hypothermic and in shock, but *safe*. Then she will have to consider how cruel it is to divorce a man recovering from near death. Because even though he is Conor's father and that this somehow endears him to her, she still wants to leave him.

'Remember we talked about coincidences earlier?' says Bernadette.

'Yes.' Bob puts out his cigarette. 'My Trish said they were little clues.'

'They definitely are. There were all these curious things happening to me. Richard went missing, and so did Conor, the boy you take me to see, and also this important book.' She looks at it on her lap, touches the textured lemon cover. 'I thought none of it had anything to do with the other, that it was just some bizarre fluke. But it was all connected.

I should have known.' She pauses. 'Bob, tell me more about this woman who was with Richard when he fixed your computer. Did she tell you her name?'

Bob appears to think. 'If she did, I don't recall. But I'm a bugger with names – faces, yes, names, no.'

'Did they seem like they knew each other well?'

'It's hard to say.' Bob glances at Bernadette and she knows he doesn't want to say the wrong thing. But wrong things are what she needs to know. 'She didn't really say anything, just seemed keen to get out of there to be honest. Glamorous creature, red lipstick and that. She looked about thirty but I felt like she was actually younger. He didn't acknowledge her particularly, just said she was his sister, staying here for the weekend. That was it.'

Bernadette actually wonders for a moment if Richard *does* have a secret sister. There have been so many revelations tonight, what would one more matter? But no, it isn't possible. His mum never talked of a daughter and there was never such a female at Christmas gatherings or at their wedding. Why would he hide one? She has to remember that Richard didn't hide Conor. She was the one who did that.

'When they find your husband,' says Bob, 'it's maybe best to ask him.'

'I will do.' Bernadette doesn't know if she can wait that long.

Bob drives down the narrow lane to the foreshore and they have the best view of the Humber Bridge, brightly lit ahead like a creature from *The War of the Worlds*. On the right – just before the bridge's north tower – thick trees and a faded sign on a chalk wall announce Tower Rise. They enter, approach slowly, and Bernadette puts a hand to her neck as though being strangled. The place has that effect, like the air alters, gets thicker, clogs up her throat.

Bob parks by the steps. 'I guess you don't need the usual receipt writing out?'

'No, thank you.' Bernadette doubts this is a journey she can claim the money back for. Befriend for Life always require receipts for meals eaten with Conor, transport to and from his home, but though this trip concerned looking for him she feels better paying for it herself.

'It's so black in there. Do you want me to come up with you?'

'No, really. I know my way in that dark.' Bernadette opens the car door.

'I'll wait with my headlights on until you're safely inside,' insists Bob. He pauses. 'I hope you hear good news soon.' He pauses again. 'I guess I'll see you a week on Saturday?'

For a moment Bernadette has to get her bearings on the dark, gritty driveway, think what he means. Of course. She'll be seeing Conor. Life will continue. It occurs suddenly to her that someone will tell Conor his father isn't Paul or Andy but her husband. Does that mean he'll be able to visit her at Tower Rise? Will Richard pursue his rights and want to see Conor? How will that affect her relationship with the little boy? What about the boundaries set in place by BFL? Is there some sort of code that states what happens when the volunteer's child turns out to be her husband's son? Can she still volunteer at all? So much to think about, but she can't now.

There is someone she has to call.

'Bernadette?' Bob is unfastening his seatbelt as though to get out, and she realises she has been standing there, lost in thought.

'I'm fine,' she says quickly. 'Thank you so much, Bob.' She goes around to his open window, not sure what her intentions are. He knows; he nods and says, 'Be safe.'

Before ascending the steps, she looks up at their unwelcoming, dark windows and wonders briefly if Richard got out of the river where it passes the end of their driveway and is sitting in the dark, waiting for her to come home.

Will he ask where his tea is? Insist she goes in the pantry to think about it? She wouldn't do it now. She's not that woman anymore. She's still a woman who prefers one thing – one child (she never dreamed of more), one husband, one friend – but she just wants one answer now.

Bernadette goes up the stairs to their flat. Behind her, Bob drives away and the light goes with him. She unlocks their door, lets it swing open and flicks on the switch. Her two bags sit by the lounge door. Does time even move on when you lock a door behind you? The stagnant air, rich with damp and old paint, sings a tired song here. She is home.

Is Richard here?

She listens. Silence.

The lounge is just as it was; bare table, no tea for Richard, no crisp napkin or polished cutlery. Cushions she sewed out of gold fabric sit symmetrically at opposite ends of the sofa, like they're sulking after an argument. Tonight the damp patch by the wall shelves looks like a drowning man. Bernadette's beloved books are all over the floor where she pulled them off the shelves in her desperate hunt for the Lifebook. She puts them back – but not all of them.

She places the Lifebook on the coffee table in full view; no need to hide it now. How guilty she felt concealing Conor, as if he didn't exist. How often words about her day with him formed in her mouth only to be swallowed again because she couldn't share them with Richard.

Now everything is where it should be. Conor is safe with Anne. The book is here. But Richard's whereabouts remain a mystery and she shouldn't be here at all. She was never coming back; she was leaving with all she could carry and going who knew where. But here she is.

Bernadette presses play on the answering machine, hears *You have no new messages* and isn't surprised.

What now?

She searches the flat, making sure a wet and exhausted husband doesn't lie in wait. However he feels about having a son, Bernadette must remember he discovered also that she lied to him for five years. He will be angry. She makes sure the front door is on the chain so she'll have to let him in, giving her time to prepare.

Then she continues her game of prove-the-monster-isn't-there.

Perhaps he is in their bedroom, has fallen asleep still clothed. No, the room is empty. Maybe he went into the place that should have been a nursery – where else would be more fitting for a man who has just discovered he's a dad? But this room is empty too.

Bernadette stands in the doorway a moment. She doesn't flick the switch, can't stand to see the daffodil-yellow walls fully lit and mocking her childlessness. How unfair it seems that Richard has a child after all. And yet it is she who has loved this child, taken him out, written about him in a book.

The baby she and Richard lost was too young to be named or be legally registered. Bernadette grieved privately, not naming him, even in secret, because that might make the loss all the more painful. She preferred to think that somehow the baby chose not to come into a marriage that was falling apart. That he made his presence known and then went to some other place. Might he have healed them?

She'll never know.

Bernadette closes the door on the nursery and checks the bathroom and the kitchen, sure she'll find them also clean, orderly and empty.

She is alone.

44

The Book

Hull Social Services Report – Yvonne Jones (Social Worker)
Conor Jordan – Access Update

Date: 16/08/2009

Conor now sees his mum every month at her new home in Doncaster, going with either Len Coupland or myself. Frances Jordan has a five-month-old girl called Kayleigh and she resides there. Conor enjoys seeing his baby sister. Understandably, there are often tensions between Conor and his mother. He swings between dramatic shows of affection towards her and swearing suddenly and asking to leave. But we're always able to mediate and calm him. Frances tries to be patient when this occurs.

Conor met his siblings Sam and George again on 18/03/09, six months after the first meeting. Sam's health has deteriorated in recent months, and the foster carer is having trouble coping. The meeting didn't go as well as previously. Sam didn't engage with his brothers and Conor lashed out at Sam's carer, calling her a dog. George got upset. An assessment will be made in six months with regards to another meeting.

Signed:
Yvonne Jones

45

Conor

I'm sleepy. So sleepy. Am I still in the water?

No. Not cold but warm and fuzzy. Where did they all go? I remember now. Paul got me out. No, not Paul. *My dad*. He let me go but then I realised it was only cos Mum had hold of me and dragged me back onto the wood. Where's Mum? I remember Bernadette was there too at some point.

Where is she now?

Anne's here. We must be in an ambulance cos I can hear the siren thing. Somewhere inside I'm excited cos I've never been in one. Yes, I have. Of course. They said I went in one when my legs burnt. But I don't remember that so really this is the first time. My legs are tingling though. All hot and sharp like they remember that time.

Anne is talking. Some of her words don't reach my ears, like they got sucked out the ambulance. But I put the other ones together and it all makes sense. That's cos we know each other. That's what you do when you know each other.

She says, *Just rest and you'll be okay*.

I want to ask where everyone went but there's this mask thing on my face. So I try and get it off but Anne stops me and says, *Let it be, you need extra oxygen to recover*.

Then one of the hospital misters says that word again – delirious. I don't know what it means but if it's sort of sleepy and happy and cold and warm too, then he's right. The bouncing of the ambulance is nice. Anne's face is blurry like she's the one in water. The misters are saying stuff about dry drowning and difficulty breathing and lethargy.

Sounds like an episode of that show *Casualty*. And it wears me out just listening.

So I fall asleep again.

When I wake up I'm in hospital. The bed is stiff and the pillow smells weird. First thing I think is that I've gone to live in some new home, which is crazy cos I haven't done that for like years now. But then I realise I've still got that oxygen thingy on my face and Anne leans over me and tells me where I am. She kisses my forehead and says that they have to do some blood tests and make sure my oxygen levels are back to normal and keep me warm and monitor me. I'll probably stay in overnight, which would be cool if I could have planned it and brought all my stuff. Like a sleepover but without the ghost stories.

I can't seem to stay awake for long. My eyes get heavy again straight away and I fall asleep.

I dream that everyone has come to see me. Sophie comes in first with a new *Doctor Who* magazine. She was in it once cos she wrote in about a Tardis she made out of cardboard and they used the photo.

Then there's Bernadette and she's got my Lifebook. I know all about it. It's not a book like you get at the library, not a made-up one. It's about me. Can't read it till I'm eighteen but I've seen it in Anne's house. The pages are all crinkly and there's things stuck in it and I wrote a note for it one time.

Mum's even in my dream but she stays near the door for some reason.

I look hard for Paul – no, my *dad*. But he doesn't come.

Is he still in the river?

When I wake up I don't have the mask on. Anne is asleep in the chair near my bed. It's dark. Suddenly I feel real dark too. Want to get up and run out of this shit place. Try and get up but there's this dumb thing in my arm. Reckon if I don't leave soon they'll put me down like they did Shana. She was so hurt they had to kill her. Was my fault. Didn't hold her tight enough.

Paul – *Dad* – held me tight.

But was it tight enough?

Anne shuffles about and then wakes up. She rushes to the bed and tells me not to struggle. I have never ever said a bad word to Anne but I do now. I say the worst one of all. And then I feel so crap cos she doesn't even mind. She still kisses me and says I'm just feeling down because I'm exhausted.

You have been through a lot, she says.

I can't feel mad for long when Anne's there.

I go back to sleep.

When I wake up she's still there, sitting on the bed. If I could have a pen now and draw her she might not like it much. She's all black lines and tomato-sauce-red skin. I don't tell her this though. She's looking at me real strange. Like as though I also changed how I look.

I don't know what time it is now.

Have they found Paul? I ask her.

Anne shakes her head. It doesn't mean anything really. He could have climbed out of the river and gone home and none of them know where he lives so they won't be able to get him. I hope he doesn't get into trouble for getting me from school. They're always going on about how you shouldn't go with anyone you don't know, but he's my dad. Wait until I tell Stan Chiswick.

Anne says that she just spoke to Bernadette and there's no news yet about Paul. Then she grabs my hand and her eyes get all watery. She says that she knows about Paul. That he is my dad. She tells me I've been very brave dealing with it all but I don't know what she means. The hard part was when I *didn't* know.

Anne says she has something else to tell me but she will wait until I feel stronger. I am strong. Didn't she just say I was brave?

I hate waiting to hear about stuff. Done it lots. Waiting to hear if I'll go and live here or there. Waiting to hear if Mum will see me or not. Waiting to find out if dogs are dead.

So I turn away from Anne and close my eyes.

When I open them again there's a nurse looking at the bleepy stuff near my bed and she smiles at me and calls me little soldier. When she's gone Anne says she'll explain a little bit about the something else.

She says that Paul isn't called Paul, or even Andy.

I tell her, well, of course I know *that*. He's called Dad. And then I go, *Doh*, cos he will have a proper name too of course.

Anne says his real name is Richard and that Bernadette knows him very well. Wow. That's cool. Bernadette will know where he lives. I tell Anne they can go and look at his house then in case he got out the river and went home.

She shakes her head, says he isn't there. Bernadette called from the place he lives and he didn't go home.

This is so mega. If Bernadette can get to his house she'll be able to take me to see him. She'll know which bus to get. So when he gets saved and stuff we can like all hang together.

Then I get my detective head on and ask how did Bernadette know she knew Paul if he's still in the river? Anne reminds me about the pictures I drew in the car. She says Bernadette saw one I did of my dad and told the police officer she knew him. I always knew my art would do good stuff.

That's what Mrs Connelly said once when we used to do lessons together. It was just me and her and she didn't have any rules like the other teachers. She let me draw what I wanted and we just looked at all this art in her books. One man actually cut his ear off. Totally did. But it didn't matter cos he was good. He had a weird name and started drawing when he was a kid and then painted sunflowers. No one liked his stuff till he was dead. Mrs Connelly told me that it didn't matter cos if a work of art makes a difference to just one person then it succeeds.

So I guess my art succeeded cos Bernadette has seen my dad in it. Don't feel tired now. Want to go home. Want to ring Bernadette. Anne tells me it's the middle of the night and they won't let me go until morning and Bernadette might be sleeping. I bet she isn't.

Doesn't feel like the middle of the night. When you're in a room with no windows you get confused. Never gonna get back to sleep with all this cool stuff in my head. Wish I could watch one of my DVDs. When I watch Muhammad Ali go side to side on his feet it makes me all relaxed. Anne is always amazed cos she says it makes her feel jumpy.

But not me. When I lie in bed and watch him dance like that I fall asleep.

So I close my eyes and picture him.

And I see Mark who was my mate when I lived at Georgina's and showed me how to punch a cushion when I was mad. I see Shana the dog and she's wagging her tail like she did when I said I'd take her for a walk. She's not mad at me. And then at last I see my dad. Don't even call him Paul. He comes into the room and I'm not even sure if I'm just picturing him now or dreaming or awake.

Doesn't matter.

Dad comes and sits on the bed and his hair is all wet. It's gone a bit wiggly like mine does after a bath. He talks in his slow soft voice that's not like people round here. Says he's real tired and can he just lie next to me for a bit while he gets his breath. Of course I let him. Don't even care if the sheets get all wet.

And he goes to sleep. Next to me. I even dare touch his wet hair dead quick. He doesn't move, just breathes and breathes, and I do too and go to sleep.

When I wake up he isn't there and they must have changed my covers cos they're not even wet. Doesn't matter.

I know he was here.

46

Bernadette

Bernadette goes to Richard's desk and hunts through the drawers for sticky tape or pins. Then she takes the two pictures she has brought with her from the riverside to the wall where her bookshelf is and unrolls the one Conor drew of her face. Carefully she pins it above the books and stands back and admires the mastery of Conor's lines and shading, thinking, not for the first time, that his ability makes her heart ache. The sketch of Richard she puts on the coffee table, beneath the Lifebook so the creases flatten; perhaps Conor might like this one for his own wall.

There is someone Bernadette must call.

But first she must know how Conor is, so she rings Anne to find out. Anne explains that he'll be on a ventilator for a while, and that they're keeping him in until morning, but he's fine. Bernadette has been telling Anne her stories all evening and now she has to tell her the most incredible one of all – that Richard is Conor's real father.

The silence on the phone line is a clenched hand letting go of Bernadette's neck. Eventually Anne says, 'I really am lost now.'

We all are, thinks Bernadette. We all are.

When they finish, Bernadette hangs up. A sound. The trees? She goes to the window, half expects a shadowy Richard to be crawling along the gravel. Nothing. Her heart takes minutes to slow down.

She goes back to the phone and calls the number she usually avoids. After three rings the woman called Ruth answers, and asks, 'Is that you, Richard?'

'No, it's Bernadette.'

'Has he come back yet?'

'No. But I know where he is.'

'Is he okay?' asks Ruth.

'That I don't know,' says Bernadette. 'But I want you to tell me who you are and what your interest is in my husband.'

'Just tell me he's okay.'

'I can't. You said you know where I live, and that you'd come and explain it all to me if Richard still wasn't back. He isn't so you should come. I'm here and I'm not going anywhere. Bring his phone with you please.' Bernadette hangs up before Ruth can respond; she should keep the line free now in case anyone calls with news.

Now she must wait and see if Ruth comes to Tower Rise. Wait and see if Richard is found. If he returns. Waiting is much harder than searching. At least when she was out looking for Conor with Anne they were occupied, had purpose. Here there's nothing but time and that's never kind to a waiting woman. Bernadette must fill it.

So she makes a plate of meat-paste sandwiches and eats them in the lounge window, looking out at the trees silhouetted against sky. She feels surprisingly strong. It's like the preceding evening has prepared her, just as running six hours a day might ready a runner for the big marathon event.

If Bernadette does leave Tower Rise – with Richard's absence she's even less sure what the future holds – she will miss the trees. If only she could uproot them and plant them elsewhere. She'll just have to get new ones and watch them grow from babies into adults. Conor will love the Tower Rise woods too. He may finally get to see them, to collect their leaves and climb onto their lower branches.

A strange feeling of jealousy envelopes the thought, like an itchy coat on bare arms. Conor was hers, but now she must share him with Richard, must understand that their bond is one she might never have with a child.

A knock on the door. Bernadette freezes. Richard? No, he'd rattle the handle, try to get in, demand why the chain is on. She puts her empty plate down and goes into the corridor. The police? Surely they would ring first.

When she opens the door she knows immediately that this is the woman who Richard took to Bob's house. Bob's description fits perfectly; she's glamorous in an overly colourful way, decorated with gold earrings, butterfly hair attachments and sparkling bangles, as though dressed for a role. Perhaps at home she peels off the costume and puts on jogging bottoms and a T-shirt, but here she is ready for a show. Red hair, too bright to be natural, is pinned up in places and hangs free in others. Crimson lipstick gives her thin lips fatness, and pink gives her cheeks a blush. Her skin says early twenties but the eyes are older. Conor, with a pencil and sheet of paper, would have much to work with.

Bernadette realises that because she's standing in the light she'll appear shadowy to this woman. She's glad of the protection. She imagines how dull she must look in comparison, hair not brushed since the morning, face dull with the night's worries and dirt. Should she care? She can't help it.

This woman should be her rival, but she feels more like she must prove she is stronger than Richard.

'Ruth,' says Bernadette.

She nods. 'You don't look anything like I expected.'

Bernadette wonders what this woman did expect. She wants to say that strangely Ruth is exactly how she imagined. Instead she opens the door wider and says, 'Come in.'

She leads Ruth into the lounge and offers her the sofa, asks if she would like a drink.

'I don't suppose you mean something stronger than tea?'

'There might be whisky,' says Bernadette, remembering the rush it had given her at Andrew's house earlier. The thought of that kick again is good. She's sure there's some in the kitchen but it's in the pantry and she hates going in there. 'I'll see.'

At the pantry door Bernadette waits. The dark space has had this effect on her ever since that first time Richard was late. Now he's so late it should simply be called absent. Didn't PC French earlier, when asking them about Conor, explain that there are certain types of missing? That most children eventually come home, tired, hungry and sorry for causing any trouble.

Will Richard be sorry for anything?

She opens the pantry door, reaches for the whisky without stepping into the darkness and slams it shut again. There's no mixer so she simply pours two generous portions into glasses, throws in ice and takes them back to the lounge.

Ruth is looking at Conor's drawing of Richard. 'Wow, it really looks like him. Did you do it?'

Bernadette wants to say no, his son did, but she's tired of telling stories tonight; Ruth is here to do that. Bernadette gives her a drink and stands by the bookshelf with hers. If she sits down she's making herself familiar with this stranger, consenting fully to her existence in Richard's life, and she doesn't yet know what that existence is.

'Did you bring Richard's phone?'

Ruth rummages in a multi-pocketed red leather bag and throws it on the coffee table, where it lands away from the Lifebook as though afraid of it.

'How long have you had it?' Bernadette asks.

'Since Saturday,' says Ruth. 'Thought I told you that.' She drinks the whisky like it's lemonade.

Bernadette sips her drink, enjoying the fire in her throat, and studies Ruth until she looks away.

'So where's Richard?' Ruth asks after a moment.

'No, you answer questions first. Who are you to him?' Bernadette could be unkind and say she's not his preferred type, that Richard likes his women pure and clean, but any anger she has is not towards Ruth. 'Were you with Richard when he fixed a computer in Greatfield during his lunch hour last Saturday?'

'I was. But it wasn't his lunch hour.'

'Well, his break,' snaps Bernadette. 'Whatever it was.'

'No, I mean, Richard wasn't on a break.' Ruth talks kindly, as though she knows the words will be harsh enough. 'He doesn't work on Saturdays.'

'What are you talking about? He's always worked Saturdays.' Bernadette is surprised to find that her glass is empty. She puts it on the shelf. 'Don't you think I know what my own husband does? He leaves at nine for work and every other Saturday I go out shortly after. It's how I've been able to volunteer all this time.'

Ruth puts her empty glass on the coffee table; they are equal.

'No, he doesn't,' she says softly. 'He has never worked Saturdays. But I do. That's when he's with me – when I'm working. I'm a prostitute, Bernadette.'

47

The Book

Hull City Council
Young Ferens Art Prize 2010 competition

Dear Conor Jordan's Parent/Guardian,
We are delighted to tell you that Conor has won first place in the Young
Ferens Art Prize 2010 Under-10 category for his stunning artwork. His 3ftx3ft
pencil sketch of Muhammad Ali's face unanimously delighted our judges. It
will hang in the gallery as part of an Icons collection for the rest of the year.

We hope you will both be able to attend the prize-giving ceremony at
Hull City Hall on 12th June, where Conor will be awarded £50 and a set of fine
pencils. The local media would like to interview all winners afterwards, so
please confirm if you are happy for Conor to take part.

Yours sincerely,
Peter Cloud
(Chairman of Arts Council)

9th June 2010

Dear Peter Cloud,
I'm writing to let you know that, sadly, Conor Jordan won't be able to attend
the prize-giving ceremony at Hull City Hall on Saturday as he will be at his
brother George's funeral. Conor was absolutely delighted to win this prize
and it's a great shame that, due to this family loss, he will miss out on the

recognition. Thank you again for choosing his art. I don't think any of the judges realise what this win did for his self-esteem.

Best regards,
Anne Williams

Newspaper article from 7th June 2010

Delayed Ambulance Tragedy

A social worker has called for an inquiry following the death of six-year-old George Jordan, claiming that an ambulance took too long to arrive. Barry Davies says George – who lived in a care home in Doncaster – suffered heart failure brought on by a severe asthma attack yesterday evening. By the time George arrived at the hospital it was too late to save him.

Though the nearest ambulance station is just five miles away, the 999 crew took forty-five minutes to arrive. Ambulance bosses have said it was an unprecedentedly busy night, but have admitted that forty-five minutes is unacceptable and the target response time is twelve minutes.

George regularly has asthma attacks and has been taken to the hospital numerous times in the past, where treatment has been successful. A carer at the home said, 'This tragedy could have been prevented. They're normally here in fifteen minutes. I'm utterly shocked. He was only six.'

Doncaster Coroner, Sean Mackerel will adjourn an inquest awaiting further information. George's birth mother did not wish to comment. The funeral will take place on Saturday. Any donations are to be given to Asthma UK.

13th June 2010

To Conor and Sam,

I am sat and righting this and its the night after Georges funeral and Im feeling very down and bad about it all. Then I thought if I right it all down it will feel better cos they say it does. So I decided to right it for you and Sam instead cos you both have books and can both have them in it. Also I have to think what you two must be feel like. You didnt do nothing wrong but I have. If Id been a better mum and had you all propers he might not of died. I want you both to know I am really sorry. I keep saying this word and then not doing much better. But I have been seeing you and getting to no you and that is good. I hope we can carry on doing that. Kayleigh likes you both. She asks always where is my brothers? My mum had lots of us but she managed to keep us all. Me and my brothers and sisters don't see each other now though but its cos we live all over and none of them really wants to have much to do with me. I understand this. Only my twin brother Andrew sees me. I would like him to see you too but it might not happen. One day when you grow up I might be able to tell you more stuff that I cant now. I am sad and sorry. Always am. I do love you both but maybe not how I should.

Your Mum xxx

Kate Sharpe
School Counsellor
1st July 2010

Dear Mrs Anne Williams,
I want to let you know that while we can recommend a child see a counsellor to talk with them, we cannot enforce such a thing. Headmaster Mr Grimshaw felt it would help Conor to have a few sessions following his recent bereavement, but though Conor came to me he did not engage. He did not appear to wish to talk about the death of his brother and said he had a proper home now and he could talk to the people he now has. This is to inform you that I see no need for any further sessions.

Very best,
Kate Sharpe

48

Bernadette

Conor's drawing of Bernadette comes away from the wall with a soft tearing of tape and floats to the floor, like a patterned parachute. Ruth and Bernadette watch it land by the bookshelf, face up, so that Bernadette's pencilled eyes watch them from the gold carpet.

Bernadette remembers once telling Conor about the *Mona Lisa* painting and how her eyes are said to follow you wherever you go. He then explained how it was all about perspective – spelling the word ever so slowly so she might understand better – and that if you draw eyes that look at you, they will, no matter where you go, because the light and shadow is fixed.

'Did Richard draw that?' asks Ruth, motioning to the sketch.

'No.' Bernadette wants to pick it up, can't stand to see her shaded face so contented when she isn't feeling that way, but she leaves it on the floor. She glares instead at Ruth's over-painted face, at her pinked cheeks and enhanced eyes, and demands, 'Do you expect me to believe that every Saturday my husband has been with you and that you're a—' She can't say the word.

'It's the truth. I'm a prostitute.' Ruth looks at her empty glass on the coffee table. 'It's a funny word, isn't it? Kind of long and official. I prefer escort, though I don't do much of that.' She sighs. 'What do I have to gain by lying about something like that? Look, you wanted me to come and tell you how I know Richard. I said I'd explain it all to you and I am. Is it better if he's with me because it's just some everyday affair?'

'No – I...'

'I don't want your husband for myself. I don't love him or anything, though I am...'

'What?' asks Bernadette.

'Well, I do have some affection for him. That happens after time I suppose. When you get to know someone and you see them every week. He's often kind to me. Has this gentleness, though I'm sure there's a deeper reason for that.' Ruth shrugs and pushes a strand of hair behind her ear.

'How long?' asks Bernadette.

'With me?'

'Yes.'

Ruth thinks. 'Maybe three years.'

'So you're telling me that Richard...' Bernadette picks up the drawing now and puts it face-down on top of the books. She turns back to Ruth. 'You're telling me he *paid* you to, you know, be with him?'

Ruth nods. The flat is too quiet, like Andrew's house earlier where no fridge or radiator hummed. Bernadette imagines the trees outside standing to attention, raptly awaiting Ruth's story. Andrew's house was a twin to Frances' house. Frances. She is a prostitute too. Richard was with her eleven years ago; they made Conor. Ruth isn't the first. It must be true.

It's too much.

Bernadette runs from the lounge, not sure where she will go, and is surprised to find herself in their bedroom. She views the bed with repulsion. How many times in the past have they had sex on a Saturday night? Not often recently, but once upon a time Richard might, in his own chaste way, kiss her neck and suggest they retire early.

She feels sick.

Ruth is behind her, asking if she will be okay, saying sorry.

'Don't come in here.' Bernadette ushers her out of the room and closes the door. 'Isn't it enough that you've had my husband God only knows where?'

'I know it must be a shock,' says Ruth. 'But you wanted to know.'

Bernadette goes to the kitchen and Ruth waits by the lounge door, as though nervous about entering other rooms she may be banned from. Ruth looks at the two packed bags by the door.

Bernadette brings the whisky bottle into the lounge, feeling like a cliché, the wronged wife in a crime drama turning to drink after learning sordid secrets about her God-fearing husband. She pours the liquid into her glass anyway and gives some to Ruth, who sits back on the sofa and thanks her.

'I thought prostitutes only worked nights.' Alcohol makes Bernadette bold. She paces between Richard's desk and the bookshelf, sipping her drink.

'We work all hours,' says Ruth. 'It's not like you imagine at all.'

'But how can you walk the streets in broad daylight?'

Ruth swirls the brown liquid around the glass and her bracelets echo the tinkle of ice. 'I don't work on the streets – I work with other women from a house.'

'You mean like a brothel? But they don't have places like that around here.'

'Of course they do.' Ruth laughs, but not unkindly. She studies Bernadette and seems momentarily surprised by what she sees. 'Some are called massage parlours and they have a website and that. But where I work, it's just a woman's home, Gina, and we all do it from there. She takes care of us. She's been doing it years. I knew her before I even got into it. She was my mum's neighbour.'

'So you're never on the streets?' Bernadette feels it's somehow better that Richard did not drive up and down alleys looking for a quickie in his car.

'God, no. Too dangerous. I've never been a street prozzie.'

'But how does someone…?' The question dies.

Bernadette thinks of Frances, the sad story of how her own father sold her to friends for a few pounds. If a parent treats you with such little value, places importance on what you can sexually give, wouldn't that lead to a lifetime of believing it was all you were worth? She wonders if that vulnerable girl from Belfast looked to Richard for help all those years ago.

But what did *he* look for? Why is she more curious about these women than her husband's disloyalty?

'How does a woman get into it?' Ruth pauses. 'Money usually. For a lot of girls it's because some guy gets them hooked on drugs. Lots of them come from broken homes, foster care. They're vulnerable to start with, sadly. I'm single with two kiddies and it means I get to be at home with them all day and then my neighbour babysits them in the evening and on Saturdays. The money's so good I couldn't do anything else now. Wouldn't get the same working in Asda. My kids have the best shoes and all the modern gadgets.'

'But don't you...?

'What?'

'Don't you ever feel, like, dirty? Used?'

Ruth sips her drink. 'Sometimes, of course. I can't pick and choose who I see and most aren't exactly what I'd choose for a date. Richard though...' She glances cautiously at Bernadette. 'He was different. Some of them are. They don't want the same as the others, you know, a quick hand job or a blowie. They want a sort of relationship. I know it's hard to believe. Richard ... Look do you want me to go on? You're leaving him anyway.'

'I need to know. How did Richard find you?'

With the creased drawing of Richard on the coffee table in front of her, Ruth tells Bernadette the story of her punter of three years. How he came to the house, upon the recommendation of a colleague, because he had heard about Ruth, the girl with red hair who was a good listener.

He was kind of shy, though he had clearly been to other prostitutes before, and he insisted the arrangement had to be on a Saturday because his wife might suspect untoward things if he were to go out in the evening. He was always smartly dressed, in a suit and polished shoes, and always paid extra. Ruth and he would at first talk for hours, while he held her hand.

Sex when it happened was simple, no kissing, no words, of course a condom. He showered afterwards, vigorously.

'He often tries to persuade me to get out of the job,' says Ruth. 'For the sake of my children. He used to sometimes bring me application forms for other jobs, but he hasn't in a while. Gets annoyed with me when I tell him I'd have to work twice as many hours to make half of what I make. Talks about his mum sometimes, how she raised him alone and didn't have to turn to prostitution. He gets me to wash my make up off before we do it.'

Bernadette believes this. Richard hates her in any sort of garish colour or lipstick. She is surprised he even sought Ruth out, with her glitzy jewellery and obvious hair dye. She is the kind of woman that he would point to in the street and say quietly, 'She has no self-respect.' Bernadette remembers sharply how in their early days Richard would sometimes touch her cheek and say that she had skin like an angel. Those are the things that have kept her with him: the tenderness that was as acute as his occasional cruelty.

'So he always uses a condom?' Bernadette asks the woman he has paid for sex.

'God, always. I insist. We can't not in this job.'

'So how might a woman, you know, *like you,* get pregnant then?'

Poor Conor – he's not only in the care system but was born of a prostitute and a man who pulled Bernadette's arm so hard it broke, simply because she disagreed with him. Bernadette recalls reading once that two geniuses are unlikely to make a genius and decides that two damaged people can perhaps only make something very special. Then she is angry that Richard, despite treating her so badly, is lucky enough to have fathered a child; one she loved first.

'Condoms split,' says Ruth. 'Happened to me before. Even got pregnant once, but got rid of it. Wasn't Richard's – some other punter.'

'Did he ever give you a different name? Andy, or Paul, perhaps?'

'No, just Richard. Why?'

Bernadette ignores the question. 'So he only sees you on a Saturday?' she asks instead. 'What about weekdays, during work?'

Ruth shakes her head, reaches for the bottle and pours more into her glass.

'Is that normal?' asks Bernadette.

'There is no normal. Men who hide it from wives will come whenever best fits their lives. They love their wives, you know. They do. I know that might sound crazy. I think I often help marriages last and I think sometimes, on some level, these women know what their husbands do. They know they can't change it so they ignore it. They're grateful we give their men something they can't.'

'Wait until you have a husband,' says Bernadette. 'And see if you feel like that.'

'Richard loves you,' says Ruth. 'You should stay with him.'

Bernadette studies her crimson mouth. 'He talks about me?'

Ruth looks very young suddenly, like a schoolgirl wearing her mother's make-up and high heels. 'Says you're the only one, with this mournful look on his face. I'd like some man to look like that when going on about me.'

'Richard isn't all he seems.'

'No,' murmurs Ruth. 'I think he has a personality disorder.'

'Who are you to say that?' Bernadette is surprised she feels so defensive.

'Really, I think he does.' Ruth pauses. 'He's obsessive, that's clear. I read this article in my mum's psychology magazine. It was about this narcissist disorder thing. And I thought of Richard when I read it.'

'What did it say?'

'People with this disorder thing have an extreme ... what's the word? Preoccupation, that's it, with themselves and lack empathy for other people. They can be really obsessed with control or power and need constant attention. They'll be kind if they need to but they don't really feel it. A difficult childhood often makes things worse.' Ruth looks a little sad. 'But underneath they're very insecure.'

'You think you know Richard after seeing him once a week as a *prostitute*?' Even though what Ruth is saying rings painfully true, Bernadette is annoyed that the woman seems to know him so well.

'No, not at all. Look, it was only an article. But I know him a little. I know—'

'What? What an earth do you know?'

'Nothing. Sorry, I've no right.'

Bernadette looks at the clock and can't believe it's half past four already. Usually by now she's been sleeping for hours, with Richard breathing peacefully at her side and the sound of the foghorn ghostly on the water.

'Why were you with him last Saturday when he fixed that computer?' she asks. 'Surely that's not part of your job?'

'No, that was a one-off. He said I should go with him because we had an hour left together. I wondered if he *wanted* to be seen for some reason.' Ruth pauses. 'So can I ask where he is now? You promised to tell me.'

Bernadette puts her empty glass on the mantelpiece. 'The last I know, he had jumped into the River Humber to save someone. They haven't found him yet. I'm waiting for news.'

'Fucking hell.' Ruth knocks back the last of her drink. 'Who was he saving?'

Bernadette is too tired to tell the story again. Too tired to say it. Too tired to think of it all anymore. 'No one you know,' she sighs. 'Look, I'm grateful for you coming here and being honest. I really have no issue with you at all. I hardly even care anymore what Richard has done. But now I have his phone and now I know who you are, I just want to be alone. Okay?'

Ruth nods. 'I understand.' She pulls a card from her purse and put it on the table. 'Here's a number we use. Can you call me when you know Richard's okay – please? Ask for Ruth Davey.'

'He can tell you himself.' Bernadette takes the card anyway. 'I'm sure he'll see you on Saturday.'

Ruth stands, knocking the coffee table with her bag and then straightening it up again. 'But he must have been in that water ... how long?'

Bernadette just wants Ruth to leave now.

But as she follows her into the hall, she realises something. Something Ruth said. *You should stay with him*. And before that, *You're leaving him anyway*.

Bernadette takes hold of Ruth by the shoulder. 'How did you know I'm leaving Richard?'

Ruth shrinks away a little at Bernadette's touch. 'I...' She frowns. 'I didn't ... I don't...'

'You *said* it.'

'Um, I saw your bags.' Ruth nods at them, standing at their feet.

'Ah,' says Bernadette.

'Don't tell him you're leaving him,' says Ruth again.

'I beg your pardon?'

'When he comes home, you should stay. He does love you. He *really* does.'

Angrily Bernadette says, 'You know nothing. Now please go.'

She opens the door. There are no more words. One full story and one summary have been exchanged. Ruth walks down the stairs, heels click-clacking, and Bernadette keeps the door open so the light guides her. When she has gone Bernadette closes and locks it.

Then she goes into the bedroom, sits on the bed and pulls off her shoes and puts her face in her palms and waits and waits and waits.

And then she cries.

49

The Book

Hull Social Services Report – Yvonne Jones (Social Worker)
Home visit to Conor Jordan (D.O.B. 10/11/01)
Date: 01/02/2011

Summary
I visited Conor at home, where he has been living with Anne Williams for three and a half years. He presented as a happy, mature and healthy nine-year-old boy who spoke with me at length about his schoolwork and latest drawings, which he collects in a big folder. Anne expressed how proud she is of his progress, and told me how close they are. Bedwetting hasn't happened since the months following the death of younger brother George, who he had only seen twice.

Access
Conor continues to see his birth mother Frances regularly at her home in Doncaster, where she lives with her two-year-old daughter Kayleigh. He recently began seeing her twice a month. Anne reported that he looks forward to these visits, though he expresses how he is annoyed by all the supervision and wishes they could spend time together alone. I assured Anne that this is something we will look into once Conor is twelve. Conor still shows affection for his mother while also getting angry that he doesn't see her more. I feel that this relationship is a positive one in Conor's life and that visits should continue at this level.

Schooling

Conor is now in Year Four and making good progress. With Anne behind him, he enjoys the work and is improving in all main subjects. He was a big part in painting the scenery for a school play after school and talked animatedly about this to me.

Assessment

I am happy with Conor's progress in this placement. There are no plans to change it. Twice-monthly access with mother Frances will continue. Future meetings with brother Sam are to be discussed since the last one did not go well. George's death has affected them both deeply.

50

Conor

I'm home.

Didn't like being in hospital. Was glad when I woke up and Anne told me the doctor was going to see me and do some paperwork stuff and I'd be leaving. I asked if she had heard anything about my dad. I actually said it like that – *my dad*. Anne shook her head. I told her that old people always say no news is good news, and asked if it was true. Anne said it depended.

Adults always say that when they can't think of an answer.

Anne said my mum had rung. That was nice. She wanted to know if I was okay. She knows all about who my dad is and how he knows Bernadette. She's back home with Kayleigh now. I'm glad. I hope she's not in trouble. It was really cool to hang with her last night. Even with all the big drama stuff going on it was dead good to be on my own with her finally. That's my special private stuff that I'll think about when I'm in bed.

I won't tell anyone about it.

Maybe just Sophie.

Mum told Anne to tell me she's real sorry for shouting in the car and she wants to make it up to me. She's going to see if they will let her take me and Sam to Hull Fair. I couldn't sit still to put my shoes on when Anne said that. All of us together. Ace.

Anne ruffled my hair then and said, *I know you saved up to take your mum on holiday. She told me. You're a lovely boy, Conor, you really are.*

So I'm home now. Anne's house looks kinda different. Not on the outside. That just looks like normal. There's the front garden with some flowers at the edge and the wall I always climb on cos it's just the right height and a gate that squeaks when you swing on it.

But inside everything looks bigger and brighter. It's like this time when Anne took me to Scarborough to see these sharks in a museum and on the way back she said there would be a surprise at home and there was. Her daughter Amber had painted my bedroom. Bright new-jeans blue. Was just white before that. Everything else seemed better just cos of the walls. My stuff looked brand new. More interesting.

But nothing has been painted today. I even check. Still eggy yellow kitchen. It's still toffee beigey brown in the front room. Minty green in the hallway. And my new-jeans blue bedroom is the same, just how it was when I went to school yesterday morning.

I stand in the doorway and that seems like it was weeks ago.

Anne shouts up that she'll make me a cup of tea and see what cake's in the tin and says I can have a nice warm bath soon. I just want to be in my room a bit. Get my brain around what's happened.

It's Friday today. Everyone will be at school later. They will be well jel that I got two days off. Bet they'll all wonder where I am. Anne said last night they were worried about me. Her and Yvonne and Bernadette and the police. I was officially missing. Kind of cool to have been missing. Like an unsolved *CSI* episode. Everyone searching and analysing the evidence.

But I wish I hadn't upset Anne and Bernadette. And I feel so mean that I swore at Anne last night in the hospital. I swore at Mum too, in the car.

Can't help it sometimes.

Those words won't stay inside all the time.

I've never seen Bernadette on any day but Saturday and it's definitely never been in the dark. I can sort of remember last night when I was out of the water and I saw her face and it was all kind of shimmery to me, maybe cos of this silver thing I had round me. Thought for a minute she was an angel. Scared I'd died like poor George. But then there was Anne and my mum and these ambulance misters and I thought, *We can't all have died.*

I lie back on my bed and get my Muhammad Ali book from under the pillow. I always read it before I go to sleep. It's not like a book you buy. Better than that. It's one I made. A bit like my Lifebook.

So I thought I'd do the same thing for Ali. A Lifebook. Its pages are the best kind, all crinkly and make this scrunchy sound when you turn them. Most of the pictures I drew myself. Some I cut out of magazines. I stuck articles in too and wrote my own stories, what he means to me and that. I did a real good bit about his match with Frazier that they called the fight of the century, and how it was his first time really losing.

I would've told him you never lose in my eyes. He only had fights with people that wanted to fight and that's important. There was this big war he wouldn't go in cos he said he wouldn't drop bombs on innocent people.

But the best thing in my book is the autograph Bernadette got me for my birthday. He actually wrote it himself. His name. His own pen. Maybe when I'm eighteen and I get my Lifebook I'll send this one to him.

Anne brings me my *Doctor Who* mug with tea in and a bit of carrot cake and I look through my book. I heard Anne once telling Bernadette that she thought I saw Ali as a father figure. They didn't know I was listening. Never knew what they meant. He couldn't be my dad. He's black and I'm not. But then I figured out that they meant I looked up to him like that.

But now I have a real dad to look up to. Now I'll be able to find out about him. I can remember how his jacket smelled last night. I remember the moment he said he was my dad and it was as if I had known all along. And he jumped into the water to get me out and didn't let me go. He only did that when Mum had got me.

I can't wait to say thank you to him.

Anne suddenly shouts up that someone's here to see me. I jump off the bed. Have they found my dad? Is it Bernadette? I go to the landing and in the hallway is Sophie.

She's grinning and wearing her white coat with the fur hood that makes her look like an Eskimo and I reckon her mum made her do her hair cos it's plaited all neat, which she hates. She's got her school bag wrapped round her and it's covered in badges and doodles I did on it. Anne tells me she can come up for a bit and then she's got to go to school at ten.

In my bedroom Sophie looks at me all weird and says I look different. And I say, *I know, I thought the house looked different*! She looks like she's been polished. We sit on the bed and grin at each other. Then we don't say anything else for ages. We're just with each other like after one time I got upset cos my mum cancelled our meeting.

Then Sophie tells me dead serious, *I never ever told the police you rang me*. She says after I rang her from the service station she didn't even tell her mum. She just went upstairs and tried to go to sleep but couldn't. She was worried about me but knew that friends keep secrets for each other no matter what.

Did you get to see your mum? she asks me. *Who was the mister that took you there? How come you fell in the river? Did you really go in an ambulance?*

So I tell her it all.

Sophie's eyes get big like two shiny moons. When I say it out loud it sounds better than when it actually happened. I love telling it. It's a bit like how I feel when I draw. It must be how writers feel when they do stories. I don't even have to make stuff up cos the drama is better than on *Casualty*. Sophie finishes my cake and sips my tea and listens and listens. When I'm done my voice is all croaky.

I'm so happy you have a dad, she says. *It's brill*.

And I just nod. I feel as proud as I did when I won this Ferens Art Prize thing. But then little George died and I would have given it up in a minute if I could have made him alive again. Poor George. When I think about him – cos really I didn't know him at all – I feel more than sad. Want to go back in time and tell all the social workers I want to see him more.

Don't look so gloomy, says Sophie. *This is happy news*.

I tell her I was just thinking how poor George died without knowing his dad.

And she says, *But I bet he's happy for you up there in the sky*.

Sophie always says the right thing. I don't even mind that she scoffed all my cake.

Anne shouts up then that Sophie has to go now.

You're so lucky to miss school, she says. *I only get to miss first lesson. Mum said I could come and see you for an hour and then go in*.

I tell her I'll be back on Monday.

She says she's going to tell everyone how I got rescued out of the river but not the rest cos that's just between us.

I can't wait to tell Stan Chiswick about my dad though. Tell him he can stop saying my family is weird cos it's just like his now.

Downstairs Sophie puts on her Eskimo coat and I watch her go down the path. She waves and says, *You are ace, Conor Jordan*! I laugh loads and when Anne closes the door I miss her already. I hear her shouting them words even when she's gone.

You are ace, Conor Jordan!

Maybe I am.

Bernadette

Bernadette must have fallen asleep because something wakes her.

The bedroom is light; she's sure Ruth's perfume still lingers on the air, proof that she *was* really here. Sitting up, Bernadette rubs her neck and remembers. There was a dream; in it she, Richard and Conor were walking along the foreshore, hand in hand. Instead of being its usual coffee brown, the river was all shades of red, like someone injected it with food dye. Conor ran towards it and Bernadette warned him about the dangerous currents. Still he ran. He cried out that there were leaves, lots of leaves. *The leaves are leaving!* Richard walked away and when Bernadette called after him, asked if he was going to rescue his son again, he turned and said, 'Now it's your turn.'

What has woken her? The dawn light?

No. A soft tapping on the door.

Richard? Perhaps he's exhausted, unable to knock any harder. Despite the dream in which he appeared gentle, like the early days, Bernadette feels sick with nerves; even a weakened Richard is daunting. She goes to the door, opens it slowly, heart hammering.

It's Ruth.

Bernadette blinks, wonders if she's dreaming still.

'I had to ... I couldn't...' Ruth stammers.

'Couldn't what?' demands Bernadette. 'Haven't you said enough?'

'No, I haven't.' Ruth pauses. 'I haven't told you everything.'

'*Everything*? How can there be *more*?'

'I'm sorry for any hurt I've caused,' says Ruth, looking back down the shadowy stairway.

'That's what you came back to tell me?' asks Bernadette.

'No. But I am. Please, just give me one minute, and then I'm gone. I had to come back. I was...'

'What?'

'Afraid.'

Sighing, Bernadette opens the door. 'Five minutes,' she says.

They return to their places in the lounge. Ruth doesn't sit. She swallows, hard, then says, 'Richard knows.'

Bernadette frowns. 'Knows what?' What's left to know? He knows she has gone behind his back with Conor. He knows he is a father. He knows about the Lifebook. What more *is* there?

'He knows you're going to leave him.'

'He knows...' Bernadette drops onto the sofa. '*How?*'

'He senses it. Told me on Saturday when I went with him to fix the computer. Said you're different. Withdrawn like. There was nothing he could pin down exactly, no proof, he said. But he *knows*. He said your heart just isn't there anymore. He can't stand it. It's breaking him.' Ruth looks at Bernadette. 'I wanted to say, earlier, but I...'

Bernadette thinks back to the previous morning at Tower Rise; how she studied Richard's morning ritual for clues of his possible knowledge that she was leaving. There had been the strange question – 'What will you do today?' – that she'd simply dismissed. The almost kiss. The one she was sure he thought about giving. It makes sense. Richard knows. And Bernadette knows now that he would not have let her leave if he'd come home at six.

'He said...' Ruth starts.

'What did he say?'

'No, nothing.' Ruth goes to leave.

'What did he *say*?' demands Bernadette, jumping up and grabbing her arm.

'Look, he might not've.' Ruth runs both hands through her crimson hair. 'We all say stuff when we're upset, don't we? I can't be *absolutely* sure he meant it. I tried to tell you not to leave him earlier, in case...'

'In case what?' Bernadette shivers. Tower Rise seems to wait with her for Ruth's reply. The wind drops. The trees still.

'In case ... he killed you both.'

'*What*?' Bernadette laughs; it is shrill.

'He said...' Ruth sits now, as though a weight has been lifted from her. 'He said he'd never let you leave. He said he'd kill you both rather than lose you. The river. He said ... it would happen ... there. From the bridge.'

The words are ludicrous, the threats of a mad man. But much as she tries to resist them, they do not surprise Bernadette. She wants to defend her husband, scream her outrage at the audacity of this prostitute saying such things. But she can't. The words make sense. They enter her heart with ease. They sting but they do not lie.

'He told me about this hedgehog he looked after when he was a kid,' says Ruth, looking to the empty glass on the mantelpiece as though hoping for more whisky. 'How he loved it to bits and then it just left him anyway. Said that wouldn't happen with you. He wouldn't let it.'

Bernadette shivers. Richard is the real monster; he is the creature she goes hunting for when sounds wake her in the night. Though he sleeps beside her, perhaps some part of him wanders the huge rooms of Tower Rise, making sure she hasn't escaped.

'I'm so sorry,' says Ruth. 'I should've said earlier but just didn't want to scare you. I kept thinking, no, he was just mad, he'd never *really* do that. Then when you said he was in the river ... well, I thought he won't be in any state when they find him. So she's safe. I tried to tell you not to say you're going! Then after I left, I thought, but what if he comes home, and he's fine, and...'

'It's been hours,' says Bernadette, suddenly exhausted.

'Yes. But ... well, what if he managed to get out of the river ages ago and he's...'

'Wouldn't he be here by now?' Bernadette is trying to convince herself more than Ruth.

'Maybe. Are you okay? Should I stay? Shall we call the police?'

'No, no.' Bernadette sits next to Ruth. 'What would I tell them?

They can't act on some threat. And he only said it to you. Not to me directly.'

Ruth looks at Bernadette, her face kindly, make-up cracked at the corners of her eyes. 'You know him best of all,' she says. 'Do you think he's capable of ... of *that*.'

Bernadette's head says no; no, in his own strange way Richard loves her. But her heart. Her heart says different.

'Maybe you should go and stay somewhere else,' says Ruth. 'Just until he's back.'

Bernadette shakes her head. 'This is the only place anyone can get hold of me. It's okay, really. I'll lock the door, leave the key in, put the chain across. I'll be fine.' She thinks of Conor suddenly. Pictures him running along the foreshore, arm raised to throw stones into the water. Will learning of his existence have muted Richard's rage? Will meeting him today, spending time with the boy, have softened him? He tried to rescue Conor; surely he wouldn't still want to hurt her after that. Would he?

'You go,' Bernadette says to Ruth. 'All I can do is wait here for news.'

'I'm so sorry.'

'It isn't your fault.'

Ruth stands, awkwardly squeezes Bernadette's arm, holding her gaze a moment, and they head down the corridor.

For the second time Bernadette watches her disappear into the shadows. Then she locks the door, pulls across the chain, and leans against it. What if Ruth is right and Richard escaped the river hours ago? She can't know for certain his whereabouts – or his intentions – so she drops to the floor and sits with her back to the door, where she resolves to wait until there is news.

What she does know is how far Richard will go to keep her. If he had come home last night, and she'd told him she was leaving, as she had planned to, right now they might both be in the river.

The Book

10th November 2011

Dear Conor,

It's your tenth birthday and I'm taking you to Ferens Art Gallery again and we'll lunch afterwards wherever you like. I can't quite believe I'm writing about your tenth birthday. How long it seems since you turned six and I hadn't known you long. I sometimes think the happiest things are the easiest to get used to; just as they say that time flies when you're having fun.

People think that adults teach children. I think it's the other way. You've taught me to look at leaves as more than just green or orange. I try and find a better word, perhaps buttery or fruity. This morning the trees are mostly leafless now it's November. Those with some still clinging on made me think of you. You're not evergreen because you change colour, but you are a leaf that won't just drop like all the others.

Anne asked me to come and visit at Christmas. I'm sad to say that it's hard for me to see you over the festive period. I feel bad because it's such a special time. On Saturdays at this time I can't get away. But we'll have an extra Christmas day in January. Anne said she'll make turkey and everything one Saturday. How great is that?

But that is a while off yet. So happy birthday, Conor. Enjoy every moment. Looking forward to seeing you in two days.

Love,
Bernadette

53

Bernadette

Someone is coming up the stairs.

Bernadette starts. She has fallen asleep against the door. Her legs, curled beneath her bottom, are numb. The only light comes from under the lounge doorway, casting a thick line of gold across the corridor as though saying, *this way*. Her bags are still waiting there. *This way*, says the light. *Take us*, say the bags.

Someone is coming up the stairs.

Richard? It must be him.

He knows, she remembers. *And he's angry. Beyond angry.*

Bernadette gets clumsily to her feet, her legs almost giving way. *Must get out.* But how? Where? This door is the only exit. Having one entrance to their flat always brought comfort to Bernadette – less chance of an intruder. Now it has her trapped.

The footsteps are coming closer. She has no time.

She heads up the corridor, not sure where to go. At the lounge doorway, she pauses. In there? The light is inviting. Escape through the window? No, way too high. She sees herself in the mirror, hair dishevelled, clothes crumpled, eyes wild. Someone is behind her. She spins about.

Nothing.

The footsteps have stopped. Silence.

Then a knock on the door. Slow, heavy, taunting.

It's Richard, she *knows* it. He's toying with her. He has walked here from the river and he's cold and wet and angry.

She stumbles on, past the yellow room where children never sleep, and ends up facing the kitchen. There's nowhere else to go. She looks back along the corridor. More knocking. She's sure the door shakes under the force. Why isn't he just opening it? He wants to tease her.

Bernadette goes into the kitchen, to the window. It's painted shut. Should she break it and jump? Again, too high. This draughty old house, with its high ceilings, means a bone-breaking drop from their upstairs flat. Where now?

There is only the pantry.

Bernadette's nemesis. Her greatest fear. Being alone in the dark. Being alone. No, not alone. *Lonely*. Now her only choice is Richard or loneliness.

He won't think she'll dare go in here. She doubts he'll even check inside. He'll remember her reaction the other time he came home late.

Along the corridor, slowly, the door handle turns.

Bernadette opens the pantry door.

Someone heaves against the main door.

Bernadette slips inside.

The black is so intense she can't see her own hands. Her other senses sharpen with the lack of vision; bleach fills her nostrils; dampness hits the back of her throat. But sound is muffled within the thick walls so she puts an ear to the door. Everything is quiet.

Suddenly, Richard's breath is at her neck. She turns, feels about, heart pounding. Nothing. But he's here. She *feels* it. He's part of the dark. The Richard she fears is next to her. So maybe the one on the stairs is the one she first married, the sweet man who could be kind, who sometimes held her gaze so tenderly.

But Bernadette can't get Ruth's words out of her head: *He said he'd never let you leave. He said he'd kill you both rather than lose you*. She sees Richard's pale eyes colour with rage. Sees him dragging her down the stairs, to the waiting river. Feels the ice cold water around her feet, then her knees, her waist. Higher.

A crash outside. Something broken. The door. She puts her ear back to the wood. Richard is inside.

Half a day late, he is home.

Silence again. Bernadette waits, breath held. If she keeps quiet Richard might explore all the rooms and, finding them empty, think she isn't here. He might leave, search for her elsewhere. And then she can escape.

The last time, in this enclosed space, Bernadette was sure she'd seen Conor. They exchanged shoes. But she won't think of him now. Doesn't want him to be any part of this horror. He's been through enough. She backs away from the door, cowers in the corner. As she does, her sleeve catches on the shelf.

Something metal hits the stone floor with a horrifying crash.

No.

Richard will come now. She's cornered in the dark. Everything she's been through today has led to this. At least Conor is okay. At least they found him before this. He'll survive whatever happens and he'll know they all tried.

The pantry door opens.

54

Conor

Anne sniffs my hair and says I still have the river in it and she will run a bath. I kinda want to keep the river there. My dad might still be in the river. Makes him part of me. Anyway, I hate baths in the day. Reminds me of my legs hurting.

I'm really tired suddenly.

Anne says I can have a nap after my bath. Like a baby. She puts loads of her blue bubbles in the water and I watch it froth and fizz. Then the telephone rings. Anne hurries downstairs and I follow. I wait on the stairs in case it's anyone interesting.

Anne says, *Hello*, softly like always.

Who is it?

I can still hear the water splashing upstairs. Maybe there is news. I bet they found my dad. I want to stay and listen but I'm worried the water will overflow. I hear Anne saying *oh goodness* a few times and I want to know about it. But the water will ruin the bathroom rug and I think Anne has forgotten the taps are on.

I run back up and turn them off. The bathroom's all steamed up. I feel a bit dizzy after running so fast. Can't fall over now though. Don't want to drown in the bath when I managed to come out of such a dangerous river. So I hold the bannister going back downstairs in case I fall.

Anne is waiting for me in the hallway and her face is full of news.

55

Bernadette

they wouldn't be right. What kind of patience does she have that one has? He all the a nurse, driver and the home maker of a child the culminates life?

Bernadette shields her eyes from the invasion of light. Just as a child thinks he is invisible because he can't see, she hopes it will delay the inevitable. That somehow Richard won't see her.

'Mrs Shaw?'

Bernadette opens her eyes. It's PC French. In the harsh light she is all lines and creases; like the drawing of Richard.

Bernadette steps into the kitchen, looks up the corridor, confused. The front door is open, hanging lopsided, the chain swinging like a noose.

'I had to,' says PC French. 'I knew you were here and was concerned when you didn't answer. In light of all that's happened. I did call to you.'

'You did?' Bernadette frowns. 'It's just you?'

'Yes. Are you okay? You look terrified. Why were you in...?' The police officer pauses and in the silence Bernadette hears other quiet times. Waiting times.

'Isn't Richard here?' she asks.

'No.' PC French pauses. 'I think we should go and sit down.'

'I don't need to sit down,' says Bernadette. 'Where's Richard?'

PC French takes a breath and sets her mouth. 'I'm sorry to tell you that a body has been found in the river. It was pulled out near the south bank early this morning.'

A body; not a named person.

'Is it...?'

'We can't be sure until someone identifies him officially, so he's been taken to Hull Royal Infirmary mortuary. I'm very sorry.'

Very sorry – is this better than just sorry?

Richard is *dead*?

'Is there someone who could come with you to identify him, Mrs Shaw?'

There isn't. Bernadette won't call her parents. Anne is with Conor. For a foolish moment she imagines asking Bob Fracklehurst, but no, that wouldn't be right. What kind of pathetic life does she have that her only friends are a taxi driver and the foster mother of a child she volunteers for?

'I don't have anyone,' says Bernadette, simply.

'I can take you now,' says PC French. 'Identify him with you.'

'Oh.' Bernadette doesn't know what else to say. She looks at the clock; five-twenty. The intense emotions of the last few hours have left her feeling like a ghost, like she might fall through the floor if she moves, be able to walk through a wall if she tries. If there's supposed to be shock from this news, that too is weightless, has no effect. Can Richard really be dead? Why doesn't she feel anything?

'I'll get my coat.'

In the bedroom Bernadette picks out a smart, tailored one, as you should to identify a husband; it's heavy so maybe it will stop her from floating away. She wore it once, to some funeral.

They head downstairs, to PC French's car. Bernadette does not look at the river.

*

Despite the suitably heavy coat, Bernadette floats from Tower Rise to the hospital lobby. Inside it's as if she's come to and PC French is asking if she is ready. She nods and they walk down a corridor with gurneys and metal trolleys parked along the walls. Two women grumble at a broken coffee machine and a security guard tries to retrieve their money. The corridor goes on and on, like when the horizon at sea never comes any closer, no matter how much you swim.

Then there is a door.

Inside, the room is chilled. Like a pantry. Bernadette looks only at

PC French as she introduces a colleague, PC James, and he says he'll show her the body. He asks for her full name, date of birth and how she came to know the deceased. He explains that the body might be quite a shock to see because the skin has loosened after having been immersed in water for longer than two hours. He wants her to tell him if the man is Richard and if she can point out any specific marks, like a mole or scar, to verify identification for the record.

Then there is a gurney and something beneath a white sheet. Bernadette recalls suddenly the entry in Conor's Lifebook where he got wrapped in a yellow blanket at birth because there were no blue ones. It's curious that new babies are labelled pink or blue but in death all is white.

PC James pulls the sheet back slowly, as though it's a gift on a birthday, and asks if she knows him.

Bernadette looks down; the body is wearing Richard's newspaper-grey suit (Conor will be pleased she specified what kind of grey) and his shoes with the metal bar across. They're dark with damp. The face is white and bloated and has Richard's hair; the one curl he can never tame is finally flat.

'I know him,' says Bernadette. 'He put those shoes on this morning for work. Though he didn't go – he picked his son up from school. He has a son now, you see.'

Bernadette glances at the two officers but they don't respond.

'That wasn't his best suit,' she says. 'He said the trousers were like cheap school ones. If you look at his lower back you'll find two moles side by side and he has a scar below his knee from when he fell out of a tree when he was nine.'

Bernadette can't seem to stop talking. She wants them to cover him up again; but she doesn't. This is the only goodbye she's going to get. It isn't the planned one; that should have been in the flat yesterday, just after six. But that goodbye could have ended her life too. She should feel safe. Sad. Relieved. But she's numb.

'He was rescuing his son,' she says. 'That's why this happened.' She pauses, suddenly embarrassed about her verbosity. She still has so many questions but she'll not get answers now. 'For your records,' she says, 'this is my husband, Richard.'

'Thank you for your assistance,' says PC James.

He pulls the white sheet back over the body. Bernadette stares at it, still seeing the metal bars across Richard's shoes. She hated them, but of course she never said so.

'We have the things retrieved from his pockets,' says PC James. 'The wallet is ruined I'm afraid. We removed his wedding ring too.' He hands Bernadette a plastic bag, which she puts in her pocket without looking at it.

'Can I give you a lift home?' asks PC French.

Bernadette nods and allows herself to be led from the room, back along the corridor that now doesn't seem half as long. The coffee machine has been fixed and the two women sit on plastic chairs near it, sipping paper cups. Bernadette's coat is still too heavy and she wants to take it off, but she's so cold she can hardly get her breath.

Outside the light behind the rooftops is changing – it is subtle greys, like someone pressed gently with their pencil. PC French doesn't drive back along the river; she takes the route through the back streets and Bernadette realises this is intentional.

By the time they reach Tower Rise, the light over the trees is different enough to be given a new colour title – the grey of eyes. PC French parks by the front door and looks up at the house with what Bernadette is sure is distaste.

'There'll still be an autopsy,' she says. 'It's normal procedure in a death like this. It will happen in the next forty-eight hours and then you can claim his body.' She pauses. 'Then you have to register his death within five days and you'll get the documents you need to arrange a funeral.'

Bernadette nods. These are just words about things that don't matter yet. She opens the car door.

'Can I call someone for you?' asks PC French. 'You'll be in shock even if you don't realise. I don't like to leave you alone.'

Bernadette wonders if she is lonely or just alone now.

'Don't worry,' she says. 'I'll make breakfast and sleep a bit. I'll call my parents if I need anyone. Listen, don't call Anne Williams, will you? She should hear this from me.'

PC French looks concerned but doesn't push it. 'Take care,' she says.

Bernadette watches the car disappear beneath the archway of trees and around the drive's curve. She stands a while, waiting for her feet to decide where she'll go. She must depend on her body because her mind is untrustworthy. Images of white, bloated faces and over-dyed red hair and smashing doors blur into one watery painting that disintegrates as quickly as it forms.

Bernadette goes to the trees.

When they moved to Tower Rise ten years ago she had explored the woods on the second day. Richard watched from the window as she stepped over dead branches and rotten logs. He asked later why she was bothered about the trees and – as though knowing what was ahead – she said they were probably going to be her companions for a good while.

Now she looks up at the window as though Richard might be there; it stares back. The morning light is hazy, and against it the trees are half-dressed for autumn. She hears the river moving past the end of the drive.

Richard is dead.

The husband she intended to leave only yesterday can't be divorced. She can't tell him that she loved him at the start, for a long time. She can't tell him that Conor – his own son – is partly why she was going. She can't ask why he visited prostitutes or how he felt about Ruth. She'll never know how he felt when he discovered he was a father.

Richard is dead.

His car will never again pull up on the gravel at exactly six o'clock. She need never abandon whatever she's doing half an hour before to prepare his tea. She won't have to worry if Anne rings at six o'clock or Carole from Befriend for Life on a weekend. She won't have to reject Conor's drawings.

Richard is dead.

He cannot hurt her. He cannot kill her. She is safe.

Bernadette sits on a log beneath an evergreen and waits for the inevitable tears. The traffic on the bridge builds to the eight-thirty rush, then slows again, and the sun moves higher over the trees. She takes the plastic bag from her pocket. The fusty smell makes her wince as she opens it. Inside, Richard's wallet is damp; within the money and one photo of her are ruined. There are his car keys and wedding ring.

And a locket.

A gold locket she has never seen before.

She moves the fine chain between her fingers, turns over the ornate heart. Inside is a picture of their wedding day, barely spoiled despite the water, perhaps protected some by its case. On the back is an inscription: *Together in death as in life.*

What on earth?

Did the people in the mortuary mix Richard's items up with another body's? But their picture inside. It must have been his. *Together in death as in life.* As though the inscriber had foreseen death? She shivers. Was it to be some sort of final gift? Had Richard intended her to wear it when he … She shakes her head. The day has been so long, with so many revelations, Bernadette can't face any more.

She realises how cold she is. The coat is no longer too heavy and the tips of her hands are blueish white. Her anticipated tears have proved too shy to show.

She goes inside and puts Richard's things on the coffee table to worry about later. There is a message on the machine – Anne's tired voice lets her know Conor is fine and they are on their way home if she needs to get in touch. It's ten-fifteen. Where has all the time gone?

Bernadette picks up the phone and calls Anne's house, imagines it disturbing the soft, safe calm there.

When Anne answers Bernadette doesn't know how to word it. Paul is dead? Richard is dead? Conor's father is dead?

'They found him,' she finally says.

'Oh goodness.' Anne's voice is joyful. 'You must be so relieved.'

Bernadette feels bad for accidentally misleading her friend. 'No, they found his *body*.'

Anne doesn't speak for a moment. 'I'm sorry. Oh goodness, so sorry.'

'I just identified him.'

'On your own? Oh Bernadette, I'd have come.'

'No, Conor needs you there,' insists Bernadette. 'I did what I had to; it's all recorded, official and everything.'

'Oh goodness,' says Anne. 'Shall I come now?'

Bernadette shakes her head even though she knows Anne won't see. 'We have to tell Conor … I should help you.'

'I'll do that,' says Anne. 'You must look after yourself. Have you eaten? Slept? Is there anyone I can call?'

'I couldn't eat if I wanted to,' says Bernadette. 'I'll call my parents soon. Can I see Conor later?' She doesn't tell Anne Richard's final intentions; she couldn't voice it if she wanted to. But seeing Conor will erase the darkest lines of this ghastly day.

'Of course. Promise me you'll eat first? Lie down even if you can't sleep.'

Bernadette promises, knowing she probably won't.

'I don't know what to say,' says Anne.

'There isn't much *to* say, but it means everything to me that you tried.'

Bernadette hangs up after Anne says she'll go and tell Conor now. She turns and looks at the creased drawing of Richard, his damp wallet and the locket, all next to Conor's Lifebook and Ruth's empty glass on the coffee table; frozen in time, as if they're waiting to be photographed as evidence.

She sits in front of them but can't bring herself to look at the locket again. Should she stick the drawing inside the Lifebook? Should she write something now on a fresh page for Conor? It will be good to have purpose, something to do with her hands.

Bernadette makes a strong tea and places it beside the glass on the coffee table. Steam rises, somehow comforting. Autumn sun filters through the window. Though it lets in light, Bernadette is still cold, still feels like she could float above the sofa, the table, the pictures, the locket.

Now is the perfect time to write in the Lifebook. Everything has just happened. That's what social worker Yvonne suggested when filling it in: it's best to write up what you've done with Conor right after you get home.

But what on earth should she write?

She looks for a pen in Richard's desk, ignoring the familiar aroma of his half-empty aftershave bottle. Then, feet tucked beneath her on the sofa, she opens the book like a child might before bed. Writing in it might help her sleep.

She flicks through the pages; they crinkle like old parchment paper under the weight of all the handwriting and stuck-in notes. She finds a new page and pauses there. Sometimes it helps to read previous entries, as you might reread the lines of a book's last chapter to remind yourself where you're up to.

So she does.

Bernadette finds a letter three pages long. An entry that wasn't there the last time she looked. Why is it familiar even though she's never seen it before? The writing is tall and angular with no dots over the i's. She knows it. She looks at the date – last night.

Where was the book last night?

With Richard.

The entry is his. Bernadette shuts the book again. It's Conor's and surely he should read whatever Richard has written for him first. But she can't wait. She has to know Richard's last words. What if they were intended for her too? Doesn't she as his wife have the right? Isn't she, as his widow, having discovered he'd cheated on her for three years and threatened to kill her if she ever left him, allowed to read his final thoughts?

She finds the page again and reads.

When she is done the reluctant tears finally arrive.

56

The Book

19th September 2012

Dear Conor,

I hardly know where to start as my life has changed in the space of twenty-four hours.

I haven't met you but I feel like I know you. It seems like I've been reading this book for days but I've just been sitting here for an hour or two.

I found it by accident yesterday. I was looking for our wedding album, which is also yellow, and found this instead. I read a few pages but had to put it away when Bernadette got out of the bath. I know from her entries that you know Bernadette. I'm stunned that I didn't know about her relationship with you. It seems I don't know her at all.

But I was even more shocked to learn about <u>my</u> relationship to you because I didn't know you existed. Sorry if I'm rambling. I'm sitting here in the semi-darkness while Bernadette is sleeping, digesting all the pages. I've read over and over the part where I realised who you are to me. <u>A son</u>. I keep looking at the letter your mum wrote to you in 2004. You may not have read it because I don't know if you've seen this book. Your first social worker, Jim Rogers, didn't seem to think you'd get it until you reach eighteen.

There's a note stuck in that you wrote when you were eight. I've just looked at it now. The writing is so similar to mine at that age. I wonder how else we are similar.

In case I'm not around when you grow up – which I fear I might not be – I want to write some things down, so you know me a bit. I'm trying to understand this huge coincidence whereby Bernadette has known you for five years, but I haven't had a clue. She won't have known you were my son. There isn't anything that would have told her. She doesn't know I knew Frances.

The part in your book where I realised you were mine was in Frances' first letter to you. She said we walked by the water and talked about *The Blues Brothers* film. Her photo confirmed it all. I don't know what Bernadette might have told you about me. I understand from her entries that there are boundaries she must obey when with you and this includes not talking about her own life.

Things have been difficult sometimes in our marriage. I imagine some might think I've been unkind to her. But I love Bernadette very much. Some might call it old-fashioned how Bernadette loves being at home and looking after my needs while I go out and earn the money. We will <u>never</u> be parted.

Frances and I only knew each other a short while. My time with her began a curiosity with women who work nights. I'd hear my mother's voice say, 'Let he who is without sin cast the first stone.' Frances kept me company when I was new to Hull, after moving from Islington. She comes from a tough family, but there was something about her that made me want to rescue her. That's my weakness. I want to rescue such women. They have lost God and themselves. I like to try and help them see how they might find it all again.

Frances was in the Minerva pub, an old place on the Marina. I was meeting a man about a flat and he didn't turn up. Frances came and chatted to me. I don't like pushy women, but she had a very sincere way about her. When I realised what she did to earn money I was surprised. Jesus forgave such a woman once.

I didn't give her my real name. I panicked, regretted within hours giving a false one but couldn't then retract it. I felt it might be better that I was a stranger. We met at the Minerva a few times. I'd finish work and she'd be starting. She wanted a man that would make it all better. I knew that wasn't me and I didn't mislead her, but I think she hoped I would be.

I walked away after a week. It was because she told me she'd had a baby (Sam) four months earlier. She didn't look after him because of her issues. As a boy who had an absent father, this angered me. We argued and I left. I've thought about her sometimes, wondered what she's done with her life.

When I read about you being bullied at school I was angry. I felt alienated at school too. I always had my hair cut differently to the other boys and wore cheap clothes. It wasn't my mother's fault that she had little money. I got picked on for going to church and because we said prayers before our tea. But she loved me and just did her best. She's dead now and I miss her.

I'm angry too that I've missed out on knowing you. My father left my mother when she was pregnant. He had a wealthy family that owned land and big electrical companies. My father was training to be a psychiatrist and they expected him to marry someone from a good family. So when he met my mum they were disappointed because she was from a poor Catholic family. Apparently my father loved her and they were going to elope. Then she found out she was pregnant. At first he was delighted.

But his family hounded him. They threatened never to speak to him again. He chose his own family, even though the baby growing inside my mum was also his family. My mum was alone at six months pregnant. Her family weren't happy either, so she was left with just a baby and God. In some ways God was my dad when I grew up. He was the only other man in the house.

I'm thinking what I should do. I'd like to meet you. It says where you go to school and where you live. I should be the one to tell you who I am. I always longed for a son and to be the kind of father mine never was. I hope I can do that ~~before~~.

I hope I can do that.

Your Dad.

57

Conor

This doesn't feel like when my brother George died.

I think it *should* feel the same cos I only seen George twice, just an hour each time. I didn't know him much – and I didn't know Paul much neither. My dad I mean. Still hard to call him that.

But Dad Paul (that's the best name I reckon) did come and lie on my hospital bed for a bit, all wet. So I saw him twice too. I think it's more about what you do with your time than how much time there is. Like with my mum there's always someone else so our time is shared. With Dad Paul it was just us two for our bit of time. That's when people are their proper own selves.

It feels like someone is standing on my chest in them big workman boots.

It feels like when Shana died. Shana was a dog at Georgina's. I loved being at Georgina's cos I met Mark there. I miss Mark. I took Shana for a walk when I was real grumpy and wasn't concentrating proper and she got off her lead and went on the road. This black car hit her and there was this horrible yelpy sound and Shana's legs were mushy red and I was sick. They all hated me for that. Mark said he didn't but I know he did. I never went back there.

I hated me too.

I didn't cry when Anne told me Dad Paul is dead. I'm not a baby now. She came off the phone and got me to sit next to her and put her arm around me and so I knew it was something crap. Like when she hugged me and said George wasn't with us no more. She said it's okay to be sad cos everyone gets sad. I know that. I'm not a twat. She was being nice but adults talk shit sometimes.

I wanted to know the proper stuff. Like how did he die and what did he look like and did it hurt lots. Anne didn't know all the answers and she just said he had drowned and only Bernadette had seen the body. I know she'll tell me what I want to know cos she doesn't talk to me like other adults. So I pushed Anne off me and told her I wanted Bernadette.

Now I feel bad about that.

Anne's downstairs on the phone to someone and her voice is wobbling. I'm up here with my bed against the door. Don't want no one. Don't need supervision. She tried to come in. Said she'd leave a cup of tea and some cake outside the door but I'm not stupid, it's just to get me to open it. So I didn't. Not hungry. My belly's churning loads, like a washing machine.

Today started so good too. I always get happy too quick. Won't next time.

Right after I won a big prize George died.

Should have known.

Anne's outside my bedroom door again.

Conor, just let me in, she's saying. *I'm really worried about you.*

I tell her she doesn't need to worry. I will come out tomorrow. On TV they always talk about how they need space and that's what I want. There's lots of it in my bedroom.

I hear her go back downstairs. Maybe it's not so good being on your own with your space. I don't like hearing the watery sound in my ears. Maybe the river is still stuck in there. I don't like how loud my Muhammad Ali alarm clock is ticking either. Someone turned it up to annoy me. I don't like how small I feel when I sit on the bed or how high the ceiling is.

I wonder how Bernadette feels. She knows Dad Paul too. I think Anne said his name is Richard to her. She must be sad. She must be in her haunted house, behind the trees, all sad.

It's my fault. He went in the water cos of me. Just like Shana died cos I let go of her lead. Bernadette might not want to see me again. She might hate me too. Bet she tells them volunteer idiots that she wants to cancel me. I'm not bothered. I'm *not*. I'll be eleven soon and won't need her. Won't need any of them soon. They can all fuck off with their boundaries and supervision and reports.

I'll move to Bournemouth with Sophie.

But it hurts. My chest hurts so bad. Reckon I'm having one of those heart attacks. I might have to open the door to be resuscitated.

Anne's back. Except it's not her. It's that social worker Yvonne. Don't like her. She talks to me like she's a teacher. Bet she's got that folder with her. She always has it.

She says, *Conor, I know you've had some very sad news but we just need to know you're okay.*

I tell her I'm just having a nap.

I hear her and Anne talking quietly. Then Anne says, *We don't mind you sleeping a while but will you promise to come out when you wake up? I'll make some lunch and you can have it when you're ready.*

I tell them I might and they go back downstairs.

I bet Yvonne is writing it all down. I bet I'll have to go and see one of those head doctors again. Last time I made all sorts of stuff up. I didn't go for long so I reckon they knew. But I don't lie to Anne. Feel crap that I'm ignoring her now.

I go in my desk and get out my biggest sketchpad. It's as big as my desk. Got it off Anne's daughter Rose for Easter instead of an egg. It's lasted ages cos I only use it for my best pictures. I get out my pencils, proper art ones, all soft. Sometimes my fingers tingle just holding one. I only ever told Sophie that cos I reckon even the head doctors would laugh. I don't always know what I'll draw.

All I know is that when I do it my heart jumps.

So I pick up a pencil. It's like the big workman boot lifts off my chest and I can breathe again. So I put the pen to the paper and wait with my eyes closed. I could draw in the dark. If I see it inside my head it goes on the paper.

I smell something cooking but I don't know what it is. Maybe noodles. I move the pen a bit. Always love the sound it makes. Not scratchy like Yvonne's pen but kind of like how it sounds when Anne sweeps up in the garden. I only open my eyes to swap colours.

Clock's gone quiet now. Water in my ears has melted. The ceiling isn't miles away anymore.

When I'm done I look at the picture and start to cry. Not cos it's crap but cos it's so real. It doesn't matter about crying cos no one knows I'm being a baby. I've drawn George and Shana and Dad Paul. Dad Paul has his arms around George and Shana is sitting next to them with her tongue out. They're sitting on a rock near the river. The water's blue like it's got Anne's bubble bath in it. And it's like they're really there and I can hear the water swishing and Dad Paul is saying, *Don't you know? Can't you feel it?*

I can feel it now. He was my dad.

I cry a bit more.

Didn't realise I'd fallen asleep. It's cold. My head hurts. Someone is tapping on the door. Am I dead? Feel like I am. Feel like I've been in the freezer with the chicken.

Tap, tap, tap.

Who is it, I ask.

It's Bernadette, she says.

So I get off the bed and my legs are a bit shaky. I'm not in the right place. The desk should be over there and the window should be next to the bed but it's moved. Then I remember. I pushed the bed up to the door so no one could come in. I move it back where it goes and open the door.

Bernadette is there, wearing this coat I've never seen her in, and she's got two cups of tea. Don't like the coat. It makes her look too tall and she doesn't smell like she usually does. Reckon it's been in some stinky old cupboard. She smiles at me even though someone has died and holds out one of the cups and says it's got lots of sugar in how I like.

Suddenly my legs go all crazy and I fall in a messy lump on the landing. Bernadette sits right down next to me. Anne comes into the downstairs hallway and looks up, but Bernadette tells her we're okay and she goes back in the lounge.

I ask Bernadette what the body looked like. Can't help it. The words just come out like swearwords sometimes do.

She says it was just white. Then she says she can't think of a better colour word. I don't mind. She gives me a cup of tea and tells me to drink it cos the sweetness will make me feel better. I drink some and it does. It goes right down to my toes.

I remember when I first saw Bernadette. When she came into the front room with this other lady from her voluntary place and she talked lots to me. She talked and talked and talked. I was in a real bad place then and didn't want to like anyone. So I was listening and I wanted to answer all her stuff about TV shows when she was little but couldn't open my mouth. It was stuck shut.

But it's open now.

Loads of words come out. I ask if it hurts when you drown and if she is mad cos I made Dad Paul go in the water and what it was like to see a dead body and can I still tell them at school that I have a normal family now and was Dad Paul like her best friend or anything.

Now Bernadette's mouth is the one stuck shut. She puts her cup of tea down and she looks at me for a long time. Then she squashes me to her stinky old cupboard coat and holds me there. I don't move.

I never want to move.

I will stay here forever.

This is where I'm supposed to be.

58

The Book

Hull Social Services Report – Yvonne Jones (Social Worker)
Home visit to Conor Jordan (D.O.B. 10/11/01)
Date: 29/09/12

Summary

Following the death of Richard Shaw (Conor's birth father) I visited Conor at home where he has been living with Anne Williams for five years. Yesterday (28/09/12) was the funeral. Conor attended with Anne and his volunteer Bernadette.

Richard Shaw had picked Conor up from school on Thursday 20/09/12 and took him and his mother Frances to Hull Marina, where Conor fell in the water and was rescued by Mr Shaw, who was sadly unable to climb out himself and was later found dead.

Frances confirms that Mr Shaw is Conor's father. Mr Shaw's own entry in Conor's Lifebook (see previous page) indicates that he had a brief relationship with Frances. Bernadette (Mr Shaw's wife/Conor's volunteer) confirms that there's a physical resemblance between them and that she has 'no doubt Richard is his father'.

Last time I visited (21/09/12) Conor would not come out of his bedroom, but this time he sat downstairs with us. Anne expressed how proud she is of how he has handled the tragedy and told me he's been eating small amounts and sleeping on the sofa for now, watching his DVDs to wind down. Conor looked healthy and spoke about how glad he is that he has a dad now and asked if he can have a photograph of him, which Anne said Bernadette is going to arrange for him. I spoke with Anne about whether

Conor might see a grief counsellor and she said she will see how Conor goes, as he is handling everything remarkably well and he said he feels sad like he should but not angry like when George died.

Access

Conor will continue to see his mother Frances regularly at her home in Doncaster, where she lives with her three-year-old daughter Kayleigh. He still sees her twice a month. Anne reported that he continues to enjoy these visits. Conor has expressed deep affection for his mother following the experience at the Marina on 20/09/12. I feel the knowledge of his birth father has strengthened things. This relationship continues to be a positive and visits should continue at this level.

Assessment

When I was with Conor for ten minutes he asked whether he will ever be able to go and stay at Bernadette's house, since this is where his father lived. I understand this will overstep the boundaries BFL have in place. A further assessment will be made as to whether Conor might visit Mrs Shaw's home. Anne said she wishes to continue fostering only Conor for as long as he needs her. I'm happy with Conor's progress in this placement. There are no plans to change it. Twice-monthly access with mother Frances will continue. Future meeting with his sibling, Sam, is to be in two weeks when Frances will take them both to Hull Fair, with respective social workers.

29th September 2012

To Conor,

I hope your doing ok. Im glad you now know who your dad is and that you met him even though all this horrible stuff happened. Im sorry I didnt tell you about your dads name. I shouldve told you more but I never thought hed come back again. It wasnt his name anyway. All this time I thought he mite have the same name as my brother. Your friend Bernadette rang me up yesterday and we talked a bit, shes nice I see why you like her so much. She loves you a lot, its just mental that she ends up married to your real dad. We had a long chat about something she mite like to do. I cant say here cos I don't know wot mite go on. I have to think real long and hard about it though. My mum kept us all even when it was really hard and I havent been a mum like her. Had five babies one stillborn one dead a few years ago. Only been really there for one. Im sad ~~Andy~~ Richard died but Im glad he got you out of the water. I was so scared wen you fell in and I feel so bad that I didnt go right in after you but I cant swim, God I wanted to I was going to I really was. Then ~~Andy~~ your dad did. He got you right back to me and I pulled u up but when I reached back for him he had gone. I yelled and yelled and couldnt see him anywhere. Then the police turned up. He mite of been wrong to have took you from school like that and take us both to the marina but he wasn't thinking right cos hed only just found out about you by reading your book. Wen he come for me he told me I shouldve gone n told him wen I got pregnant with you but I didnt no where he was. And I never thought hed be bothered. Now he is and its too late. Hull Fair comes soon and I said Id take you and Sam and I will. You can go on all the rides you like. I think I shouldve done more in your book. I never seen it cos they just take my letter n stick it in. Bernadette told me ~~Andy~~ your dad wrote something for you in it. Im glad and I hope it helps you know stuff and that you got his own words from him. I dont no what will happen in the future but I do want you to no that I really really love you I really do and always will.

Love,
Your Mum xxx

59

Bernadette

The funeral is small, intimate, and the church much too big for the few guests. In a wooden pew near the coffin Bernadette's parents sit on either side of her, quietly supportive. She embraced her father tightly when they arrived last night, letting his familiar wool and hard-boiled-sweet scent wash over her. Both remained in the hug for a good two minutes while Bernadette's mother fussed over how Tower Rise was much too large and cold, how she'd never liked it and thought Bernadette should find somewhere smaller.

Now Bernadette's mother doesn't fuss or ask questions; she whispers Amen at the end of each prayer. The word makes Bernadette reach into her pocket and touch the gold locket. *Together in death as in life.* She couldn't wear it, instead hung it from the bedpost so the late evening light caught it and reflected a gold heart on the nearby wall. All she knows is where it belongs today.

Brittle leaves blow in through the back doors, like children leaving school in a tumult of excitement. Bernadette turns to look at Conor, sitting in the pew behind with Anne and Frances. He's wearing a burgundy waistcoat just too big like he's borrowed it for the day. Anne must have brushed his hair the opposite way to usual because it rebels and is stuck up, just as that one stubborn strand of Richard's always did. Bernadette watches him follow the words of the prayer on his service sheet, frowning at the ones he probably finds alien.

Frances said earlier that she will stay only for the church service, to pay her respects, but that she's not family enough to attend the party later, despite Bernadette insisting she is. Bernadette is touched that she appears to have chosen her best suit, a sharply ironed lead-grey one that Richard might have admired. Anne comforts her when she cries at the choice of hymn. Bernadette hears Frances admit she is just sad because she should have done more.

Don't they all feel that way?

Conor looks up and sees Bernadette watching him. She smiles but he doesn't. Instead he shakes his head solemnly and puts a finger to his lips. Later he explains it is because you mustn't smile at a funeral as it's mean to the dead, and Bernadette assures him you can do whatever you want when it's your own family. She wishes she could be described as Conor's family; Frances is his birth mother, Anne his foster mum, and Richard his father. Bernadette is merely his volunteer friend.

How can *she* be more?

The leaves at the back swirl fiercely about the stone floor. Following their dance leads Bernadette's eyes to a figure by the farthest pillar, near the font where new babies are christened. Ruth. She's wearing black clothes and less make-up, though her red hair still stands out like fire on a dark night.

Bernadette guesses she has read the obituaries in the paper, or seen the brief news coverage of Richard's death. Bernadette couldn't bring herself to let the woman know he'd gone. She kept looking at her sugar-pink card. It was a colour you might pick for announcing a baby or wedding, not give to men wanting sex. But she didn't call her.

Now, surprisingly, she is not angry or put out to see Ruth. She supposes she has a right to say goodbye too. They lock eyes for a moment, two women whose only connection is via a man left scarred by his fatherless, God-fearing childhood. They are not likely to see one another again and yet they have each been living their lives in the shadow of the other for three years. Without Ruth, Bernadette would never have fully known Richard, and for this she is sad but grateful.

Bernadette returns her eyes to the front of the church, to the priest, to the flowers, and the coffin containing her husband. None of the people here really know him, not like she and Ruth do. Not his work friends, not an ex-neighbour from Tower Rise, not Richard's

Uncle Tom and two adult nephews. But she's glad. She doesn't want them to.

This is where she's supposed to say goodbye to him. But she already said goodbye. Really, she's been very slowly saying goodbye to Richard from the moment she met Conor.

This is just the Amen.

At the cemetery Conor throws his drawing of George, Shana and Richard on the coffin as it's lowered into the ground. He cries a little and Bernadette kneels down and puts his head on her shoulder. This is no time for boundaries. There is no rule in a book to dictate what is or isn't right when comforting a small boy at the graveside of the father he's just found.

Finally, Bernadette throws the gold locket onto the coffin. *Together in death as in life.* No words. No Amen.

Knowing she's still officially Conor's volunteer and can't invite him to her house, Bernadette has chosen to hold a small party in the upstairs room of a local pub, offering sandwiches and quiche to guests. She tries to be a good hostess. People who don't know each other make small talk. Conor collects cups and asks who wants cake. Bernadette's parents – who know him only as the boy Bernadette volunteers for – fuss about his overly polished shoes and waistcoat. There will be time when things settle down to explain to them who Conor really is.

Who will he be to her when she can no longer be his volunteer?

Bernadette sits on a stool in the corner of the room and watches everyone. A thought planted itself in her head recently; at first it floated about as though unsure where to go, but now it takes root and grows a little. It came in the days following Richard's death and it blossoms as she now watches Conor fiddle with his rebellious hair strands. She doesn't know how likely it is that it could happen, or exactly how to go about it. But for now it makes her smile and forget all the unpleasantness of the last week.

People begin to leave. Conor goes with Anne, taking a box of left-over cake. Bernadette says goodbye to her parents. Suddenly she wants to run after the car like she did the time they went on holiday without her as a child.

But she just waves, and goes home.

The Book

* Please stick in this letter received from Jim Rogers – thanks

1st October 2012

Hi Conor,

Messy handwriting alert!

Some things never change. My writing is no better than it was when I used to write in your book, perhaps it's worse with my arthritis. It's now eight years since I was your social worker but I have never forgotten you. (I learned from Yvonne that you sadly lost both your brother George and your real father.)

I read about George's death in the newspaper and wanted to write something then. Instead I came to the funeral but just stood quietly at the back of the church. I watched you put a picture you'd drawn on the coffin. (I'm glad you still draw.) Gosh, I'm glad you have lived for a long time with a good foster carer.

Of course I'm glad too that you finally know who your father is but it's such a shame that your time with him was cut short. Still, perhaps some time is better than no time at all. I remember once writing to you about how so many things make us, like our family, our history, and circumstances. Even though tragedy has taken him from you, I think this will make you too.

Anyway, I just wanted to send a short note and express my respects for your loss. I know you will be eighteen when you read this (and it may all seem far in the past by now) but I can say good luck in your adult life, whatever it brings or doesn't.

Jim

Bernadette

Bernadette's routine has changed.

It's not that she intentionally altered it, it's just that her natural rhythm is off, like a winter snowdrop flowering in July. When Richard was alive she could barely keep her eyes open after ten. Now she can't sleep before midnight. It's then that she sees him. In dreams he comes from the river, locket clutched in dripping hand. He rattles the door handle to get in and Bernadette wakes, bathed in cold sweat, crying, 'No, I won't stay!'

Unsettled by stillness interrupted only by a change in weather or danger on the river, Bernadette then gets up in the dark, makes tea and sits by the lounge window. Only when the sun appears over the trees does Richard disappear; he is a ghost that the sun melts.

In the days after last week's funeral she broke things. She smashed the thin-rimmed cup he always drank coffee in. She threw his laptop in the bath, where it cracked with a satisfying crunch. She went through his suits, pulling them off hangers and ripping them, before lying amongst them, sobbing.

This morning Bernadette doesn't return to sleep after sunrise, despite dreams of Richard's damp footprints around the flat leaving her exhausted. Today there are things to be done. In the kitchen she makes a boiled egg with bread soldiers, just how Richard liked them; the egg almost too hard to dip into, the toast cut in small, neat squares. As soon as they're on the plate she realises what she's done; she crushes the soldiers into breadcrumbs and throws them in the bin. She makes milky coffee and eats a banana.

Taking her coffee into the lounge, Bernadette sits by the window. She looks at the bookshelf, skimming paperbacks for that lemony spine with no words to identify it. It isn't there. Of course not, it's back where it belongs – at Anne's.

Will Conor want to know everything? Certainly not now, aged ten; but what about when he's eighteen? Bernadette supposes he will figure it out himself. He'll work out what kind of women Richard talked about in his letter and he'll likely find out that his own mother is a prostitute too.

Perhaps Bernadette should simply tell Conor what his father liked: walks by water, movies from the seventies, sometimes singing quietly in the shower. And how he never forgot a birthday or anniversary. Maybe those are the truths you give a child who never had the chance to know a parent. The other truths – his last threat – are gone. Cannot hurt anyone now.

The phone rings, intrusive.

'It's just me,' says Anne. 'How are you?'

'It's so quiet,' says Bernadette. She hasn't told Anne about what Ruth revealed to her. She will never tell anyone that.

'When Sean died I missed his snoring,' says Anne. 'It kept me up for hours, but when he'd gone I longed to hear those grunts again.'

'Anne.' Bernadette pauses. She looks at the trees. *The leaves are leaving.* She smiles and it hurts her face. 'There's something I've been thinking about ... but I'm not sure...'

'Tell me?'

'I've looked into it, read some websites. I have to know what you think first.' Bernadette pauses. 'I'd like to adopt Conor.'

'That's wonderful,' says Anne, immediately, her voice full of smiles. 'If it was something you could do, I'd back you. I can't think of anything better. But Frances – she'll never say yes. Never has all these years.'

'I rang her after the funeral – I copied her number from your book. Maybe wine made me brave or maybe something happens when you bury someone?' Learning Richard's final intention had somehow compelled her into action too. 'I suddenly felt I can't waste the next ten years like I have the last. It might not be possible. I've read how difficult the process can be.'

'What did Frances think?'

'She said she'd have to think and I understand.'

'Goodness,' says Anne. 'It's such a lot to take in.'

'How's Conor?' asks Bernadette.

'He's doing fine. It's like the joy of finally knowing a father has lessened the fact that he died – as if the bereavement hasn't taken him away but given him something. Does that make sense? He's excited for Hull Fair with his mum.'

'Children are so wonderfully simple,' smiles Bernadette.

'All he talked about at breakfast was which rides he'll go on and what colour candy floss he'll pick.'

Bernadette puts her forehead against the window's cool glass, needing the wake up. 'Richard's haunting me,' she says. 'His ghost is here.'

'Then leave; it would be easy. You don't own it. Hand in your notice.'

Anne is right. There's nothing keeping her at Tower Rise. The things she loves – her books, the soft furnishings she made – are portable. But the view she's enjoyed for ten years isn't. The treetops like rows of children in green school uniform. Perhaps Conor might paint them for her. Even though he can't come here she can photograph the scene and ask him to draw it. Financially, moving is possible. Bernadette was surprised to find that Richard had a life insurance policy. And even without it, she can work now. Though her CV is sparse, she has volunteered for the last five years, which always makes an applicant look good.

Bernadette's coffee has gone cold. She must get dressed, call a taxi. 'I'm seeing Carole at BFL in an hour. Even if I get Frances' consent to adopt, what about in the meantime? Will I still be able to volunteer until it goes through?'

'Surely it won't matter,' says Anne. 'You're a huge part of his life.'

'But I have to make sure. Carole might tell me how good the chances are for adopting him.' She pauses. 'That's if he wants me to. I can't mention it in case he does and it doesn't happen, can I? I couldn't let him down.'

'See what they say.'

'I'll ring you soon. Give my love to Conor. Tell him...' She isn't sure what Anne should tell him.

'I'll tell him,' says Anne, knowing.

They hang up.

Bernadette pours her cold coffee down the sink and leaves the cup on the side. It feels good not to wash it, not to feel she must immediately dry it and put it away; yet she still half anticipates Richard's admonishment. After a quick shower and a phone call to Top Taxis, she waits by the window. She hears Richard's voice in the rustle of leaves – *I'll never let you go*.

When Bob Fracklehurst pulls up, she smiles. She didn't request him, but the universe sent him anyway. She moves away from the window where she has waited so many times for Richard to come home, and puts on her coat.

'You're going to *have* to let me go,' she says aloud, angry. 'Because I'm leaving. Maybe not today, or next week. But I am!'

She heads downstairs.

Anne said everything happens the way it should.

Bernadette really hopes so.

When she gets to the driveway Bob Fracklehurst is finishing a cigarette and drops the end in a takeaway cup. Life goes on. For a moment after she gets in the car, he doesn't speak. The song on the radio crackles.

'I read about your husband,' Bob says eventually. 'I'm really sorry.'

'Oh, yes.' It's all Bernadette can think of to say.

'You didn't book the usual trip on Saturday.'

Bernadette nods. 'I'm not sure if my Saturdays will continue.'

Bob looks sad. 'So where do you want to go today?' he asks.

Bernadette directs him to the BFL office and he drives under the archway of trees and emerges by the river. She can't escape it. The water travels east, past Tower Rise and out to the North Sea, a constant. She hears it when their window is open and sees it every time she leaves the house. She knows she'll only ever think of Richard while it's there, picture him trying to crawl out, clawing the muddy bank, over and over and over.

It suddenly occurs to her that this image could be wrong. What if he didn't claw? Didn't try. Didn't fight. What if he surrendered to the current once Conor was safe? What if – knowing she was leaving him – he simply gave up?

'You okay?' asks Bob.

'You know, I *think* I'm fine; then I feel so angry I could scream, and so sad I cry. I was going to leave him and I didn't love him anymore. So why am I bothered at all?'

'It's called grief, Bernadette,' says Bob, kindly.

She nods. They pass Walton Street where Hull Fair's rides are being built, and then the stadium. She realises that Bob has taken a route that avoids the rest of the river, like PC French did that night. But sometimes you need to look into the current to see the truth. Ruth's suggestion that Richard had a personality disorder has been stuck in Bernadette's head, the way things that make sense do.

Last week she went to the library and read up on narcissistic personality disorder. The low hum of noise in the building disappeared as she read words like 'appearing unemotional' and 'easily hurt' and 'requiring constant attention'. Her eyes filled with surprise tears as she read that a parent's absence or excessive criticism in childhood was often a background factor. How often Bernadette had felt Richard's mother was cruel, but not wanted to say?

Another trait she read was that, in an attempt to hide feelings of insecurity, the sufferer sought to control others' views of them and their behaviour. Wasn't that what Richard had done throughout their marriage? Hadn't she felt she was merely there to make *him* feel good, strong, happy?

It was like having an explanation for why you'd got cancer: it didn't make it fair. And did it justify threatening to kill someone because they wanted to leave?

Bob turns left at the lights and stops by the pharmacy that's below

BFL's office. Bernadette looks up at the sash windows and imagines the team coordinating volunteers and writing reports and changing children's lives.

'How much do I owe you?' she asks Bob.

'Don't worry about it,' he says.

'Don't be silly.' She offers him ten pounds and when he won't take it she sticks it in the glove compartment. 'I don't need a receipt.' She might never need one again; might never fill out a monthly expenses report, sticking on bus tickets or café receipts.

'Take care,' says Bob. His radio crackles and Barbara's voice tells him he's needed elsewhere. Life goes on.

'I'll still need a lift somewhere soon.' She gets out.

Bernadette watches him pull away and goes into the building. She hasn't been here since a two-day training course on 'challenging behaviour', which luckily was during Richard's work hours. It occurs to her that his is the only behaviour that has ever been a challenge. Passing posters for youth clubs and fostering help groups, she remembers her first interview and telling Carole why she'd like to volunteer.

At the top of the stairs is an open-plan office where plants wilt near a radiator, a half-empty vending machine flashes blue lights and staff type away on keyboards. Carole is at the reception desk with Bernadette's folder; one of her pearly pink nails is chipped.

Carole turns and her expression changes from up to down, as though someone has flicked a switch.

'Bernadette,' she says. 'I'm sorry to hear about your loss. Come on in.'

She follows Carole into a separate office and sits opposite her, the grey desk dividing them like a frown line between eyes. The heating is turned up too high.

'This must be such a difficult time for you,' says Carole. Her black hair is so sleek it reflects the overhead light. Bernadette remembers her habit for pushing it behind her ear repeatedly. 'Coffee?'

'No, thank you.' Despite the dry air, Bernadette thinks a drink will make her sick. 'I'd rather just talk about Conor.'

'Well, it's a unique situation; we've never had a volunteer in such a predicament.'

'I suppose it *is* a predicament,' says Bernadette sadly. 'But I'd like to continue here. I'm considering taking other steps in Conor's life…'

Carole interrupts. 'As you know, the primary concern for us is the child.'

'But can I still volunteer?'

'No.' Carole studies Bernadette, frowns. 'Boundaries would inevitably be overstepped. As you know, he can't know your surname or where you live, and he does now.'

Bernadette knows that confidentiality is to protect both volunteer and child; a child might turn up at a volunteer's home unannounced, causing upset for both the youngster and the volunteer's family. They might make allegations against a member of a volunteer's family that would be hard to prove or disprove. Anonymity helps volunteers remain detached, something Bernadette knows she's never succeeded at. She knows the words: *Detachment is so the volunteer is there as an independent in the child's life, distinct from regular carers or the professionals paid to support them.*

But Richard has changed it all.

Carole opens Bernadette's folder and says, 'Conor will naturally seek more information about his father, leading directly to you and your life.'

Bernadette feels tears welling; she fiddles with her bag, wishes the heating would go off. 'You see, I'd like to adopt him. But that could take years to get off the ground. And in the meantime, if I'm not a volunteer, how will I see him?'

Carole says kindly, 'But Bernadette, don't you see? You're his family.'

'I am?'

'Yes. No boundaries. Why would you need to volunteer with us? You're more to Conor than that; you're his step-mum, you don't need to volunteer anywhere.'

Bernadette hadn't thought of it. Why has it taken her so long to see? It's like when she found out Richard was Conor's dad. Shouldn't the similarities have been obvious? Yet she missed them. Like you might a yellow book on a full bookshelf.

'So I'll be able to visit him?' she asks.

'Of course. And being his step-mum will help an adoption application.'

Bernadette puts her bag on the floor. 'So what do we do here?'

'You just have to sign our leaving form, relinquish all association with us.' Carole pushes a form across the table and Bernadette signs after skim-reading. 'You've been a wonderful volunteer. Conor has thrived and I'm sure it's down to you. I can drop you in Hessle if you like. I've to see a new child there.'

Carole drives along the river and Bernadette is glad. She doesn't need people to decide on her behalf whether she can face the water. Now sunlight dances on the waves, turning muddy swirls into hopeful blue. Conor would say that *hopeful* isn't a way to describe blue, but Bernadette would insist that since blue is often associated with sadness it's nice to make it joyful for a change.

'You can leave me here,' she says as they approach the foreshore.

Carole hands Bernadette her folder. 'You might want it as a record of your time with us.'

Bernadette closes the door and watches Carole head into the village. She walks down the hill to the foreshore, then along chalky white stones that merge into mud and eventually water. Three children chase a wet dog towards the bridge, their wellington boots coated in slime and their cheeks aglow. Bernadette loves dogs but Richard never wanted one. Said it would stink the flat out. She had wanted to argue that the place smelt of damp anyway but of course never said a word.

Life goes on.

Looking out across the water, Bernadette suddenly remembers being stuck in that abandoned fridge as a child. When her mother eventually opened the door, the sun stung her eyes like the drops her doctor used for infections.

Her mum had helped Bernadette out and said, 'It was only a short time,' and hugged her tightly.

Bernadette insisted it had been *forever*. Without light, time has no measure. Children respond less well to darkness. But even with an abundance of light, it's the absence of human contact that damages. The fridge's cold insides hurt Bernadette more than not being able to see.

Life goes on.

Bernadette approaches the water, her shoes sinking into the mud. She came here with Conor a handful of times, watched him chase the water, always feeling it was too close to Tower Rise, wondering what might happen if, by chance, Richard came home ill and saw them.

But everything happens the way it should.

She stands where the waves gently lap at her feet, letting them wash her ankles and calves. The cold is invigorating. With one hearty thrust she throws the BFL folder out across the river; white papers scatter like homework from a child's school satchel. They sway on the wind and land in separate parts of the river; two stay joined, maybe held by a paper clip.

They float the longest.

When all the papers have sunk Bernadette turns and starts walking towards Conor's house. She knows she will one day come to terms with Richard's flaws – with his occasional cruelty and that final threat – because everything he was and everything he did led to Conor. She's going to see Richard in the boy more and more as he grows up. The best part of him remains. So she must remember him, not as the husband who might have killed his wife, but as the father who rescued his son.

62

The Book

16th November 2012

To Conor,

I hope your doing ok. Theyre gonna give your book to Bernedette soon to keep for you so I just wanted to explain proper why I did what I did. I mean I can tell you when I see you and you can ask me anything you want but I want to put it in here for you. I didnt just let you go easy I promise. I thought and thought about it all I really did. I talked lots with Bernedette and with Ann too and the social workers. It went round and round in my head. Then there was something I saw on the telly about kids in care being worse off than ones who stay somewhere forever even if its not there own real mums. Maybe I should of done that to start with. I feel bad all the time that Ive been there for Kayleigh but not you or Sam or George. I don't know if its cos shes a girl and I see the me when I was small and want to change it all by making her ok somehow. It hurts so much to talk about George. I dont really do it much. When I do think about him I know I do right by lettin you go with Bernedette forever and maybe if Id of done that with him hed be here alive still. I dont know if someone might want to do the same for Sam one day. I dont know if he has anyone as nice as Bernedette. But if there isnt Im gonna try and see him more and be a better mum to him. Im gonna try and do things rite so he can maybe live with me one day. Ill still see you after all this like I do now so really nothing much changes its just that youll not really be my son youll be Bernedettes son now officially. That makes me real sad. Im crying now sorry. But it does make me feel kind of releived too cos I know deep down Im doin this for you and only you. With Bernedette youll kind of know your dad too and she can tell you all his stuff and that way your still close to him even without him. I do love you little boy. I hope you enjoy your new home and Ill see you soon anyway.

Your Mum xxx

Grace Bryan
Hull Social Services
Ref – New Adoption Application

5th December 2012

Dear Bernadette,

I'm the social worker who will guide you through the whole adoption process for Conor Jordan, and though I'll be calling you later today to arrange a first home visit I just wanted to send a note outlining exactly what will happen now.

As you know already, it can take several months to be assessed and approved. The recommended maximum time from your formal application is eight months, which means for most people it will not take longer than this. However, just to let you know that occasionally it can, though I see no areas of concern in your application.

This might be an emotional few months, so do make sure you're getting lots of support from family, friends and colleagues.

I would like to invite you to your first preparation group, where you'll have the opportunity to meet experienced adopters and foster carers, as well as having the chance to speak to some adopted adults. I understand your situation is different to most, in that you have known the child for five years and he is your stepson, but these sessions can still be helpful.

I will go through the whole process with you. I'll visit your home over the next several months, both to assess you and how the living arrangements are going. I understand you have just this week moved into the more suitable accommodation we looked at, and this will look good in your assessment. I will also meet your family, friends, neighbours and general support network. It seems very thorough, but we have to make sure we're making the right decision, and that you are too.

I will then write a report called a Prospective Adopter's Report, which will include your assessment, some personal references, all checks, and a medical report. You will have the opportunity to write some of this yourself. Then finally you'll sign it and it goes to the adoption panel.

When you have been approved – and 94% are – it is official. You apply to the court for an official adoption order and your new life with Conor will begin.

This is a lot to take in, but I wanted to make sure you have all the information before we meet for the first time. If you need to know anything at all, please contact me on the above number.

Best regards,
Grace Bryan

63

Bernadette

The cottage is the last in a row of five, painted feather-white like the other four but with an extra window as though trying to stand out. It does, at least to Bernadette. Upon first viewing the end-of-terrace house a month ago she had thought it benefited from the company of a neighbour on one side and the solitude of a small field on the other. The best of both worlds. Like when, as a child, she pushed a chair against the bedroom door to read alone, knowing her parents were just on the other side if she wanted them.

Now Bernadette has the key to this two-bedroom house with a sloping back garden and bramble bushes that tangle like fruity spider webs about the fence. Snow covers them all today: the windowsills, the bushes, the grass, the roof. It's hers. It will be Christmas in three weeks and she'll spend it here.

The removal van isn't here yet, but Bernadette unlocks the door and goes in. Only her breath fills the space, like that first day at Tower Rise. Then Richard had called the removal company and complained that they were late. Bernadette doesn't mind this time. It means she can explore and imagine in peace. She can sniff the air like she always does in a new place and claim it properly.

The estate agent said the place had been empty for some time.

Waiting for her.

She goes up the narrow staircase and looks into the bedrooms. Both are in the roof so enjoy a sloped, attic feel. Bare floorboards mean Bernadette's heels click intrusively as she crosses the first room, to a window flat against the roof. It opens onto a school playground and a row of shops. She imagines that if a bed were beneath the glass, at night the sleeper might be able to see the stars. The other bedroom looks onto the back garden. There are no trees, but she can plant new ones in spring.

Bernadette hasn't chosen a bedroom; it isn't for her to decide. Anyway, she doesn't mind which view she has. She only knows that neither room will be painted daffodil-yellow like the nursery at Tower Rise.

Back downstairs Bernadette stands for a while watching snow blow against the kitchen window, then fly off like dandelion seeds seeking new soil. Bernadette's parents came with her for the second viewing. Her dad nodded, silently confirming his approval; her mum opened cupboards and said it was much cosier than Tower Rise.

'Include us more,' she added, without judgment, just kindly. 'I know you've always been a loner – I used to say to my mum, little Bernadette, like a closed book, she is. What is it they call the boy Conor's book? A Lifebook. Well, yours is closed. Open it now and again. Let us see *your* life.'

Bernadette nodded, promised she would. She had visited for a weekend to tell them about Conor. She spent time with her father in his greenhouse, with her mother in the kitchen, and with them both in the conservatory as the sun set over the distant church spire. It was such a long story, one that made Bernadette cry as she spoke. Both parents said they would get to know Conor, that she mustn't think she had to protect them from everything.

'You know what it's like to be just one child,' her dad said in a rare gush of words. 'You'll understand each other.'

Rumbling wheels and screeching breaks outside draw Bernadette to the front window. Her things – the few items she selected to come here. She had to let a lot go because the flat was bigger than this two-up-two-down cottage. So she brought what was essential and what she loved: the table, her bed, one sofa, the bookshelf, pots and pans and crockery, books, pictures, and other mementoes.

Two men bring the boxes and furniture into the living room, stamping snow off their feet and asking where she wants things. For now, she asks them to put the bed in the back room – she can move it if needed. The rest she shuffles into half-decided positions, before finding the kettle and making tea.

Grace Bryan, the social worker dealing with the adoption, said the house was ideal. Less isolated than Tower Rise and not damp or draughty, she confirmed that it had all the space necessary, was in good proximity to school and friends, and that the garden was perfect and the area low on crime.

Bernadette sits and opens the box labelled PERSONAL STUFF. Inside, on top, is a handful of Conor's artwork. There are sketches of Muhammad Ali and Anne and Sophie and Frances. There are coloured pictures of her and Richard and Sam and George. She finds drawing pins at the bottom and tacks the papers to a corkboard in the kitchen. All her people, shaded in light and dark, flaws subtle, beauty emphasised, stare back at her.

There's just one face missing.

A soft knock on the front door, and Bernadette smiles. She opens it on the missing face, the artist – Conor. He's wrapped up warmly in a quilted jacket and bramble-purple scarf, his cheeks and nose pink. Anne follows down the path with a bunch of equally colourful flowers.

'It's like one of those olden-day houses,' says Conor.

'Come and see inside,' says Bernadette.

He runs straight upstairs. Anne hugs Bernadette and says, 'He was up at five this morning. Couldn't wait to see your "not haunted" house. I haven't told him the rest.'

Bernadette puts the flowers in the sink and runs cold water over their stems. 'Grace said he can come and stay here once I'm settled in. I can apply for the court order once he's lived with me for at least ten weeks. Then it'll be official.' Bernadette pauses, studies Anne's face. 'Are you sure you're okay? He's lived with you so long. I'm so happy, but when I imagine how sad you must be...'

Anne shakes her head vigorously. 'No, you mustn't think that way! I knew I was only having Conor until he found his true home. And now he has.'

They hear footsteps above them, back and forth, back and forth. Bernadette goes upstairs and finds Conor on the landing, grinning, his scarf in a snakelike curl on the wooden floor.

'Which bedroom would you pick if you could?' Bernadette asks him.

'Is it a game?' he wants to know.

'No, it's for real. If you stayed here, where would you sleep?'

Conor goes straight to the front. 'In here of course,' he says. 'There's more sun. And I can spy on that school and the kids at the shops.' He pauses. 'Do you mean like a sleepover?'

'Would you want to stay here longer than that?' Bernadette asks.

It's the first time she has actually asked him. She didn't want to talk about it at all until everything looked certain and Grace agreed. He's had enough let-downs. She feels sick – he might not actually *want* to be with her.

'Longer?' he asks.

'Live here,' says Bernadette carefully.

'Like, not at Anne's?' He stands in the sunlit window and purses his lip. 'I suppose you are my step-mum and all that. Would Anne mind?'

'No, she'd be happy for you.'

'Can Sophie come over?'

'Yes.'

'And my mum?'

'Yes.'

'And Kayleigh and Sam?'

'Yes.'

'And you promise me Anne doesn't mind? She won't be sad? I can't go if it'll make her sad.'

'I promise,' says Bernadette. 'She's excited about it. She wants you to go where you'll be happiest.'

Conor smiles. 'Well, yeah, *totally* then.'

Bernadette goes and stands next to him. She recalls their chat on the wall at Anne's house, about scientists looking for the smallest thing in the universe; how Conor had explained that the centre of the universe was everywhere.

Perfectly in tune with her thoughts, Conor tugs on Bernadette's arm and says, 'This will be the centre of the universe if I live here because I'll see *everything* from this window. I'll be in the centre. And you'll be there too.' He grins and pauses. 'And Muhammad Ali of course.'

64

The Book

9th May 2013

Dear Conor,

I want to write a last note here. Since Bernadette has applied for an adoption order this week I'll hand your Lifebook to her so she can give it to you when she wishes, which she said will be on your eighteenth birthday. Once a child finds a permanent home we no longer need to record their life since they will get the background info they need from their parent or parents.

I'm delighted that you have found a home, especially when it has such special significance. Bernadette assured me that she'll encourage you to continue seeing your birth mum, which Frances is happy about. Also your long-term foster carer, Anne, is a good friend and will stay in your life.

You will see your siblings regularly. Your brother Sam has been seeing more of your mum and there's hope that he will live with her sometime later this year. She is doing much better and we feel that, with continued support and the changes she is making to her life, she can look after Sam fulltime as well as Kayleigh.

All that really remains for me to do is to wish you well in the future, and I know those good wishes come also from all the social workers, carers and support workers who have got to know you and been part of writing in this book. I hope one day it helps you put together your history, everything before now that has led to me being able to stick just one more document in here (see below).

All best regards,
Yvonne Jones (Social Worker)

Application for an Adoption Order
Section 46 Adoption and Children Act 2002

I/We the undersigned **BERNADETTE KATHLEEN SHAW**
wish to adopt **CONOR JORDAN**
and give the following details in support of my/our application
I/We want my/our identity to be kept confidential and wish to apply for a
serial number **YES NO**

Domicile and residence
I am domiciled in the United Kingdom, Channel Islands or Isle of Man.

Status
I am the partner of the child's **FATHER** MOTHER
I am not married/do not have a civil partner.
I am a widow.

About the child
The child is a **BOY** GIRL
The child was born on 10/11/2001
The child has had his/her home with me/us continuously since 23/02/2013
I/we have notified in writing my/our local authority of my/our intention to
apply for an adoption order (see details)

Parent/guardian consent to adoption
The child's parent(s)/guardian(s) has/have consented to the making of an
adoption order.

Child's name on the adoption order
If the adoption order is made I/we want the child to be known as
CONOR RICHARD JORDAN

Statement of truth

I believe that the facts stated in this application are true

Signature of applicant

Bernadette Kathleen Shaw

65

Conor

Today is my birthday – my eighteenth birthday.

It's supposed to mean something. I'm an adult. But I don't feel any different to yesterday. Still got red pimples all over my forehead that don't go away no matter how much Clearasil I use. Still got out of bed this morning and ran around the living room with our dog Jasper for five minutes like crazy.

I can legally go to the pub now and buy my own drinks. Not that I'm really bothered. Don't like beer much. I can vote too, though I'd not know who to pick. They're all as bad as each other. That's what Sophie said. She was eighteen two months ago and read a website about what we can do now as adults. Not that we'll do them all.

I'm waiting for Bernadette, in our favourite place.

It's this café near the town centre and it's been here years, even though it's changed name and owner lots of times. We come here for two reasons. The first is that she met my dad here years ago. They weren't even supposed to meet – she was actually on some blind date with this other man called Richard. I love that weird shit. Coincidences you couldn't make up.

The second reason we come is that they do the best freakin' steak and ale pie in the world and it's only three quid with loads of chips. I'm a pig and love my food, but I swim lots so I stay fit that way.

I just started training to be a lifeguard.

Wasn't sure about it for a long time. I mean, I was sure I wanted to do it, but not sure I was good enough. The careers staff in sixth form harass you all the time about what you want to do when you grow up, but who the hell knows at sixteen or seventeen? When they asked what I like most and I said drawing they said that wasn't useful and I'd just end up teaching it. They kept saying pick a trade or profession and stick to it.

Bernadette said go with what's your calling.

Tried boxing once. Went to this club off Hessle Road that my mate Mark runs but I was shit. I knew him when I was fostered once and he said I could go for free. But I found out that just because you like watching a sport doesn't mean you're good at it. I've got two left feet or something. Probably two left fists too.

But it doesn't seem to matter in the water. I feel good there. The scars on my legs tingle when I first dive in.

The waitress comes over with this big smile and asks if I know what I want to order. She knows us so knows I'll want pie. I tell her I'm just waiting for My Bernadette. I call her that. My Bernadette. I've never called her Mum because I see my real mum. Also it's hard to change what you call someone and I'd known her a long time before she became my adoptive mother.

She's not late though, I'm early. It's a bad habit I have. I'm scared I'll miss something so I always get places a half-hour too early. I went to my first lifeguard lesson so early I was asleep when the others got there. I've had one session and we didn't do much except sign forms and learn about what it involves. I have to be able to swim fifty metres in less than a minute while wearing shorts and a T-shirt. I can already do that. Took loads of practice.

The café door opens – you always know when it does because this wind chime slams against it and annoys you. All the customers look up. Bernadette comes in with a blue bag in one hand and some envelopes in the other.

Happy birthday, she says, and kisses my cheek.

I used to hate kisses when I was about fifteen. Would wipe them off. But you're an arsehole at that age. These days I let her, and sometimes even kiss her too. I do now. She smells of our house. It's weird how people do.

We live in this small house a bit like a cottage, the last on a row. She said it was what she'd always wanted. Not big or cold like her haunted flat before. But she misses the trees. Always goes on about the friggin' trees. We planted a line of them but they take so long to grow that we'll probably be old when they're full trees. She said maybe my kids might enjoy them one day.

That's if I ever get married.

She sits opposite me and the waitress takes our order. Bernadette says she's got a full hour for lunch because she told them it was my birthday. She works in this travel place. Sells posh cruises and stuff. Said once that if she can't actually get to see the world she's happy to sell it to other people, and she gets discounts and we went to Mexico with Anne last year. If she makes enough sales this year we might go to New York in January. Sophie might come.

Did you talk to your mum? asks Bernadette.

I did. She rang before I came out. I spoke to my sister Kayleigh too. She's eleven and got attitude, but I don't take it. I'm always telling her to be kind to her mum and that she's lucky to have her. My brother Sam lives with them too but he was out with his mates today.

My mum has had loads of issues. She used to do stuff I don't like. Now she works in a care home, which is nice. She gets depression big time and probably always will. I reckon my brother Sam has that too. He's also got mild autism and it makes it quite difficult to talk to him, but I can. You just have to be patient. You have to talk about the boring stuff so he gets to the good stuff.

When my mum cries to me I get this awful feeling in my stomach and can't cope with it. Sounds mean of me I know. But I have to get away from her when she's that way cos I'm scared I'll fall into that blackness too and never get out. That's when I draw.

I always have. As far back as I can remember. Probably always will. Doesn't matter if it's not what I do as a job because it's much more to me than that. I couldn't just do it because someone told me, *Oh you have to draw this building or this boat or that thing*. I have to feel it. Don't reckon I could teach it neither. Don't have words to explain, so how could I?

I can't believe you're eighteen, says Bernadette. *Where has the time gone? How did you get to be six foot tall? What happened to my cute-faced boy? I wish I'd taken more photos or counted every minute or something.*

She goes on and on, and I just laugh.

The waitress brings our pies. Loads of gravy on them and even more if you ask for it. Whatever Bernadette doesn't eat I will. She says I should have it while it's hot and then open my present. So I do. I tell Bernadette what I'm gonna do later. Me and my mates from sixth form are going out.

Sophie's coming too. They always do my head in, winding me up that I should just ask her out once and for all. But my relationship with Sophie isn't like that. It's hard to explain. It's more than that. I don't need to ask her to be something to me. She just is. We kissed. Just recently. It felt right. But it's no one else's business. No need for anyone to be interfering or labelling us.

When we're done eating Bernadette pushes the gift bag over the table, but I say I'll open the cards first. I don't want to – everyone likes presents most. But it's good manners.

There's one from Anne with a huge eighteen on the front made out of paper tissue. She's written inside how proud she is of me. I get so embarrassed about shit like that. There are cards from Anne's daughters and then one from Bernadette. It's got a black-and-white photo of Muhammad Ali on the front. He died in 2016 and I was heartbroken. One day I'm going to Louisville to see where he was born and grew up.

Open your prezzie, says Bernadette.

She's more excited than me. So I take out something wrapped in tissue. It's a book, I can tell. So I get ready to fake excitement at an Ali biography I've already got. But it isn't. I mean, it *is* a book, but this one is yellow and old-looking. At first I think she's made me a photo album but inside there are handwritten notes and stuff.

And then I remember.

It's not like I forgot, more that I haven't thought about it in ages. Not since before I lived with Bernadette. But it comes back now. There was this book they were all doing. I think I even wrote in it once. It got passed around to all the people that knew me. They'd write stuff in about whatever was going on in my life. Someone said it was with my dad the night he died. I don't think you forget things, do you? I think I put my memories away for a while just like Bernadette did with this book.

When I look at her she's crying.

I'm sorry, she says. *I don't mean to be gloomy on your birthday. I'm not sad. It's just, well, there's so much in this book for you. It's going to explain loads. They call it a Lifebook. It might make you sad. Might bring back painful memories. I'd put it away and not looked at it in years and then I read it last week in bed. I remembered how it was, what a lost boy you were and how hard we all tried to do the right thing. But also I felt so joyful that you've survived it and that you're with me and we're here on your big birthday. So I think it will make you happy too. You look like your dad, you know. You've his eyes and way of moving. It's just uncanny.*

I drew a picture of him once. We've still got it, though it's all faded and the wrinkles in the paper have made his face age like he's still alive. It's hanging over my bed. I talk to him sometimes. Just tell him private stuff.

The waitress comes back and I reckon Bernadette is glad she interrupts. So we get mugs of tea. I put loads of sugar in mine. Then I look at the first Lifebook page, at my birth certificate at the bottom of it and a photo of me when I was a baby wrapped in a sweetcorn-yellow blanket.

Bernadette smiles and says they didn't have any blue ones that day.

I look at the words at the top of the first page, but don't read them.

Maybe read it tomorrow, Bernadette says. *Enjoy your friends today.*

That's when I tell her that I went to see my dad's grave earlier, and George's. I go there a lot, she knows that. Sophie comes. But today Bernadette's real emotional and her eyes fill up again. I tell her it was just what I felt I should do today. Poor George never got past six. He'll be a kid forever. Never get to pick his spots or listen to careers people lecturing about doing something useful.

It's a bigger day for you than most kids, says Bernadette. *Not everyone gets their life handed to them in a book. There used to be a TV show when*

I was little called This Is Your Life. *They'd have some celebrity on and invite all kinds of people from their past. Muhammad Ali was on it once. Didn't stop talking.*

I'll have to watch it sometime, I say.

I remember reading that his bike was stolen when he was twelve and he wanted to beat the thief to a pulp. That was when a police officer told him to learn boxing. It was when I was eleven and after my dad drowned that I started thinking about rescuing people out of the water. I used to get Bernadette to take me down to the rescue boat station all the time. Used to watch them preparing their gear. Saw the boat go out once.

When Bernadette realised why I was going she said the river was cold, and one of the most dangerous in the world for its currents. I reminded her that I'd been in it. I knew. I can still remember it now. How the temperature took my breath away. How quick you get tired and then don't care and want to sink. So someone's got to go in and rescue people. If my dad hadn't gone in for me I'd not be here.

I only wish I could have gone back for him.

Bernadette looks at me quietly for a moment and then says, *I've got one more thing for you.*

She goes in her bag and takes out a small velvet box. She holds it for a minute as though she doesn't want to give it to me. But she does. I open it. Inside is a gold ring. Bernadette tells me it was my dad's. His wedding ring. She says they gave her it after he'd died and she put it away, not knowing quite what to do with it. But now she knows.

Thank you, I say.

I'm really happy to have it. I hold it in my hand. Bernadette tells me to try it on, says to put it on my right hand or people will think I'm married. It fits just perfect. Never had owt so valuable. Don't think I'll ever take it off.

Like she knows what I'm thinking, Bernadette says that my dad never took it off from the day they got married until the day he...

She won't say the word died. I don't want to say it today either. I went to see my dad and George's graves earlier, but sometimes you just go and see people who have gone so you can then enjoy the people who are still here.

I have to go back to work, says Bernadette. *Will you be okay?*

I tell her of course I will. *It's my birthday remember*.

She kisses my cheek again and squeezes me. I can tell she doesn't want to go.

Then she says, *I think I'm just emotional because you're not mine anymore. You're grown up. You'll go soon. And I'm glad for you and excited about all the stuff you might do. I just have to let you go.*

The waitress gets our mugs. Bernadette sniffs and messes my hair and leaves. The wind chime bangs against the wall again.

I decide to sit for a bit cos this is where she met my dad and I like that. Maybe he's watching, who knows? Maybe he somehow made me choose to come here today. It's hard sometimes to remember him exactly cos I only met him once. He put his coat around me. I remember that. Bernadette's told me about him but I get this feeling she leaves stuff out. Like she doesn't think I'm old enough or something. Or that it's not good.

But I don't care about that. I'm not perfect.

When I leave the café it starts raining. Doesn't bother me. I like getting wet. I love the water. So I walk slowly and let it soak me. But I don't get far because there's something in my trainer. Does my head in so I stop under a bus shelter, take it off and shake it. This stone falls out. So small I can't find it on the ground. Makes me smile though. Just a tiny thing can stop you walking.

Like a whole mountain in my shoe.

I carry on walking in the rain. I've got a new ring on my finger and my life written in a book under my arm. I don't know what the words to my future will be. Eighteen doesn't mean shit really. It's just a number. I won't read my Lifebook and be twice the age afterwards. You have to be okay with the child you are. That's who I'll always be inside. I can look back and I can look forward and it's just the same.

So I open my Lifebook and read the first line – just that one – and then close the pages again to keep it dry.

This book is a gift.

Acknowledgements

First I want to thank Karen Sullivan (Orenda Books) for making my lifelong dream come true when she published my debut novel *How to be Brave* in 2015. For her passion and support. For having such faith in me that she said she would publish *this* book even before she had read it. I'll never forget all you've done.

Thanks to my early readers who helped so much. Sister Claire sat with me one August afternoon and we talked out the full plot, from beginning to end. Sister Grace was a passionate and impatient-for-the-next-chapter reader. The wonderful Cassandra Parkin too. And I met friend Lesley Oliver because of this book and how she loved it. Thanks also to my fabulous nephew Tom for making the amazing book trailer.

Thanks Mark Swan of Kid-ethic for designing both covers, and Karen and West Camel for the fantastic, patient edits. Thanks to Martin Doyle at the *Irish Times* for his support.

Thank you to the bloggers who reviewed *How to be Brave*, and for your continued support – Anne Cater, Anne Williams, Liz Barnsley, Sophie at Reviewed the Book, Stephanie Rothwell (stephbookblog), Sharon at Shaz's Book Blog, Louise Wykes, Janet Emson, Karen Cocking, Vicki Goldman, @janeaustenrulesok, Marina @chick-catlibrary, The Book Trail, Live Many Lives, Stephanie Cox, Brian Lavery, Mumbling About Music, Vicki Leigh-Sayer, Jack Croxall, Trip Fiction, Jackie Law, Sarah Hardy (By The Letter Book Reviews), Poppy Peacock, Jacqueline Grima, Louise Hector, Shaz at Jera's Jamboree, Leah Moyse, Christine at Northern Crime, Melinda at the Discerning Reader, The Last Word Review, Nick Quantrill, Lisa Adamson (Segnalibro), Hilary Farrow (thinkingofyouandme), Melissa Rose, Pam

McIlroy, Joanne at Portobello Book Blog, Ana at This Chick Reads, Lisa Hall (ReadingRoomWithAView), Safie Maken Finlay, Adrian Murphy, Jules Mortimer, and Abbie Headon.

Thanks for the lovely messages I've had from readers, some of them great authors – Sue Bond, Jeanette Hewitt, Ian Patrick, Jane Isaac, Vicki Bramble, Gill Paul, Lor Bingham, Richard Littledale, Fiona Cane, Richard Gibney, Yusuf Toropov, Amanda Jennings, David Ross, Paul Hardisty, Rebecca Stonehill, Katie Marsh, Matt Johnson, Nicky Doherty (Black), Rita Brassington, Annie de Bhal, Carol Lovekin, Sarah Jasmon, Tara Guha, and Mari Hannah.

Thank you for the support from Helen Jn Pierre and Dave Mitchell with the cakes, crazy photos and events, Simon Shields, Janet Harrison, Chris Watson and the Willerby/Kirk Ella Reading Group, Shane Rhodes and Humber Mouth/Head in a Book, Sue Wilsea, Ian Judson, Lisa Martin's Beverley Book Group, Pat Lawrence and the Best Supper Ever Book Group, BBC Radio Humberside, Vicky Foster, Ian Winter, The Women of Words, Hull Libraries, Beverley Folk Fest, and my favourite team, Fiona and Pete Mills at Hull Kingston Radio.

A big thanks to the Book Connectors group started by Anne Cater for all support. Thanks to the Prime Writers, an amazing group of writers who arrived at this later in life like I did. Also thanks to the vast Facebook TBC (The Book Club), especially Helen Boyce and Tracy Fenton, who are so passionate about books. Thanks to all the many wonderful (too many to mention) members (friends!) there.

Hello to Aston from the 'girl who writes all the books'.

I wanted to include a quote from my great friend Johnny Ennals, the kind that would never likely make it to the cover but deserves to be included here. He said of my first play – 'Better than Shakespeare cos I didn't fall asleep'.